Crucifixus

Belinda Tobin

Crucifixus

Copyright © 2024 by Belinda Tobin

All rights reserved. No part of this publication may be reproduced, distributed, or transmitted in any form or by any means, including photocopying, recording, or other electronic or mechanical methods, without the prior written permission of the publisher, except in the case of brief quotations and certain other non-commercial uses permitted by copyright law.

Published by Bel House Books

Paperback ISBN: 978-1-7637246-7-9

EBook ISBN: 978-1-7637246-8-6

For permissions or enquiries, please contact:

Bel House Books

Email: bhb@heart-led.pub

Website: www.heart-led.pub/bel-house-books

First Edition: October 2024

A catalogue record for this book is available from the National Library of Australia

Other titles from Bel House Books:

I'm Sorry Juno

The Love Life of a Chameleon

The Emptiness Algorithm

To The Heart of The Man

I acknowledge the Yuggera and Ugarapul peoples as the Traditional Owners of the lands and waterways where this book was written. I honour the wisdom that lives within the cultures of our First Nations peoples and celebrate its continuity. I pay my deep respects to Elders past, present and future and send my greatest gratitude for all they do for the life of this land.

Always was, always will be.

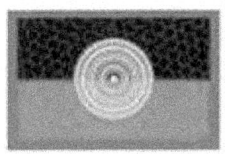

To my mother, who bore so much pain so that I may have the privilege of sharing this story.

Prologue

A room rich with Raphael frescos, the walls adorned with wisdom.

At its heart is a huddle of Fathers in flowing robes of scarlet, purple, and pure white. Their chests are adorned with precious crosses and their hands with heavy rings.

They are there to listen to a song, and then to speak of what has been stirred in their heads and their hearts.

The castrato is ushered into this sacred space. There is no commandment needed to attend to this guest. His appearance was an aberration, yet his psalm was perfect.

Some close their eyes to allow the voice a swift journey to their souls. Some eyes are shut to block out the misshapen body; to stop disgust from destroying their sense of dignity.

Some ears hear the song of the heavens, others, the siren that would send them to hell.

Yet all are witnesses to the purity and power of the castrato. All hearts were pierced by his performance.

There was no applause. The Pope gave no permission. The castrato was simply escorted away, replaced by a silence, a settling.

Soon, the only divinity remaining was the daylight streaming through the windows, illuminating the dance of the dust spiralling downwards.

The sun warmed the women observing from their sanctuary in the ceiling, circled in gold; Theology, Justice, Philosophy and Poetry, their distance from the table below precluding participation and offering protection.

The Pope arose from his sumptuous seat.

"Venerable brothers in Christ, esteemed Cardinals, and devoted servants of the Holy See. We gather here under the watchful guidance of the Father, The Son and The Holy Ghost. I address you in this blessed assembly with a heart uplifted by our shared faith while also burdened by our great responsibility.

As the Vicar of Christ on Earth I am tasked with the shepherdship of our Lord's flock. In this solemn duty I call upon your wisdom and discernment on matters of profound import. Brothers, you have heard the voice of the castrato. Now, a decision must be made as to whether we, as the voice of our Holy Church on Earth, will condone such a practice. There is much to consider. May the Holy Spirit guide us, and the forefathers we see here before us, Socrates, Aristotle and Plato, counsel us to a conclusion that is right and just.

Cardinal Mancini. You have already expressed your concerns to me in private. I call on you to share them so that we may begin this debate."

Mancini cleared his throat and stood, one hand clinging to his rochet, the other placed on the table.

"Your Holiness, and my venerable brothers. There is no doubt that the song we have heard was sublime. For this reason, I understand the castrato's growing popularity. However, Canon Law, as decreed in the Councils, expressly forbids mutilation of the human form. We are stewards of

God's creation. Our bodies are not our own. They belong to our Lord. How then, can we justify such an intimate and torturous alteration of the sons under our care?"

The Cardinal resumed his seat, glad for its support. The Pope rose in reply.

"Indeed, Cardinal Mancini, the laws of our Church are clear. Yet, we must also consider the spiritual service these voices render unto God. Is there not, perhaps, divine grace in the sacrifice made? A sacrifice made for the greater glory of the Holy Mother Church? Cardinal Bellarmine, you have a view on this?"

Bellarmine burst upwards.

"Yes, Your Grace. What my esteemed brother has failed to consider is the example provided by Jesus himself. Our Lord made the ultimate sacrifice to save us from sin. Similarly, our monks and nuns renounce a worldly life, and the honour of reproduction to serve God and his people here on Earth. These boys are but making a choice to consecrate their bodies, to offer them up so that through them we may all become closer to God. Who are we to deny them this act of service?"

Mancini hesitated, but his heart screamed for him to stand.

"Brother, how can you believe that these boys, of no more than seven years of age, are able to choose the life they want? It is their parents, facing poverty that push them into this. It is not a choice but a necessity for hungry families looking for any shred of hope for their future. You have been witness to the profit from their pain, but your view of their suffering is short-sighted, as is all those who send them to this fate."

Bellarmine's own voice became blustery.

"And who are we to take away any source of sustenance and hope from the families under our care? Brother Mancini, I also think you best be careful lest you insult the mystery of our God. He calls upon all ages to serve Him. Have you forgotten Dymphna, Tarcisius and Agnes, all saints who held the sign of God from such early ages. Brother, I think it is you who are displaying impudence in daring to speak for the children of God."

Both men sat and the murmuring began. Bishop Savelli arose and spoke directly to the Pope, whose dark eyebrows were forced into furrows.

"Your Holiness, my fear is for the soul of the castrati. Does the Church not risk burdening these young men with a life that neither heaven nor earth can fully accept? They are betwixt and between both man and woman. So, what do they become?"

The Pope rubbed his ring and pressed his lips together. In seconds, they turned from a serious straight line into a smirk.

"Angels. They become angels."

All others considered this answer final, but Bishop Savelli continued.

"My Eminence. Ours is not the power to make angels. Are we not stepping into the shoes of our Almighty God and Saviour?"

"And if I may add to this, Your Holiness", said Cardinal Rossi, standing beside Savelli.

"This debate takes us back to the original sin. Our first father was presented with such a choice by the serpent—a choice that promised divine-like knowledge yet was fraught with disobedience to our Creator. Corruption of God's creations is outlawed. That is clear. By allowing ourselves to be tempted by these sublime voices, are we not repeating the same mistakes that led to Adam's downfall?"

His pause may have made his point. But his passion was not satisfied.

"If all we seek is a heavenly melody, would we not be better to be away with the Pauline Dictum and allow women to sing in our churches? For their glorious voices are God-given."

The proposal was met with gasps, which grew into growls and swelled into calls of sedition and shame. The Pope allowed the commotion to continue towards anger, awaiting the crest before raising his hand for silence. His temper was calm, but his ruddy cheeks and shaking hands were a testament to his fury.

"Careful, brother, you skirt dangerously close to heresy. The teachings are clear. Need I remind you?"

This question was rhetorical, the Pope pushing forward, reciting passages ingrained in every inch of his identity.

"In Corinthians, let your women keep silence in the churches: for it is not permitted unto them to speak; but they are commanded to be under obedience. It is a shame for women to speak in the church.

And Timothy instructs, let a woman learn in silence with all submissiveness. I permit no woman to teach or to have authority over a man; she is to keep silent.

Go, Cardinal Rossi. You are excused. You have nothing further to contribute to this debate. I shall forgive your foolishness, but I cannot be assured that God will be as merciful towards your insolence. Leave now and find one who will take your penance."

It was a hateful hush that pushed Rossi towards the door, but from above, he heard a gentle call. It was Fortitude, from the fresco, encouraging his endurance. Rossi was glad Raphael had placed armour over her flowing pink gown. As he passed underneath, he sent a silent apology to her for his naïve and stupid attempt. And then, he wondered, how much longer could she placate the lion sleeping in her lap?

When the drama of the departure had diminished, Bishop Vincenzo took his turn.

"Your Holiness, the moral complexities of the castrati are vast. However, we must not overlook the profound spiritual impact the castrati have on our congregations. The people, our flock, come in greater numbers and their souls are drawn closer to God by virtue of hearing them. Surely then, this is the sign of the Holy Spirit's work among us. These castrati, through their sacrifice are helping us fulfill our deep and divine responsibility, to bring our people to God. Your Holiness, so many of our people are suffering. Do we not do them a great service in providing a beauty so profound that it stirs them onwards to the paradise that awaits? This I believe is no small matter."

Savelli stood once more, adjusting his cloak and speaking confidently.

"Neither, brother, is the matter of wilfully destroying the gifts that God has given."

Bellarmine, with his tiny stature, turned to face Savelli, tormented. His voice belied his body, and he bellowed.

"Savelli, you forget that they contribute to the greater good. These are no sacrificial lambs simply providing a single meal. Their bloodshed is in the realm of saints, delivering spiritual sustenance. Your Eminence, Brother Savelli, would see their courage censured when it should be consecrated. These men are not monsters. They are martyrs."

The enthusiasm with which Bellarmine put forth his beliefs left spittle sitting on the table's intricate inlay; the lack of inhibition conveniently ignored.

The Pope showed his hands, and stillness resumed among the ranks. He stroked the red velvet armrests, weighing what he had heard.

"Thank you all. I have heard enough. I will adjourn now and make my deliberations. May the Holy Spirit enlighten my mind and guide my heart, that I may act justly and rightly in the eyes of God."

All stand as the Pope shuffles away to the adjoining room. The Pontiff's eyes are cast to the floor, yet he pays no heed to the magic in the mosaics at his feet.

For hours, the bishops and cardinals clung to their factions, sustained by their secretaries, servants, and sense of self-righteousness.

All rose again when the Pope returned and then sat with anticipation for the answer to the solution the castrati posed. After the sign of the cross, and with hands clasped over his ring, he began.

"Venerable brothers in Christ, I thank you for your diligent contributions to this debate and your patience during my deliberations. All of your arguments have weighed heavily upon me, as does my duty to adhere to the Holy Scriptures and the sacred traditions.

I have decided on behalf of our Holy Mother Church that castrati will not only be condoned, but due to their ability to engage our people and lift them up to our Lord, they are to become a pivotal part of our church choirs. I shall set about immediately restructuring the choir here in St Peters to mark their place and set a precedent.

I do acknowledge the law around bodily mutilation, and it stands. There are to be no forced castrations. However, if a boy wishes to sacrifice his body to God, then we shall accept his offering. We will stand by him, to support him and honour his service.

Therefore, I order all of you, devoted servants of the Holy See, to care for all castrati within your parishes.

I also uphold the law that castrati must not wed, for this goes against the sole purpose of this sacrament, which is procreation. As the castrati cannot multiply, they must not marry. Let their song be their service to God.

Esteemed brothers in Christ, let us move forward on this issue in the spirit of unity. Unless there are significant shifts, I will hear no more on this matter.

The session is hereby adjourned. Deo gratias."

With this, the crowd forms a line and files past the Pope, bowing as low as their ageing bodies would allow, and kissing the hand that held their future.

The Pope, weary, wandered back into the room where the decision was made. The wine was poured, and feet were placed on pillows. The castrato entered and was commanded to sing again and again. The Pope took his place amongst the angels. And the women on the walls wept for the boys that their own fathers had fated.

CRUCIFIXUS

Rosa

Rosa wept in well-practised sobs, strong enough to expel her despair, weak enough to remain within the thin wooden walls. It was hard to separate the source of the stinging tears. There were some falling heavily for the loss of her husband. It was a year since he had been taken by God, but the grief was still raw. It stabbed at her whenever she saw her son Antonio, who had his smile. But both Antonio's father and his smile were now absent. The weight of work and worry had taken away any last remnants of his childhood. At eleven he was the man of the house, a role he took seriously, shown by his constant, straight lips and sombre eyes. How Rosa wished she could have protected him. Now, she could only try to heal his battered hands until the callouses would come in. There would be no respite for either of them as long as there was a farm to tend and a family to feed.

Rosa grieved for the laughter gone. Her husband was a hearty man who knew how to celebrate the cessation of each day. While Rosa feared how his indulgences would be seen in the eyes of the Lord and scolded him for the silliness he shared with the children, he brought a lightness, a levity to their long days and dark nights. Outside this home, he would abide by the conventions of manly decency, but his love and laughter would loom large inside.

Was it this excess, this lack of righteous restraint, that took his life? Rosa knew of the rumours. The priest had shared the whisperings when he came to provide solace to this widow and her six children. There had been no period of illness, no signs of decay. Simply, in the field, after the Feast of St Peter and St Paul, he fell dead. When Rosa found him, the crows had already fed on his eyes. One stood defiant, staring at her as the sickening mess of her husband's earthly humours stained its chest. Such a sudden death was fraught with fear, and suggestions of evil intervention were to be expected. No matter her intense faith and unswerving devotion to the Church, there was always suspicion. Had Rosa caused his demise?

Rosa's case was not aided by her recent reliance on Giulia, the herbalist, who walked a fine line between being supported by the Church and being burnt at the stake. She followed the rigid rules, concocting and creating within the Church's prescriptions and adding prayers to her practice. She had been baptised and bore the burden of regular interventions by parish priests. She did so for the women and girls who would have otherwise been left helpless. And for Rosa, she put herself at risk.

Rosa had declared to her daughter, Francesca, that there was no more that could be done for her pain. But Francesca was fierce. She did not listen. Francesca finally went to get Guilia, returning to find Rosa huddled on the floor, pleading to God. Since the birth of Maria five years ago, it had hit her so much harder. Before, with her husband's help, a heat pack and some rest, she would recover quickly. The greater age and exertion since his passing meant each month, she was mauled from the inside, a searing stabbing testing the limits of her strength and her sanity. In the quiet moments, in the weeks between the blood and the torment, beside the fire, Rosa would explain to Francesca the gift she would herself, soon receive. Any day, Francesca would be blessed with the signs that she was ready to bear a child. To fulfil her duty to God was an honour. Yes, there would be crosses to bear, but His will would be done, and she should accept it with dignity.

And so, Rosa called on the saints to show her the way. Francesca did not share her view that faith should be the final answer, and fetched Giulia with her tinctures, teas, poultices and prayers. The latter were the same as those Rosa had been reciting daily to herself and those she shared with the Nuns who came to offer charity. The incessant chanting made no change to the condition. However, the remedies Giulia applied brought relief. The torturous cramping did not end, but it did calm enough for her to cuddle Isabella, who came crawling to her, not satisfied with her sister's arms. And the heat in her heart cooled allowing her to carefully cling to the little hand of Maria, crying with concern for her mama. Slowly, the fog in front of her eyes cleared and she could see the mess around her that would need to be cleaned.

As the pain subsided, Rosa's pride took its place, and a panic ensued about how payment would be made. Rosa instructed Francesca to fetch some eggs, flour and figs, which the Giulia had taken with gratitude. She left with the promise to return for the next stage of treatment.

These tears staining the sheets were also tinged with fear. Was the aid Rosa had accepted of a form that could be forgiven? Or would her weakness continue to condemn her children with punishments still to pass? Rosa knew the women and the clergy would have their own views, and this helplessness added to her heartache. She would bow her head in church to show her respect and reverence and avoid those eyes seeking any evidence of evil.

Another grievous spasm made Rosa want to cry out, to cut through this silence and share her suffering. She wanted to let go of the hurt she held so tight, to show her daughter the extent of this affliction and threaten her with spiteful words that this, too, would be her fate. These thoughts added to her distress. While part of her heart knew it was merely the voice of weariness, the other half worried it was wickedness. Had her daughter, in her desperation, invited in the Devil, and was he now woven into her words? For in this state, sometimes, for a second, her faith would falter, and she would become confused. Where was the Christ she loved? The one she worshipped. Had He abandoned her?

A moment of misery would pass and then Rosa would be again sound of mind. He may decide she was not worthy of his mercy, but she would not abandon Him. Rosa would fight for her faith and the right for her children to be seated with Him in Heaven. If this was her hell, then she was determined to continue honouring her Lord within it. Her will would not be found wanting. Christ received the lances on the cross with dignity, and so would she. Preparing for the next onslaught, Rosa began to hum a hymn she had heard so often in church. Her mouth made the music, and her mind sang the words.

Sing, my tongue, the Savior's glory,

Of His flesh the mystery sing;
Of the Blood, all price exceeding,
Shed by our immortal King,
Destined, for the world's redemption,
From a noble womb to spring.

With this song, she was transported to the sanctity, her sanctuary, the church. Her inability to speak in the sacred space was never a source of concern. The silence of the service was a respite and provided the chance for her to listen. In the hymns, she found hope, and as the choir's voices rose, they took her to a land of beauty. She would breathe deeply and surrounded by the scents of frankincense and myrrh; her breath would become blessed. The strength of the songs offered support she could not find elsewhere, and they lifted her beyond her bodily torture.

She pictured Paulo, her son, standing in the centre of the chorus, and her pride momentarily took the place of the pain. Her little boy, her youngest son, had the voice of the heavens. So how could she be cursed when God had given her this child?

Perhaps Francesca had heard her stirring or the macabre mix of melody and moaning. Beneath this girl's wild will was a warmth, a light that led her to wherever there was need. And tonight, she knew that need was here. Francesca came with a pillow of heated grains and herbal tea, helping her mother slowly sit and sip. She knew she would soon find relief as her darling daughter rubbed the lotion of lavender and sage around one source of her suffering. Surrounded by Francesca's solidity and scents, Rosa found soothing.

Francesca was so soft, so gentle, just like Paulo. Between them, they made generous guardians of their younger sisters and a counter to the bravado of her older boys, Antonio and Luca. But these girlish ways would be gone soon enough. Francesca would realise the rough reality of being a woman and a wife and how moments of joy would slip away hurriedly between hours of hard labour. Rosa knew it was her duty to prepare Francesca and all her children to bear their trials with bravery, and she would do this with a strong hand, better hers than someone else's. She may be weakened now but would readily return to provide the discipline that would put her children in good stead and allow them to find favour in the eyes of the Lord, their Father in Heaven.

Francesca

Francesca, satisfied that her mother had settled as much as the condition and the remedies would allow, and on her mother's orders, returned to her room. She tucked into the mattress she shared with Maria, fatigued and frustrated. What father could ever allow his child to suffer so much? What possible sin had prompted this punishment? Francesca knew her mother as a God fearing woman and found it impossible to conjure the notion of her breaking any commandment. Was there something in her childhood that God had decided to delay vengeance for? Or was there a malevolence in her mother's mind that Francesca could not see? There was another possibility. Perhaps her mother's faith was misguided.

Francesca would never suggest that to her mother, though, for she would surely receive another of her monstrous slaps. The last one was brutal, leaving a red welt on her cheek for hours and making Francesca wonder whether her mother's hand was hurting too. The crime was simple. Francesca was caught singing at the stove, boiling the water to wash Isabella's soiled clouts. Before her father died, indecencies like this were overlooked. But since the rumours began about the sinfulness that may have taken him so suddenly, her mother had become hardened. Nothing could be out of place, and with her family, no fault should be found. The sale of their produce relied on the priest's favour. Therefore, the Contadino women must not sing where anyone may hear. It was simply a matter of survival.

But Francesca was sustained by song, and so she sought out the places that were safe. Walking through the open spaces on the way to the market, she sang to her baby sister, sleeping in the sling on her back. Standing in the field, her family at a distance, she would find joy in the vibrations of her voice, shielding this with sombre looks. She made the most of the storms that would swirl around the cottage, cuddling with the little children and calming them with hymns that could not be heard over the winds.

Each Sunday, Francesca would witness the castrati in the church. Some stood behind her brother Paulo in the choir, and their voice was perfect. She would try to listen but was often distracted, supervising Isabella and Maria, minimising their fussing and trying to secure the little girls' silence. In the small moments of peace, she would pine to have the life of a choir boy or a castrato. To spend her day in song was her greatest wish, but one that was futile. On their long walks, Guilia would tell of noble families where daughters would learn all manner of music and make glorious careers in the opera. Their parents, patrons of the arts, would surround them with support and outside the confines of the Church, they were free to find their voice. But Francesca's family was far from genteel. And as the eldest daughter there would also be no chance for Francesca to join a convent, to sing with the other sisters, and compose within the cloister. She had promised herself that one day, she would travel to the convent in Milan, attend an audience with the nuns and hear what was possible; one day, when the children were older and her mother was well. Until then, her place was here.

Her place was no longer at school, but that thought brought her no sadness. She would much rather have the freedom of the farm, with all of its labours, than be locked up learning things that brought little light to her life. She found more inspiration in the fresh air than in learning letters, and more knowledge in her imagination than in numbers. With her father gone, it was expected that the two eldest children would withdraw and provide four small hands to replace his two large ones. Luca, Paulo and Maria would still attend; their futures to be very different from their firstborn sister and brother.

Francesca did feel angry sometimes. Although this was soon tempered with the smile of the toddler, or the peaceful moments with Paulo listening to him practice. She felt happy when she could help, so she would visit Giulia, often without her mother's permission. If she could not sing, then she would find another way to stir souls, and so she was learning from Giulia how to use the gifts of God's land to heal. Giulia was a firm friend, understood her plight and offered her protection. Her mother never questioned the time it took for Francesca to return from the markets, meaning there was always the chance to take a detour and, if Giulia was home, continue her lessons. She was now proficient at the treatments for pain, practising these regularly on her mother. Francesca also knew what to use on wounds, which was important on the farm where any infection could be deadly. And she had begun lessons on how to care for women during childbirth.

Giulia promised that she would seek Rosa's permission for Francesca to assist at the birth of their neighbour's next child, only weeks away. Besides, at thirteen, she would soon become a woman herself, and witnessing a birth was essential education. She had been too young to see the birth of Antonio and at school when her younger siblings arrived. But now, with Giulia as an ally, she would see miracles. In this, she found meaning.

For Francesca found no sense in the teachings of the Church, especially the decree that demanded women's silence. The Pauline Dictum was but one of a long list of liturgical lessons she was forced to remember at school. She found it almost idiotic that she had to repeatedly recite the rule that prevented her from speaking in any sanctified place. Could no one else see the hypocrisy? But there was no reason provided, and no questioning allowed. Corinthians and Timothy had given the order, and her duty was simply to obey.

Francesca did not yet understand how castrati, being men, could replace a woman's voice. It confused her. Although Giulia had promised that, when Francesca became a woman, she would explain how castrati were made, for her mother would not tell her. When Francesca did ask her mother, one night by the fire, the only response provided was they had made sacrifices that should not be spoken of. This answer did not assuage Francesca's curiosity, only fuel it. To find out the secret source of their gift, she was willing to wish her menses forward. However, with this wanting came a great worry. What if she did suffer from the same ailment as her mother. How could she possibly bear this burden? Surely, she would break and scream and curse the Christ that had condemned her? Could her womanhood become the family's downfall?

For this disease did not just destroy the body; she had seen how it had changed her mother, from one calm and gentle to guilt-ridden and cautious. There was once singing in the home, while sewing, cooking and cleaning, and bathing the babies. Her father would congratulate her on her heavenly voice, and her mother smiled at the compliment. Now, her father was no longer there, and the joy from her song was forced out by baseless Church concerns and constructed commandments. Francesca was now being forced away from being a girl and towards being a role model. This required that she do only those things that were deemed good in God's eyes. There were things that she agreed were good in the future set for her, like caring for children, watching them play, their incredible progress, enjoying their embrace, hearing their little laughs, and finding ways to ease their tears. These parts of her future role felt right.

She also saw how Paulo shared her love of these moments. He would often join her to help with Maria and Isabella and sing to them in his sweet voice. Paulo would practice his scales while he did his chores, but even these simple flows were pure and perfect. Even though he was only a few years older than Maria, Paulo took his job as older brother very seriously. He showered the little girls with a sense of silliness and security that their dead father could not, and much more than Antonio ever could. Antonio would be seen eating, working, planning or sleeping. He was too serious now for affection and too weary for games. Luca stayed away from all of them, spending each night outside, alone, watching the moon and the stars. He was adamant that he would not give up his lessons and that he would become an astronomer. This only made Antonio angry, which, in turn, made her mother agitated and sometimes aggressive. So, Francesca did not send for Luca until it was time for bed. That was best.

Francesca could feel herself slipping back into sleep. She could hear no more humming and would never admit to her mother that she ever had. She would calm herself in these few precious moments by continuing her composition. It was to be the processional hymn for her imagined mass – a mass for mothers, where everyone would be allowed to join in, even the women and children.

Antonio

Antonio had heard the stirring; Francesca moving pots to make her preparations, and the muted mutterings as she tended to their mother. He did not shift, for he had no place in the worries of women. Antonio would, though, he would transverse the rules if he could offer protection to his mother, if he could assist in taking away her pain. But he knew that in this situation, he was useless. So, he remained still, silent, with his eyes closed but awake lest he was needed. Antonio had become a master at this masked state, at pretending to be asleep. He would retire early, his body too heavy to hold him up any longer, but he lay and listened, letting his body rest, yet ready. Ready for what, he did not know, but his mind provided many possibilities. One of the little ones could injure themselves in the fire and may need to be transported quickly for treatment. A cry of alarm may be sounded by the sheep, and he may need to take up arms against a wolf. Or Luca could re-enter, riling his mother to give permission for him to find a patron and continue his studies elsewhere. Then, he would need to intervene to save his mother from further stress.

He was adept at battling Luca's body; they had been waging skirmishes against each other their entire lives. Antonio, though, could not compete with Luca's mind. Every rationale Antonio gave as to why Luca should take on more responsibility was met with retorts about how much more he could contribute to the family in an academic role. It always came down to a fight between Luca's vision for his future and what was needed now, to Luca's desire to gain support outside the family and the help Antonio needed from him here. Luca's stupid stars would not secure a sturdier shelter for the animals nor plant the seeds for the next season. But Luca wanted to learn, not labour.

Antonio did take joy in the beatings. For a moment, he had someone to blame, other than God, for his father's death and his despair. And at least here, at fisticuffs with Luca, he was assured of his superiority. Although he would never injure Luca. The family could not afford the burden of an invalid. Antonio used his fists only to stop the war of words. And then it was finished.

He could not hear which words Francesca was using tonight to soothe his mother. He knew this to be another of his mother's excruciating episodes, but more than that, he would never enquire. Thank God for Francesca though, her strength and surety. He had been fearful the day he had found the herbalist in their home, working with Francesca over the hearth. Yet he trusted Francesca implicitly. She would only ever do things out of care. Francesca always cared for him, and she would do the same for their mother. She would make him sit and eat, even when he said he was too weary. From the fields, he would see her airing his bed, using her herbs to cleanse it of bugs. Because of Francesca, he was lying here in comfort, although still crushed by the grief and guilt that came from his anger at God. Perhaps this fatigue, this fugue, was part of the punishment for the harsh words he had yelled at the heavens.

Francesca would also listen to his concerns. In their quiet moments together, he held back tears, begging her to do all she could to prevent their mother from dying. He stopped short of saying that he did not care if she had to call on the devil himself to help. However, he knew that Francesca would not judge him for this, for there were moments he saw in her eyes the same desperation.

Antonio shared the responsibility for his mother's life, each day trying to take on more so that her condition would not worsen. She was strong but was struggling. Antonio would tell his mother to take on the lighter duties and leave the heavier ones to him, but often, she would not listen. And the work did not end.

Sometimes, in his bitter moods he wondered if his mother's condition actually provided some respite. It was obvious that she was in anguish, but then so was he, just in a different way. On these days, Antonio imagined that a bang to the head would not be unbearable if it meant a day of imposed rest. He remembered his father, tired and dirty at the end of each day, but still with a smile for his children and energy to entertain. Antonio could not muster any joy for himself, and so there was none to share.

Mother had already spoken to him about taking a wife. Yes, it would be another mouth to feed, but also another pair of hands to work the farm. A wife, she told Antonio, would provide him with the care and comfort needed when Francesca was wed and moved away. In a wife, he would find support. In marriage he would find contentment. With his mother's insistence, he had already begun looking at the girls at mass a little differently. Some of the girls he knew from school. He had shared space with them before but could not envisage them now sharing his bed. The next step would be for him and his mother to meet with the priest and see if he had suggestions for a match that would suit his station and afford benefits for his family. He was in no mind to push for this. The priests were not people he wanted to be around.

Antonio had, as a younger child, admired them. From afar, at the back of the church, in their robes, they seemed supernatural. He had even thought that one day, he would like to be someone of such importance. Then he had felt their harsh hand. At school, righteous anger was used as a reason for harsh retribution. Failings were seen as faults, best flogged from a child, in the name of the father, of course. Antonio's own children would also tread this torment. In that, he could trust. For without the means to pay for a private education, there was no other way. Is this what drove Luca? To look for new paths to prevent his offspring from the same pain? Unlikely. Luca never did anything for anyone else. It was simply a selfish pursuit of his passions.

Besides, how could Antonio possibly trust the opinion of those who allowed castrati into the church? Were they not taught that their bodies were gifts from God? He understood the excuse given for their emasculation was to serve God and His people with their voices. Yet he found them horrific. He would watch as Paulo sang at the front of the choir. But it was the castrati that commanded attention, their position elevated yet pushed to the back. Seeing how close Paulo was to them made Antonio worry.

Even though he loved Paulo, he also envied him. Antonio would see him so proudly singing and then, that night, with his sisters at play. What would become of his little brother? This thought created a nauseous churning in his chest, for Antonio could see the direction in which he was being pushed. Still, he would never give his permission.

Antonio knew his mother was stirred by their voice. He saw her close her eyes and become enchanted. Only his sister shared his suspicions about how scriptures may have been manipulated to serve mortal ends. He believed in the natural order of things. How could such destruction be divine?

Although it did not stop Antonio from praying to a God that was good; his version, one that shared his values. One that could put him in touch with his father so he could ask about when to start harvesting and what strategy to use to sell the crops. On nights like this, he would seek advice on what he should do for his mother and how to manage their money better. He would plead for assistance to decide what to plant next, and how much yield to preserve. Paulo and Luca would come in and put themselves to bed while Antonio would wait, listening for answers from whatever father was willing to respond. And hoping that forgiveness may also be forthcoming for the anger he felt towards the Nun's charity and the deep hatred he still harboured towards God for his father's death.

In the dark hours before dawn, he would consider how tough he was becoming, how he was sloughing off the softness of childhood, and coming to truly take the place of his namesake. He was progressing well to this end, becoming more familiar with death; it was present all over the farm. He had watched as his mother showed him how to kill a goat that had been mauled by a fox and Antonio had carried many torn, bloody carcasses ripped apart by weasels and wolves, throwing them on the pyre. His mother had made him slit the throat of the little lamb born with a mangled leg, and then prepare it for supper. Hawks would take hatchlings, their tiny bodies flung around until they would hang limp from the talons, taken to be sustenance for this superior beast. After floods, the fields would be awash with the stink of decay, and he would be drenched in it for days. All of these things were disturbing but he could now stop it from creating distress. He was successfully becoming hardened, and for this he was glad. Because without his fortitude, his family would suffer far more than the quick fate of the animals on their farm.

Twilight was heralding in the tomorrow that was set for fixing fences for their crops and flocks and providing shelter from predators. Before rising, Antonio prayed, not to send praise but to ask, on this day, for no more punishment.

Paulo

Paulo was also awake and glad of the dark, so no one could see his tears. He turned towards the wall, trying not to stir Luca, but desperate to ensure no other person could bear witness to his weakness. There were no cries, only a silent flow cascading down his cheeks. Here, in the dead of night, he could indulge his sorrow. Tomorrow, in the daylight, he would have to hold it in. This he had learnt the hard way.

Before his father was buried, there were wails and moans, mountains of grief manifest for all to see, and valleys of tears shed across every acre. In this space between Antonio the elder, and the younger, in this momentary chaos, crying was permitted. But as soon as final farewells were said, as the last shovel of soil was placed, and the priest's prayers concluded, Paulo was no longer a child, and he had lost the protector of his papa.

The next day, Paulo declared that he would not go to school. He would stay and help at home. He begged and bawled and then was beaten by Antonio. He was accused of creating more stress for his mama and upsetting Maria and Isabella. This hurt much more than Antonio's hands. Francesca followed him out the door, cleansing his face with a wet cloth and fixing his shirt before calling Luca to lead him and Maria to school.

On the walk, Paulo had weighed up whether he would, like Luca, fight for what he wanted. His hands were as worthy as Antonio's and could spare his mother some suffering. His help could cover Luca's lack. So why did Antonio not allow it? But he could insist, take the punches as they came, and still stand his ground. He could show Antonio that he was determined to do what was right. This would mean war though, like that he saw every day between Antonio and Luca, and which left Luca outside. But Paulo was not afraid of the cold or being alone and he would happily cuddle with Nero and watch the night progress. It would break his heart, though, to give up time with the girls.

Francesca was the only one who seemed to understand and ease his confusion. She would call Paulo over to help her, knowing how much it meant to him to care for baby Isabella. Soothing her cries made him feel like he was contributing something, and making her smile eased the uncertainty about his place. He would hunt out the kittens, and bring them to the little girls to play with, teaching them how to hold the fragile creatures without causing hurt. Francesca would encourage him to sing, to free his voice through song, and to use it to bring peace.

Francesca would tell him when to sit with mama and sing to her. Paulo would snuggle into his mama's legs and float Kyrie Eleison into the fire.

Lamb of God, who takes away the sins of the world, have mercy on us.
Lamb of God, who takes away the sins of the world, have mercy on us.

Lamb of God, who takes away the sins of the world, grant us peace.

Sometimes, his Mama would reach down and place her rough hand on his shoulder, a touch that testified to her love. In the Easter months, Paulo would practice Regina Caeli, bringing his attention to the alleluia, stretching out the syllables to create a sense of space. Here, in his home, amongst his family, Paulo's song made him feel powerful. In the church, with the choirmaster and the priest, he felt petrified.

He had never questioned his place in the choir. He had been chosen from the classroom and commanded to attend practice. His duty was to honour God with the voice he had been given. So, while the other students were sent home, Paulo and the other boys battled to make their bodies do His will. Only perfection was tolerated, all else was punished. To fail as a chosen one would bring shame to his family, but to succeed meant he may be taken away.

It had happened to Marcus. His older sister had told of how a man had come on a magnificent horse, dressed in fine clothes, handed his father some money, made him put a cross at the bottom of a scroll and then took Marcus away. That was over two years ago, and not one word from Marcus has been heard since.

Paulo lived each day with a knot in his chest that only seemed to unwind when he was with his sisters, playing with Nero or singing to his mama. The rest of the time, it would wrap around his heart, pressuring for some resolution. The choirmaster suggested it could come soon, with a Vatican talent scout to be in the parish for Pentecost. With the arrival of the Holy Spirit, this man could also bring a new future for some of the boys.

This was the success that scared him, but to question it would be sacrilege. While Paulo sang out loudly, there was so much he held in. Because, if the truth were to be told, he did not want to be with these people. That became clear the day he was caned.

Paulo had noticed Lorenzo starting to lag before anyone else. He felt Lorenzo break the strict boundary, lean to the left and place weight into Paulo's arm. Paulo could not look. His job was to hold the line. But when Lorenzo fell, the choirmaster ordered them all to cease. Lorenzo's shaking came on suddenly; the bloody foam from his mouth was slower to appear, rising as the violence of the attack escalated. Everyone was frigid with fear. But Paulo could see Lorenzo's head being pummelled against the lectern. Paulo did not think, and that became his problem. He ripped off his robe and wedged it between Lorenzo's head and the hard surface, just putting it in place before he was pulled away.

Paulo did not hear much after that; some angry accusations about disobedience, about aiding the devil, and how his actions would not help his mother, who was already under suspicion. He was advised that his hands would be spared this time out of an act of charity to his family, but behind the door of the sacristy, he was told to kneel, and his buttocks were bared. A priest had come to assist, pushing Paulo's face into the cushion to muffle his moans. When the first beads of blood appeared, the weapon was wiped and retired. Paulo thought now, may come some relief. But his head was not released. It was pushed further down as his wounds were drenched in vinegar. His punishers seemed to get great satisfaction from his screams, saying that this was for his own good. They were washing away his sins, and he should be grateful that they had the courage to do their heavenly duty. They made him stand, which he did shakily. They made him redress, pulling coarse, woollen pants over hot, raw flesh. Then, he was thrust into the confessional, where the priest told him of the penance he would pay and offered him forgiveness.

That evening, the same priest accompanied Paulo home, paying no attention to the pain that the boy felt with every movement of the cart. He pushed Paulo toward his mother and outlined her son's horrific behaviour. Father left with a lesson from Proverbs, reciting that "whoever spares the rod hates their children", and advised Paulo's mother to show her son the same love that God had called him to provide that day. Paulo was sent to his room without supper but when all were asleep, Francesca brought him out to eat and tend to his wounds. She made him drink some warm spirits before pulling the fabric from the cuts and cleaning the skin. Then she put balm and bandages where she could and made him warm milk and bread before sending him back to bed. Each night, for weeks, this routine was repeated until the wounds were fully healed.

Lorenzo never returned to school or to the choir. He was not seen in church or at the local carnivals. Paulo hoped that he had not shared the same fate as their old dog, Viggo, who also had seizures. Viggo was a generous guard dog, and when he became ill, Paulo was determined to afford it the same protection it had given to their family for many years. So,

Paulo tended to it in secret. He knew a seizure was coming when the animal started to lose the support of his legs. Paulo would pick him up and hide him away, stroking his fur until the flailing had ended. Then he would wipe the dog's mouth clean, wash the waste from his legs and tail, and wait with him until it could walk again.

Paulo had thought this process was working well until he came home one day from school and Viggo did not greet him at the gate. But there was a fire and a smell that Paulo knew only occurred after death. His father had seen a seizure that day, drowned the dog immediately and burnt its body. Paulo's father, though, was not worried that there may be evil lurking, but by the hurt that this honoured family member was enduring. He could end its suffering and so, he did.

Paulo wished he had the same clarity and courage as his father. He could not choose which path to take for his future and feared desperately that it may have already been made for him. Sitting with Francesca one night, he asked if there may be any herb that might hasten the breaking of his voice or make it unsuitable for singing. She was shocked, and Paulo had been too by her reaction. He thought until then that Francesca was unshakeable, but his request had disturbed her. She reminded him of the Dictums that prohibited mutilation of the human body. It would be a sin, and it would be shameful. It would also take away a great gift. Paulo didn't mean to get angry, but his shout slipped out. He demanded to know why she would sin to help mama but not him. He was sorry the moment he had said it. He waited for the slap he knew he deserved. But it did not come. He cast his eyes to the floor and asked for forgiveness. Francesca granted it generously and grabbed his hands, holding his longing and his loneliness.

CRUCIFIXUS

Paulo

The parish piled into the church, eager to receive the gifts only available in this place. But Paulo was weary and could not wait for this mass to be over. The past few weeks had been full of preparations and practice, the longer days of late spring allowing for many more hours of training. He had been chosen to lead the choir in procession and granted the honour of some solo parts. With this blessing came the burden of intense individual instruction. His performance was said to be for the glory of God. Still, Paulo wondered how much of this effort was actually aimed at impressing the attending agent.

And there he was. When one boy spied him, whispers spread quickly, and soon Paulo was peeking through the curtain, taking turns to see the one they had been instructed to call "Your Excellency". He was obvious from his fineries and the fuss made over him by the choirmaster. For he was not merely here to secure a boy's fame but to judge the worth of those in charge. His Excellency had long, raven hair, falling far past his shoulders and joining his cloak to form one long sable silhouette, broken only by his pure white stockings. His dark, full eyebrows cast a shadow over his otherwise pale face, and his clean hands held a felt hat adorned with a single hawk feather.

His Excellency was guided to a prominent position, a privileged pew reserved only for those deserving of the greatest respect. It was beside an open window, providing the pleasure of a breeze on this balmy day and some respite from the odours of the ordinary. He sat and stared up at the stained-glass replica of Christ on the cross, its warm, coloured lights contrasting against the cool, stolid stone walls.

The boys were called to dress, delayed as long as possible to prevent such sacred clothes from being sullied. Paulo put on the red cassock, covering his common clothes and the white surplice, understanding the weight of trust placed with a colour so pure. He could not imagine the punishment that would ensue if the vestments were defiled. He placed the red cincture around his waist. Then he watched as the castrato was given a red stole, embroidered with a blazing yellow tongue of fire. Paulo had never spoken to Vincenzo, nor was it allowed. Mother had said it was because their voice was sacred and should not be spent in idle chatter. Francesca had shared her view that it was, instead, secrets they were sworn to keep that kept them isolated. All Paulo knew was that the uncertainty made him very uncomfortable.

With the priest's signal, the candles and incense were lit, and lines were formed. Paulo was third, behind the boy waving the thurible and another bearing the banner, the burning flames for the Holy Spirit. Behind him came the choir, the altar boys, then finally the cross, the holy book, the priests and the bishop, almost as if in order of importance. With the gentle clanking of the censer chains, the procession began. As they crossed the threshold, through the majestic wooden doors, Paulo pushed his fear aside and let his song flow along with the smoke, reaching across the pews, purifying the place and the people.

Come Holy Ghost, Creator, come
from your bright heav'nly home,
Come, take possession of our souls
and make them all your own.

From the periphery, Paulo saw his family, far enough back to be shielded from his fear but not from the shame that would be flung if his voice faltered. He was glad to have the choir behind him and their voices join with his for the rest of the journey.

For you are called the Paraclete,
best gift of God above,
The living spring, the living fire,
sweet unction and true love.

And you are sev'nfold in your grace,
finger of God's right hand,
Whose promise teaches little ones
to speak and understand.

Supported and sustained by the other boys, Paulo's mind could wander to his little ones, Maria and Isabella. He imagined how they would want to call out when they saw their big brother, and the tussle Francesca would have to keep them placated. Antonio would be sombrely following his mother's lead, and Luca would be surveying the crowd, eager to find a supporter for his studies.

O guide our minds with your blest light,

with love our hearts inflame,
And with your strength, which ne'er decays,
confirm our mortal frame.

Far from us drive our deadly foe;
true peace unto us bring;
And through all perils lead us safe
beneath your sacred wing.

Paulo thought about the solace this song and this service would give his mother. He pictured her closing her eyes, just as she did by the fire, his invocations providing inspiration, his voice enclosing her in a sense of calm. Here, she could again be a daughter finding support and guidance from something greater than herself. Here, she could find respite from responsibility and be held by the hymns from heaven.

Through you may we the Father know,
through you the eternal Son,
And you the Spirit of them both,
thrice-blessed Three in One.

Now to the Father and the Son,
Who rose from death, be glory given,
with Thou, O Holy Comforter,
henceforth by all in earth and heaven.
Amen.

And so it was that the choir, with the boys at the front, the men and the castrato at the back, took their positions to await their next calling. As he stood, Paulo was struck by the memory of how he had missed his chance to take control of his own fortunes. Last night, squashed against the wall while Luca slept with his legs out wide, Paulo thought about how easy it would be to bring it all to an end. He could feign laryngitis or fiddle his voice so everyone would think it was breaking. He could pretend there was pain, so much pain and in whispers plead for forgiveness. The sudden onset of sickness may be deemed yet another sign of the devil's work, but even this, he was willing to risk. He had fallen asleep with a plan in place, then was awoken by his mother in anticipation.

Pentecost was one of her favourite feasts, and she would ensure Paulo was there early to do his part. He saw the shine on her face as she served him warm broth and bread and felt her excited energy as she combed his hair and checked for lice. He could pretend to be in pain, but the result would be real for his mother. There was no doubt he would lose her respect and break her heart just a little bit more. Paulo would not be responsible for further injury. So now he stood in front of the congregation and was on display for those who would decide what he would become.

Paulo listened to the scriptures and heard of the turmoil that came with the Holy Spirit's arrival. He watched the bishop and the solemnity that never left him. Every movement, every word was done with control, with command, following the script served by God. The air had become heavy, and Paulo's vision began to blur. He sought out any little wisp of breeze to help him stay alert. He could not faint. Not today. Paulo thought about Lorenzo, an image that never left him but became hidden behind other concerns.

Sometimes, he pulled it out of its hiding place to remind himself of the punishment that would ensue if he were to fail. He would replay it in his mind, relive it, and this would make it easier to move forward. The reading delivered by the bishop though delivered a very different promise.

> *Therefore my heart is glad and my tongue rejoices;*
> *my body also will rest in hope,*
> *because you will not abandon me to the realm of the dead,*
> *you will not let your holy one see decay.*
> *You have made known to me the paths of life;*
> *you will fill me with joy in your presence.*

With these words came a flow of fresh air, and Paulo felt that he could finally breathe.

> *The promise is for you, for whom the Lord our God will call.*

And as this sentence was said, Paulo's heart shifted. He was no longer being chosen but called. He was being shown the way by the apostles. They too were afraid and yet accepted the gifts God had generously given them. Instead of allowing fear to hold them back, they heroically stepped out into the world to honour and help. He would do the same.

The priest extinguished the Pascal Candle. The light without was now invested within, and with the rising of the smoke came the responsibility for all to shed their earthly concerns and heed the guidance of the Holy Spirit. Paulo noticed, though, that the dowsing of the flame did little to dent the brilliance of the day. There was no difference between the declared extraordinary season and what came after its end – all he could behold still seemed as bright.

Through the glory endowed on the bishop and in front of bowed heads, the bread and wine were transformed into the body and blood of Christ, his sacrifice an example of what was expected from his people. The magnitude of the moment was captured by the choir, sending forth an ascension in song.

Veni Sancte Spiritus
Veni Sancte Spiritus
Veni Sancte Spiritus
Veni Sancte Spiritus
Veni Sancte Spiritus
Veni Sancte Spiritus
Veni Sancte Spiritus

With each successive chant, the cruelty of the crucifixion was cast away and replaced with a sense of elation. As each person arose from kneeling to share in the spoils of Christ's offering, Vincenzo sang.

Suddenly there came a sound from heaven,
as of a mighty wind coming where they were sitting,
alleluia;
and they were all filled with the Holy Spirit,
speaking the wonderful works of God,
alleluia, alleluia.

But this was not the sound of a mighty wind. It was the voice of man, transformed and trained to take its place. Paulo could see how much this proxy was appreciated. As his mother approached, he could see her elevated, the load lighter and her hands held out in hope. Here, she was close to heaven.

With the closing of the mass, the procession took form once again. Paulo at the lead, Vincenzo at the back. Their hymn was a reminder to themselves, and all those listening, of the task assigned to them by Christ.

I will sing to the Lord as long as I live,
I will praise my God while my breath remains.

The bells rang, the bishop dismissed the parade, and Paulo could now feel free. The boys returned to the sacristy, relieved that now there would be no retribution if their vestments rustled.

Rosa

The messenger made his way to Rosa through the close crowd and chatter of the congregation. No bow was given or apology made for the interruption; it was simply a summonsing. Rosa's presence was requested in the parlour promptly, and the messenger would escort her. There was nothing more Rosa knew but much she suspected. It had not taken long for eager eyes to spot a newcomer and for conversations to be filled with suppositions. These were being shared with those closest to her when she was called.

While Rosa tried to concentrate on the conversation, the words being spoken by others were wafting around her, not sinking through the shelter she had crawled into during the mass. She was still held by the hymns, letting their touch linger, and their legacy live just a little longer. She was holding tight to the echoes of organ and song, and the sense of expansiveness they created within. But this space had now been encroached upon, and for what she knew would be a serious reason. It could be one of several. Perhaps the fathers had found a suitable match for Antonio or Francesca or even both her eldest children. This had been a point of discussion during visits and anticipated to be advanced sometime soon. Or it could be further accusations about the nature of her husband's death, decisions made that may damn them. Or was it a way forward for Luca in his studies or Paulo in his music.

These Fathers' decisions touched all their lives, and this knowing made this meeting even more menacing.

Rosa's concern was reflected on Francesca's face as she took Isabella from her mother's arms. There were no words exchanged, only glances of worry. Antonio had noticed too, the band of boys with which he stood being insufficient to shield him from the sight of his mother being summonsed. Their bravado buoyed his superficial bravery, but beneath, his heart was full of fear. Luca was oblivious to all but the bugs his friends had found and for which they were now preparing a painful death through dissection.

But Rosa refused to rush. Her steps were steady. She would take her fate with the fortitude shown by her beloved mothers and show her children the dignity of duty. She strode behind the messenger, her mind determined not to be carried into his drama and instead inhabited by repeated prayers. Her chants only ceased when she passed Paulo, cleaning the pews. The long look they shared hid how much they both were scared for what was yet to come. Rosa's genuflection at the altar was genuine and graceful and final few steps, gentle.

The parlour was a place of light and full of fabrics Rosa had never yet felt. The rich reds and pure whites were of a world far away from hers. It smelt of warmth, beeswax and sweet wine. Wonderment was swiftly replaced with wariness. Rosa recognised the grave risk that these representatives would pose if they interpreted God's will wrongly.

Waiting for her in velvet chairs were four proclaimed footsoldiers. Three she knew; the bishop, the parish priest and the choirmaster. The stranger was introduced to her as the esteemed talent agent Niccolo Conti. At the completion of his name, Rosa curtsied, her heart sinking at the same time.

Rosa was asked to sit in a simple cotton chair, but its cushion could not remove Rosa's discomfort. How could she be at ease, dressed so simply in a place adorned with so much beauty. Her clothes had been washed well; this was always assured before mass, yet they could never be clean enough for this environment.

No food or drink was shared, the only offering being Conti's proposal. His voice was crisp, clean, round, and rolling, showing his expertise in elocution and extensive education. The high scale of his speech was contrasted by his short stature, bolstered by his heel-blocked shoes.

"Mrs Contadino. I have had the pleasure today of hearing your son, Paulo, sing. Now, I am honoured to declare that your son has significant potential. With dedicated training, Mrs Contadino, he may become the next bright star and share his gift across the country for the glory of God. And so, I am here to present to you, a proposal.

Tomorrow, I leave and I wish to take Paulo with me to the music college in the city. At the college he will receive the Sacrament of Confirmation and declare his willingness to sacrifice his body and his voice to God. He will become a castrato, Mrs Contadino, and I believe a great one.

I will pay for all food, lodging and tutelage, which will span at least ten years. As you can imagine, the cost to me will be considerable, but this is how much I believe in your son. In return I ask only for half of his wages when he is hired. I have already been seeking out placements in the Vatican, and within private opera houses, and the opportunities are vast."

Conti smiled; an expression never seen on the faces of the Fathers beside him.

"There is no need to fear, Mrs Contadino, for Paulo will be well cared for. The college is endowed with a great many resources, and he will be surrounded by boys just like him. He will be where he belongs and be blessed for his contribution to our Mother Church.

You will also be blessed, Mrs Contadino, for I understand your situation and how hard it will be to lose another pair of hands. However, I will compensate you with sufficient funds to hire labour for at least another season.

I will pass by your farm around midday tomorrow, and if you assent, I will take Paulo immediately. Time is of the essence, Mrs Contadino, for we cannot risk his voice breaking and his future being ruined."

Rosa sat in stillness and silence, for no question had been asked. Instead, the bishop intervened.

"Mrs Contadino, I have given the Signore Conti permission to proceed, as I believe Paulo has received God's gift of song. He has received the Holy Spirit today and now we need you to ready him for this great responsibility. Under Canon Law he cannot be released to the Signore and to the Church unless he declares it is his desire. Do you understand, Mrs Contadino?"

Rosa nodded her comprehension, hoping it was not held to be her final decision. She knew one required soon enough, but with her husband's death, in the haze of pain and grief, she had lost track of time. Now, she would need to make one in less than a day. The bishop seemed to have his own time pressures, standing and forcing Rosa to do the same.

"Good, Mrs Contadino, very good. Then Signore Conti will see you at midday tomorrow, with the contract at the ready. You are dismissed. Go with the grace of God."

Rosa curtsied again, knowing that this meeting was now at its conclusion. There was nothing more to be said, not here anyway. Much would need to be explained to Paulo and Antonio, and as Rosa returned to her place in the crowd, she prayed for divine guidance for the words that would come. As she rejoined her friends and family, no one asked what the meeting was about. Her dour demeanour did its job of creating distance from other's curiosity and explained her immediate departure. No doubt there would be tongues wagging when she left, but her only concern was to return home where she could be with her own thoughts. She picked up Isabella who was happy pulling at the grass with her plump little fingers. Holding her close was a comfort, and her continuous wriggling was a welcome distraction.

Rosa said her goodbyes, told Francesca to follow with Maria and Antonio and instructed Luca to wait for Paulo. This would give her time to prepare. Then she walked home, humming cautiously the whole way.

CRUCIFIXUS

Antonio

Antonio was angry. He should have been walking with his mother, being briefed about the meeting and consulted on the outcome. He should have been beside her, just as his father always was, to protect her and provide answers. Instead, he was forced to be with the girls, Francesca and Maria, being treated like a boy. He cursed his mother for not bringing the carriage and her claim that on Sundays, even the donkey deserved a rest. It would be required for hard labour during the week, and they could not risk injury for their indolence.

There was very little conversation on the journey homeward. Francesca was too busy consoling Maria, crying because she was tired but unable to sleep being carried. He would have preferred to walk alone to avoid this annoyance, but he would not do anything to stir his mother further. Antonio saw as his mother turned away that she was close to breaking. It was the same rigid stance she took before she was confined to bed on a monthly basis, bracing herself for what would be.

In a moment of relative calm, he asked Francesca to share her guess as to what was going on. But she would not. Francesca did not want to speak of any scenarios lest, through the magic of words and the mischief of maleficent spirits, they became real. So instead, they trod in silence, both carrying the weight of their worries and Francesca, the weight of a wriggling, whingeing child.

They made it home by midafternoon. Antonio had anticipated relief away from the sun, but the house was hellish from a roaring fire and his mother's frustration. He dared to ask what had occurred but was met with a simple statement – they would be told after supper. Until then, there was work to do. She turned and tended to the stew, steam rising and sweat dripping from her face. Then she headed to the door, going to salt the cheeses and tend to the garden, and giving instructions on her way. Maria would join Isabella for a nap. Francesca was to make the most of the heat and wash bed linens and babies' nappies. Antonio would secure the livestock and ensure the equipment was in order for the following day.

Antonio did his chores but with a seething anger. Why could he not be included in whatever was going on? Mama would just keep to herself, just demand and decree. But what about his role? She was now without a husband. He was the oldest male. He could make decisions, too. All Antonio knew was that it would be different if his father was here.

Antonio was up in the top paddock when he saw Paulo and Luca arrive, lumbering along silently, listlessly. The lack of Mama's greeting from the garden confirmed that whatever was yet to come would be horrible. A union would have normally come with a sense of relief that the boys had made it home safely, and there would be much praise for Paulo's performance. Today, there was not even acknowledgement of their arrival. Mama would have been moved if Luca had been granted a position for further study, but her focus on the weeds told him it was something far more morbid.

Work continued in their own separate spaces until the sun was headed towards the horizon. The coming together was tainted was troubles; nerves only allayed through attention to the little girls. Congeniality and conversation were directed to the babies, at least breaking the silence and allowing all to believe they could avoid the inevitable. There was love for these children, but at that moment, they had become scapegoats for all that was as yet unsaid. No one wanted to speak to anyone else out of fear of exposing the other's emotions.

The meal was shared, and words were swallowed with the stew and freshly baked bread. On any normal Sunday, Antonio would have basked in the stories and gossip gleaned in the after-mass conference. Mother decried idle chatter, but she seemed to allow it on Sundays, even offering some of her own. She was more gracious after the glory of the mass and more relaxed with a focus on the menial tasks that came with this relative day of rest.

This day, though, her steely face foreswore such folly. Antonio was pulled between eating slowly, to suspend himself in this safe space and time, or going at it greedily to get this over with. Mama had chosen the former, and so it felt like forever before she took Francesca to clean and pack away the plates. When the area was once again presentable, she called Paulo into his room.

Whatever was said was in whispers, and it took until darkness knocked at the door to work through. This time, Luca did not absent himself after supper to go look at the stars. It was an act of solidarity for the others' anxiety, and for once, his presence did not result in annoyance. Francesca put Maria and Isabella to bed and then came to sit beside Antonio. All of them just watched the fire, finding their own meaning within it.

When Mother and Paulo came out, Antonio could tell they had both been crying. Their eyes were red and swollen, and clean tracks ran through their dusty cheeks. With this sight, Antonio could feel his anger scratching at the bonds of its abeyance.

Mother sat in her chair, Paulo at her feet. Her exhausted emotion made her voice low and steady, and she spoke straight to the flames. Antonio heard the announcement that tomorrow at midday, Paulo would be leaving with the agent to attend music college and join the choir of angels as a castrato. He witnessed her calmly outlining her reasons. This was her son's chance to rise above his station and to give glory to God. He would be assured food, lodging and a good education, far more than she could offer. He would be a blessing to our family. And with each word, Antonio's agitation grew and the boundaries that held his chaos crumbled. Then Mother asked Paulo to speak. And he did, strongly, sturdier than Antonio had ever heard before. Here was the voice of a man in the making, and it was about to be taken away.

Over the top of Antonio's torment, Paulo testified to the honour he felt to be called and that he would do whatever was required to serve the Lord and his family. Paulo declared that it was his choice to become a castrato.

Francesca began to cry and went to cuddle Paulo. Luca looked down at the floor, seemingly now contemplating the gravity of his own desired fate. Antonio's walls crashed, commencing his frenzy. He could not hold his heartache in any longer and leapt to his feet. Flinging his hands into hard arcs, Antonio told his Mama plainly, roaring with rage, that no, Paulo would not become a castrato. That he, Antonio, forbade it. That no brother of his would be made into such a monster. No. Paulo would stay, sing in the choir, marry, and be a man, just as he and Luca must be.

Rosa waited for the words to cease and then simply told her son to sit. The decision had been made. There was no need for a show. These words did not settle Antonio. They only made his seething arise even more acrid and spew forth in sinister form. He heard what came next from his own mouth, but even for him, it was a surprise. When he called his mother stupid and told her to know her place, it was like he was possessed. When he cited the scriptures saying no woman shall have authority over a man, it was like he had gone mad. And when he spat that she was to keep silent, he felt like he had just met Satan. The energy that came with this outburst was all-embracing. Excited with this fervour, he stated that he was the man of the house and he would not allow it.

Antonio could see that he had struck a chord, watching his mother's eyes go from calm to cruel. His questioning had shaken her resolve, and it was not appreciated. She answered factually, but with contempt, reminding Antonio that he had not yet been confirmed and so was not yet a man, but still a boy. And there was bitterness behind the observation that Paulo would become a man before him and make the ultimate manly sacrifice, a triumph greater than the spouting of scriptures would ever be.

Antonio could not win this battle with his mother, so he turned to Paulo and pleaded with him to not give his permission. He goaded Paulo with guilt, saying that the family needed him here to help. He tested Paulo with the possibility that Mother may change her mind in the future; women are fickle, but by then, it would be too late. Begging soon turned to insisting. Antonio ordered Paulo to listen and heed his command not to go on the morrow.

Still firmly planted at the foot of his mother, Paulo repeated that becoming a castrato was his wish.

And then Antonio had no choice. Threatening and taunting had not worked. Now, he must rely on his physical power. He drove forward towards Paulo, hands hard, pummelling over the ears and explaining that this was done to knock some sense into his brother's silly head. Slaps came with shouts from both sides to stop it. Demands for denials were met with angry assertions until Paulo, too, was pushed too far. The younger boy arose and bore down upon his brother with the force of Atlas. Antonio was unprepared and fell back onto the floor, fanning the flames and sending cinders flying. But Paulo was not satisfied with this prostration. Hopping atop him, Paulo punched frantically, Antonio having to defend his face. Until, after some consideration of the right cause of action, Luca placed himself in the middle and pulled the boys apart.

Antonio growled, not just from pain but from the lost chance. Seconds before, he had reconciled himself with causing injury to Paulo to spare him from this frightful fate. He was about to choke Paulo, to crush his throat and make him unsuitable for singing. Antonio had no second thoughts;

he would have happily carried the burden of caring for the injured brother if it meant Paulo did not have to leave. But his ploy had come seconds too late to be considered self-defence. Instead, now, it would be judged a sin and more shame cast. Now, all he could do was to exact revenge. Antonio would have the final word, which he did, saying that such a monster would never be welcome into his home and that Paulo's choice had severed the connection between the brothers.

Amidst Antonio's despair, Rosa called Paulo away to pack. Francesca went to bed, leaving Antonio and Luca alone. They could hear their elder sister's sobbing and then sweet, innocent questions coming from a child.

CRUCIFIXUS

Paulo

Paulo gathered the clothes suitable to be seen in public. At the same time, his mother inspected the outfit he had worn to mass that day, determining if work needed to be done on it before its next display. Paulo's ears were still burning from Antonio's attack, but so was his heart. Paulo didn't want to hurt his brother, but there was no other way. Antonio would not listen. Paulo had to show Antonio he was serious but hitting him with such ill will was a surprise. As Paulo piled his few decent belongings, he stood in the shadow of a stranger. He had just met a part of himself that he had never before known. This outsider supported his mother when she had belittled her brother. It had given a rousing ovation when Paulo had landed punches. The presence of this stranger scared Paulo more than the one he would meet the next day. For this one he could not run from.

As his mother removed the belongings from his room, she ordered Paulo to bed. It would be a big day tomorrow, and he must be at his best. And so, he settled in for his final night at home. The cat had crept in through a crack in the door, and Paulo felt its cautious paws prodding and then climbing over his body to cuddle into his chest. He thought he had no more tears left, but the closeness of this creature and the knowledge that tomorrow, this would be taken away, created a whole new well of despair to draw from. He stroked its soft fur and put his head close to hear the purring, gratefully extracting some of her peace.

Antonio came in and landed heavily in his own bed, anger and embarrassment embedded into his actions. The red hot rage was still evident, even in the dark. Luca came and nestled in behind. Once he would push Paulo to make space, he now pulled his brother toward him, holding him and hearing him breathe. Luca's silence spoke so loudly, and his generous presence was a parting gift. When Luca began snoring and finally rolled over, Paulo was released. He kissed the cat and snuck past Antonio, not caring if he was awake. His big brother could provide no greater punishment than that which the dawn would deliver.

Paulo found his way through the dark to Francesca and felt her hand reach out for him. She told him to come and he snuggled in behind Maria, enclosing his little sister in the embrace. Francesca felt his face, wiped the tears with her warm hands and stroked his hair. She had no words, not even ones to convey in whispers. Maria wriggled but was settled by her sister and then wrapped within her brother's arms. In this moment there was so much meaning and so much love it was becoming unbearable. Within the adoration was anguish, and within this place of safety, he finally became scared. How could he live without the smiles of his sisters? He would soon find out.

With the first few clicks of the blackbird, Paulo let go of Francesca's hand and hurried back to his bedroom. The cat had gone, leaving just enough space for him to scrunch between the wall and Luca's wide legs. And here he waited until the beautiful song of the birds was replaced by the breakfast bell. Only one other morning had been so awkward. That was the day after his father's death, when the news was still raw, and all were still reconciling with the hole created in their home. Today was so similar, only thoughts were centred on the chasm yet to come.

Breakfast was taken in silence, save for the continuous chatter of Isabella and the instructions from Maria who had taken on matronly duties on this day. She was the one scolding her little sister for flinging bread to the floor and assisting her to spoon the sloppy porridge into her mouth without making too much mess. Even Maria knew today that the strings of this family were pulled tight and that it would not take much for them to snap. She would help ease the situation, just like she had seen Francesca do many times before. Paulo watched Maria doting on Isabella, and Francesca offering the barley water and wondered who would be there to help him in his future.

As plates were cleared, Paulo felt the stranger creeping and knew he would have to apologise to keep it at bay. He asked to join Antonio on his rounds of the fences and flocks, also providing the chance to say his final goodbyes. Antonio did not even look at him to reply, his answer almost automatic. Paulo's request was denied; it was not his place.

His mother also intervened. Paulo needed to be prepared for his journey, and they could not risk any wounds. He would remain here at home in the relative safety of these walls. And so, he sat, just outside the door, with Nero and waved off Maria and Luca as they headed to school. This came after much crying from Maria and a long cuddle in which she moaned how much she would miss him. Francesca had to come and settle her, and Mother came to shoo her away. Otherwise, they would be late. Luca gave him a look, a legacy from his father, one that said I understand, I am sorry, and I love you, all in one. Paulo stayed outside, using Nero to shield his sobbing as he watched them wander into the distance. Paulo saw Maria's twisting, turning and erratic inquisitions and Luca's response; a simple stoic posture.

Paulo thought about pursuing Antonio. As his eldest brother strode past him and towards the fields, it would not have taken much time to catch up. He could declare his sadness for the previous night's events and ask for forgiveness. He could leave a little lighter and pass back some of Antonio's rightful authority. But Antonio would not even acknowledge him now. The bridge appeared to have been burnt by both of their anger and now he was just a nuisance. No, Paulo would stay in his place, the one his mother had set for him. This would not stop him from praying, though, that one day, he may have the chance to atone.

With Antonio gone, Paulo went back inside to find Isabella. He played a game of peek-a-boo, presenting a smile that he did not think would be possible today. He passed her things so that she could throw them back at him, which made her very happy, especially when she hit him. Then he would pretend to be hurt, and she would chuckle, and he would wish he could capture the child's laughter and hold it close. It was more precious than anything else he had ever known.

When Mother and Francesca had finished their morning duties, Francesca came to fetch him. Before Paulo could rise, she sat beside him and held his hand. She was his strength. What would be without her? They waited together as long as possible until their mother's cranky call ceased their connection. Then, his mother ordered Paulo to sit upon a stool, and she shaved his head. She did not want to send him onward with a risk of lice, and so this was the only way to be sure he would not be shamed. Paulo could feel the razor scratch his scalp and winced when it went deeper, leaving a red line or tiny cut. She called Francesca to cover his head with a balm, which stung where the razor had sliced. Francesca applied the salve with the assurance that it would kill any remaining eggs and heal his wounds.

The next instruction was to Francesca, to fetch the hot water from the fire and to fill his bath. She did so, placing some lavender within it, both for the benefit of the bather, his mother and the man who would accompany him on the journey. And then she was told to leave, for seeing her brother naked was not proper. Paulo's mother scrubbed him with tallow soap until his skin was scarlet, then rubbed away any traces of his current reality. While still draped in a towel, he was fed early, and his teeth were cleaned with a cloth and salt. When he was dressed, Francesca brought him mint leaves to chew on and a pouch of crushed rosemary and sage to wear around his neck. Only then had the preparations been concluded.

In the space between the cessation and the scout's coming, Paulo was told to stay at the table and read the Bible. When Nero heralded the arrival of a horse, Mother made him expel his bladder before joining them at the door. Which he did, holding back any nerves that would have harmed his sister and his mother. He stepped outside and waited beside Francesca as his mother made her way up to the dark horse and the man seemingly dressed to blend with it. Paulo wanted to take Francesca's hand but knew it would not be helpful. Instead, he leant towards her, and she leant back, both steading each other, an offer of support, a beautiful brace.

The man dismounted with dignity, donned his hat and stood silently to receive Rosa's curtsey.

"Mrs Contadino. I see that Paulo has been prepared. He has made the right decision and will bring much honour to your family. First, let me inspect him."

Paulo was waved forward by his mother and met with cold hands opening his mouth, checking his spine, looking at his hands and listening to him sing. When he was confirmed to be in good working order, the man retrieved a rolled paper from his saddlebag. He did not bother to ask Rosa if she would read. He pointed and explained each paragraph, each term, just as he had relayed to her the previous day. She was asked to hold it as he prepared the quill and ink and then she was shown where to provide her mark. Mother made the sign of the cross on herself and then one on the contract.

"Very good Mrs Contadino. Please bring me his things and we will depart promptly."

After the paper was aired and returned to the satchel, Signore Conti turned to Paulo, looking triumphant.

"Congratulations Paulo. I already know you will make a great castrato, and bring glory to God and me the man who has heard his call. It will take us two days travel to arrive at the college. Until then, you will have plenty of time to practice and strengthen your voice."

Paulo's mother returned with a small bundle wrapped in cloth and tied with twine. The man attached it to the straps on one side and then alighted onto his animal. He told Paulo to put his foot into the stirrup and grasp his arm. With that, he pulled Paulo up behind him.

"I wish you and your family well Mrs Contadino. We will keep you in our prayers."

The rider gave the horse a nudge, turned it toward the gate and kicked it into a trot. As they worked their way down towards the road, Paulo saw Antonio up in the far field. No arm was raised in recognition or respect. Their separation was now certain.

Part way along, Paulo could already feel the bouncing causing bruising. The man stopped and passed him three straps. One would be wrapped around his chest and secured around Conti's own. The other two would join their thighs. Paulo was told to wiggle close behind, and the bonds were applied. This would reduce the movement and risk that Paulo would slip off if he fell asleep. With the human haul held tight, the finder was free to go faster. And with his mother's cross on the contract, he could command Paulo to entertain him along this expedition.

CRUCIFIXUS

College Officials

The College Committee, clergy and laymen alike gathered in a great room. They were here to do their regular review and make decisions and demands to deliver success. The Chairman ceased the idle conversation and commenced proceedings with a prayer. With bowed heads, their plea was delivered.

"Heavenly Father, who art the source of all wisdom and harmony, we gather here today, united in our purpose to nurture the gifts you have bestowed upon these young souls. Grant us, we beseech Thee, the clarity and wisdom to guide them rightly, that they might sing not only with their voices but with their spirits attuned to Thy divine will, and work hard to progress your purpose here on Earth.

Bless, O Lord, this assembly of minds and hearts. Enlighten our deliberations with Thy grace so our endeavours glorify your perfect goodness.

In Your holy name, we pray,

Amen."

At the conclusion was a chorus of Amen, and crosses were signed over the chests of each person seated. Silence allowed the words to sink in, and papers were prepared.

"Let us begin. Maestro di Capella, please present your progress."

The maestro stood gracefully, with the posture of a prince, and his voice was attuned to the audience.

"Thank you, Monsignore. I am pleased to announce that over the month past, and across all of our colleges, we have welcomed in one hundred and ninety-two boys. We have aided each one to give their generous sacrifice to God. Of this cohort, one hundred and eighty-three have commenced the castrati training.

Our graduates, those completing the ten-year program, number fifty-two, an outcome I look forward to increasing in Our Lord's name. All but ten have received paid postings within St Peter's, across the parishes, in the opera or patron's homes.

While some of those unplaced have conditions that make them more of a burden than a benefit, the number of those who are not of a satisfactory standard to receive a stipend is a personal shame.

My brothers, every boy unable to make it to a paid position I see as a failure. And for these, I ask for your forgiveness."

The maestro bowed his head in anticipation of a backlash. But the Chairman's voice rose above the murmurs.

"Maestro. We all appreciate your apology but are also aware that some are given to us simply for the sake of the finder's fee and not for the love of the boy, the Church or God. Secretary, I ask that you prepare a schedule of those boys who fail the program and, beside their name, that of the person who brought the boy to us. At the next meeting, we will see if there is systematic abuse and whether penalties may be warranted.

Is there any more you wish to discuss, Maestro?"

"Thank you, Your Lordship. Yes. I want to assure you that I am introducing a more stringent training regime to remove any recalcitrance and push the boys to their fullest potential. Their days will be extended by two hours to allow additional attention to scales and solfège, firming their foundations. I have also employed five more teachers to ensure that the instruction is fresh and that the boys do not become lazy.

Finally, Father, I must mention the changes we have made to the social regime of the castrati. Last week, we had another castrato brutalised by a senior student from the standard music school. We are unsure who was at fault, but the castrato was badly injured. It is as yet uncertain whether the castrato will make a sufficient recovery to be able to sing. This continued conflict puts the children in danger and threatens the great investment we have made. Therefore, I have now separated the meal and free-time schedules so that these two groups do not interact. I believe this should address the problem and provide due protection."

"Yes, Maestro, that is wise. While many understand the great gift these men give, others are overtaken by worldly concerns. We should ensure that they are only ever exposed to those who will appreciate them.

Consigliere, is there anything you wish to advise or ask of the committee?"

"Monsignore, my greatest thanks. Yes, My Lord. I am honoured to announce that all college contracts now contain the explicit clause that any compositions done within its walls are held within our ownership and our privilege to publish. This will reduce the risk of any further frightful incidents where patrons make profit from what was produced by the castrato while a student at the college."

The Chairman gave a deep nod and then asked.

"That is well and good. But how will such a practice be policed? How will we be sure that no great works escape?"

"My Lord, I have advised the maestro that no castrato is to leave the college with any works. Each one, on exit, will be searched and any sheets of music confiscated. And where a work is published by a Patron soon after acquisition of one of our students, proper investigations will be made to ensure it was not constructed at the college. If so, a claim will be made."

"Well done, Consigliere. We deserve to be compensated fairly for the intensive tuition that we provide.

Now, what of the episode with the mother that occurred last month?"

"Yes, My Lord, that was dramatic. For your information, brothers, we had a mother approach the college, calling for her son. She was refused entry, after which she became crazed. She kept shrieking her son's name and demanding that she see him. She calmed somewhat when a member of our clergy approached her and began to converse. However, when he advised that the contract she signed prevented parental contact, the chaos continued. It was as if she was possessed, scraping her head against the stone wall until it was shredded and bloody, and then beginning the same brutality on her hands. We sent for the police and she was promptly restrained and removed. The most recent update is that she was institutionalised, so we have no further cause for concern."

"Was the boy inside, and did he observe the commotion?"

"No, My Lord. He was one who was too weak to survive the surgery."

"I see. Well, at least the boy was spared such a display of disgusting self-indulgence.

Dottore, any news from you?"

The dottore stood slowly, his ageing body seeming to provide him with pain. Yet his bow was low and lengthy.

"Monsignore. There is not much to tell from our team. We continue to quarantine any child who displays signs of consumption. Thank the Lord there have been none last month whose symptoms have progressed. One outbreak of scabies has been suppressed, with some children still in isolation while their symptoms subside. We have had the cleaners hotwash all bedding and clothes and scrub all of the boys' skin. The proportion of deaths post-surgery has remained consistent, suggesting that we have reached the threshold of improvements at this time. However, we are undertaking further research to speed recovery so that the boys can more swiftly resume their training.

That is all, Monsignore."

"Thank you Dottore, and may God guide your hands and those of your helpers. Now, Bursar, is there anything we should be aware of?"

The Bursar had made it up before the Dottore had descended even halfway, his haste arising from his apprehension, intimidated by those in whose presence he stood. His voice started shakily.

"My Lord. All is well with our finances. Thanks to the popularity of the castrati, patrons are plentiful. And due to their relative scarcity the profit is substantial. We even receive generous payments from church postings, thanks to the support of the Pope. We are in a comfortable position to pay for the extra tutors the maestro has employed.

I would add my support to My Lord's concern, though, around the finder's fee. I, too, am worried that it may be leading to some abuse of the arrangement. I am working with the Consigliere to determine if lessening the upfront fee but increasing the payment on posting may be of benefit. We do not want to continue lining the pockets of those who are not working in the Lord's best interests."

"Yes, I agree Bursar. Well, done. Continue."

"Thank you, My Lord. Well, My Lord, while we are in a sound financial position at this time, I do worry with the growth of the program our profits will be reduced. With more castrati graduating from the college, they become less special. Therefore, the price we will be able to ask for placement is sure to dwindle over time. Also, adding boys to the program also means an increase in those who are affected by the castration and who cannot support themselves through service. Moreover, there is also the risk of outbreaks which would decimate our earning ability in the future, but not necessarily our costs."

With this, the Dottore shot the Bursar a wicked glance, a symbol of contempt received by the speaker, who sought to recover quickly.

"My Lord, I am sure that the Dottore has the best systems in place. Nevertheless, I believe it would be prudent to begin reducing costs and create a more substantial buffer for the future. With your permission, and that of my esteemed brothers here, I will work with the maestro to identify where we may begin to make cuts. I suspect that there may be ready sources of reduction, such as in food, clothing and heating."

The Chairman cast his eyes around the room.

"Are there any concerns with the Bursar's recommended approach, brothers?"

There was only silence and shaking heads.

"Then your proposal for cost-cutting is approved. Please provide an update on those areas identified at our next meeting."

"Yes, My Lord."

With that the Bursar sat, his hands moving from his back to his lap, but still showing small bursts of shaking.

"Maestro, before we conclude, please provide a summary of the significant events for this coming month."

With grandiose grace, the maestro stood, and with melodic tones, he told of a new group of boys that would arrive over the coming days, deemed suitable after their performances at Pentecost. This clutch would receive the Sacrament of Confirmation at mass on Sunday, with their castration scheduled for the following day. Somewhere between the Assumption of the Blessed Virgin Mary and the Martyrdom of Saint John the Baptist, these boys would begin their training.

There was clapping and a concluding prayer, and then, with a formal dismissal, each returned to their rooms and their roles.

CRUCIFIXUS

Paulo

Paulo was pleased for the chance to sing; having to concentrate on the words and keep his voice steady on the back of a horse was helpful to distract his heart from the world he had left. And between songs he watched as a new world opened up in front of him. At a steady pace, they slipped from the reaches of Vesuvius. Still, they remained well in sight as they passed through olive groves, vineyards, and watched farmers pulling their yields from fertile soils. They passed many merchants carrying wine, cloth and crops, ensuring that the journey was far from dull. Sometimes, they would see groups of pilgrims plodding along, praying as they walked, guided by a monk, on their way to some miraculous monastery. Carriages of the wealthy would require them to move and make way for those more worthy, their servants seeing to their security.

And then there were the poor: the full families on the move to find work, dressed in rags and covered in dirt, with few possessions packed in their cart and children who could not smile. Paulo found the homeless who lined the village entrances confronting. Some cried for assistance, others too weak to use any words. They would beg for bread, wine, whatever people were willing to give. Their empty bowls declared that generosity was in short supply.

Signore Conti assured Paulo that the road was far too busy for bandits, but this did not stop him from looking closely as they passed protective trees. Crossing mountain paths, Paulo got to view the sea, which, until now, he had never even had cause to imagine. He eyed its expanse and decided he felt safer at a distance, although a cool bath would have been a beautiful respite from the relentless heat. Through the shrubland the breeze brought them perfume offerings of rosemary and thyme to lift their spirits.

Paulo was startled when the Signore Conti slapped his legs to alert him that they were stopping. He must have fallen asleep and was angry at himself lest the man thought the worse of him for not being able to stay awake. Straps were untied, and the boy and man dismounted. The horse was held tight as he wandered deeper into the bushes, and the boy followed, relieving himself at a distance from where the man was doing the same. Paulo's legs hurt so much. He could feel the coarse cloth of his pants chafing his soft skin and yet could not complain. They took on water, ate some dried apple and aged cheese, then retied straps and set off again.

This sequence occurred one more time, strapping, singing, sight-seeing, sleeping and slapping and then a short stop before one last stretch. The seeker and his find arrived at an Inn when the sun was well down their backs, and their bellies were empty. Paulo was so glad to get off the horse. Still, he found himself giddy from the continual movement, his companion chuckling to see him stumble and sway. He was relieved to see the man capable of mirth, for his mood had descended from friendly to firm, generous to grumpy over the course of the day, at the end deriding Paulo for any move, making comfort impossible. Paulo was also pleased to be separated from the Signore's body, which began pleasant and perfumed but, over the course of the afternoon, had become tinged with sour sweat.

The stench reminded him of his father when he would come in from the fields in the height of summer, and his disgust was mixed with depression. His father was buried, and his mother was burdened with sickness. His brothers were in conflict, and his sisters were so sad. He reached for a pole to steady his legs, his head, and his heart. After the horse was handed to the attendant, he followed the man into the unfamiliar.

Coins were handed over to the keeper, and they were shown their room; a simple setting of two mattresses, a jug, a bowl and a pot. Conti pissed in the latter and ordered Paulo to wash, change and wait while he tended to the horse. He had never been alone in a place he did not know before, and the anxiety was making his stomach ache. Or it could have been the hunger. Either way, Paulo did not feel well. He removed his shirt and saw where his arms had been burnt during the day. He extracted his pants from the now peeling skin and used the chance to release some sobs to ease the sting. It felt like the back of his legs had been burnt in a fire. He wondered if the scout's fancy fabrics saved him from these same wounds.

But he did not watch when his guardian returned, undressed, washed and changed. His curiosity would have surely granted him a clip over the ears.

"Come boy, it is time to eat."

Paulo was so relieved he almost ran. He made it downstairs close behind the Signore and sat quickly opposite at the table. A chubby and colourful woman bought cups and filled them with diluted wine, which Paulo downed greedily.

"Go gentle, boy. I don't need you becoming drunk."

The woman returned with bowls of stew and bread, and Paulo began eating, but slower this time. The clip came unexpectedly.

"Boy! Are you some kind of brute? We must say grace!"

Paulo placed down his spoon and bowed his head. He would have preferred to bawl, blubber, or both, but he knew better. After the man did some mumbling, Paulo followed him in picking up his spoon and starting to eat. The stew was full of flavour, rich stock and fresh herbs. There was not much meat, and where there was, it was fatty, but it filled Paulo's belly, and for that, he was overflowing with gratitude. He even gave his guardian a smile, which Paulo thought was returned subtly.

The woman returned to fill their cups. She inquired whether Paulo was the man's son, and as she did, Paulo could see some missing and rotten teeth. Paulo knew how it could happen; his own father had two pulled after roaring in pain. His mother had also done her own when an abscess could not be healed. As much as he wanted to, Paulo could not look as she was lancing it, but he would never forget her cries.

"No, this is Paulo Contadino, soon to become one of the best voices in the land. Take stock now for when you hear of him next it will be as a star castrato."

With that, the woman's eyes enlarged, and her face quickly went from a smile to a scowl. She sincerely expressed her sympathy to Paulo but went further, calling Signore Conti a devil and saying she would be in her rights not to serve him. She presented her hopes that he landed in hell.

Hearing this exchange, her husband hurried over and profusely apologised. His wife, it seemed, was not right in the head. He would make sure they were not disturbed again, and to prove his point and his position, he gave her a strong slap. Paulo could see the mark that it had made on her cheek and the hurt in her eyes. She complied with her husband's instructions to return to the kitchen, and the scout kept eating silently.

After they were done, the Signore ordered Paulo to return to the room and to sleep. Paulo did the former, and despite the firmness of the floor being felt through the mattress, he sent his greatest thanks up to Heaven for this place to rest. He could not sleep, though; there were too many sounds, and he was so unsure about when or even if the Signore would return. What if he just changed his mind, left him there, or sold him to the innkeepers? What if he would be taken by bandits or tormented by a drunk patron. Whenever he would hear the creak of the stairs he would stiffen. And then, after two loud lunges, the door opened, and the lamp light from the corridor crept in. Paulo was grabbed by clumsy hands and hauled outside the door. A woman was waiting outside, one that Paulo had not seen before, but he had to look down for her breasts were almost showing, and to see them would be a sin. The Signore shoved him down beside the door and told him in slurred speech to wait while he and the woman went inside.

Paulo looked down at the patrons below, and some looked up at him. From the room came a raucous bellowing, and all Paulo could do was to tuck his knees into his chest, feel the scabs on his chaffing legs crack and rest his head on his arms. Paulo waited for an attack, for plenty of others may take advantage of his abandonment. Instead, all he felt was a gentle tap on his arm. There was the serving woman who had paid for the pity she had shown Paulo. She stood beside Paulo, offering him a cup of warm milk. She assured him she was watching out for him and that, given how much the man had to drink, he would not be long. She went back downstairs, giving him a wave from the last rung and went back to work. And she was right. A few minutes later, the visitor left, mumbling something Paulo could not make out.

"Boy, come."

Paulo left the empty cup in the corridor and went inside, cautiously closing the door.

"Sleep."

And he did, to the sound of the Signore snoring, but only when he was sure the man beside him was no longer a monster.

Paulo was awake well before his roommate but had a hard time rising. The muscles in his legs were stiff, his flanks bruised, and the back of his thighs were crusted scrapes. He had to hold back groans as he hobbled to the pot, pissing quietly into it, and then awkwardly laying again to listen as downstairs started to be filled with sounds of cooking and chatter. It was a long way after sunup before the Signore stirred, groggily and grumpily. Paulo was told to go and get him a tonic, advise the innkeeper that they would be requiring breakfast and that they would need a pack of provisions for a meal on the road. Paulo's departure was delayed by the difficulty of him standing. The shouts of "Now, boy!", could not make him move any faster, but he put on a serious face to show the man that he was trying and shuffled as fast as he could.

Paulo was looking for the innkeeper when his wife signalled to him from the kitchen. He entered to find steaming pots, freshly baked bread and baskets of fruit. He asked for his master's tonic and the woman prepared it for him, mixing together a strong dose of alcohol and some rosemary. Then she handed Paulo something else. A little sachet of lavender held on a string. This was not for Paulo's guardian. As far as she was concerned, the Signore did not deserve any care. This was for Paulo, to protect him and bring him peace. She put it over his head, tucked it into his shirt, gave him a quick kiss on the forehead. Then she told him to go before the Signore's impatience would result in his punishment.

When Paulo returned to their room with a small cup of herbed spirits, the man had washed and was looking much fresher. He sculled the tonic, collected his things, told Paulo to do the same, and then led the way downstairs. It was a brief breakfast, bread, cheese and apples, barley water and wine, with more placed beside them in a package for later. Paulo went to arrange for the horse to be saddled and supplied while the Signore paid. Standing by the stables, Paulo realised that right then, he could run. He could escape. The man was too hung over to make much chase, and now that he had eaten, Paulo could go quite far before he would tire.

He could. He really could just go. Now. He took a step forward to see how it would feel. It felt forceful; it felt free. And then he realised what it would mean for his mother. No doubt the Signore, scorned, would return and claim that Paulo's mother had schemed this whole situation so that she could reap the reward. He would demand the payment back and put mother into a panic. Likely, the Signore would also call the police. Besides, Paulo knew he could never return. That would bring so much shame. Instead of moving any more forward, he stood still. It was not long before the Signore came to stand beside him, and they were once again upon the horse.

Paulo tried to use his hands to create a gap between his legs and the horse's back, to reduce the hurt. And yet, it was still horrible. He could feel the film of protection woven overnight being ripped open again and the wounds starting to seep. It was so excruciating that Paulo was glad when his legs finally went numb. But when they stopped to relieve themselves and take in water, the feeling would return. It was like his legs were on fire. This time the guardian noticed, looking over at Paulo while he pissed.

"Boy! Why didn't you tell me about your legs? The college will not have you if they get infected."

The man, redressed in a huff, told Paulo to keep his pants down and reached into his saddlebag for a tin. He wiped a thick waxy salve all over the wounds and bound them up in Paulo's clean shirts.

"I would piss on them for you, but I don't want you to stink for the rest of the trip. That should help. We should be there by late afternoon anyway."

It did help. The pain was soothed, and the wounds were padded, and Paulo could relax a little. It was still too uncomfortable to sleep, but there were always the demands by the Signore for another song, and the scenery was stunning. Rugged cliffs gave way to pastures, punctured by towns and villages buzzing with a mix of merchants, markets, and military men. Always though, there was a church and a communion of clergy. Trotting through the plains, Paulo would spy the towers and domes at a distance, knowing they would soon meet much more activity.

When they reached the river, they stopped under the shade of a tree, joining other travellers who were waiting to cross. They ate their provisions and asked the others for advice. The fastest way was through the ford. One group knew the way and offered for the Signore and Paulo follow them. When the guides were ready, Paulo and the man packed up the horse and headed on foot in single file behind the leaders. The water was fresh and cool. While wading through, Paulo took the chance to drink from his hands and wash his face. This simple act restored his energy, and as he smelt the two herb patches around his neck, his spirit also seemed to ease.

Soon, though, the going was tough, with mountain passes and rocky terrain making it hard for the horse. The two had to dismount and walk themselves through the heat and over the hard stones. For Paulo, it almost all felt worth it when they arrived at the Hermitage of St Michael the Archangel. The springs surrounding it abounded with clear, crisp water, and the seats inside provided shelter from the sun. It was a respite for their bodies and souls.

To make up for lost time, they fairly flew through the forests until the bush became less dense and before them stood the abbey of Montecassino. Paulo was spellbound. Throughout the trip, he encountered many sensational buildings, but this gigantic one atop a mountain was truly magnificent. He wanted to ask what it was, but the Signore was on a mission. He sped the horse on around the base of the mountain towards the town. At the outskirts, the Signore turned into a large estate and stopped at the metal gates. A man in uniform asked for his identification, and Signore Conti provided it promptly. The gates were opened and they rode through, past a fountain to the front door. Pulling up, the man dismounted first and helped Paulo off. Paulo felt ill again, but he was not sure whether from the wild ride at the end or from the fact that this was the finish line.

Paulo held the horse hard, his heart beating and his breath heavy, while the Signore knocked and spoke with the attendant. A young boy came from behind the door, and the visitors took what they needed from the horse before the boy took it away to the stables.

As they walked through the doors, the Signore said something that gave Paulo chills.

"Boy, this is your home now, well, at least for the next ten years."

They stood in a circular foyer, stark white, spotless and lined with statues and ornate columns. The attendant who let them in, dressed in the finest attire, called another boy to take Paulo's things.

"There will be no need for these here. And we do not wish to spread disease, so these things will be destroyed. We will provide you with fresh clothes after your meeting.

Please, make your way up these stairs and wait where you see the chairs. The Maestro di Capella will see you shortly."

Stairs were difficult for Paulo with his stiff and strapped legs, but he tried to look as normal as possible. There were many to manoeuvre, and the Signore kept glaring back at him,

CRUCIFIXUS

sending sharp looks that told him to hurry up. Paulo was so relieved to make it to the top without making the man mad. But his triumph was short-lived when he saw three bald boys waiting there already, silent, scared.

A bearded guard waited by the gilded office door and signalled for them to sit. They did, opposite the other boys but closer to the door. All Paulo could do was trace the lines on the tiles in his mind and sit on his hands to stop them from shaking. On the third go-around of the geometric design, the door opened, and a man, similar to his own, and a boy only slightly bigger than Paulo walked out. The boy was sat beside the other three, told to do his family proud, and his patron left. And then there were four.

Before he could fully comprehend what was happening, a booming voice called "next", and the doorman pointed to the Signore and Paulo signalling them to come. Walking into that room, Paulo forgot all of his pain. It was truly wonderous. There were stained glass lamps, leather seats, foreign fabrics and a smell of sage. Initially, Paulo was astonished, his awe keeping him stuck. With one push, the maestro shocked him out of this state and into anxiety. Paulo had landed in front of a tall man, dressed magnificently, but as terse as twine. The two men bowed to one another and exchanged pleasantries, although it was clear which one held the power.

Despite the heat, the maestro's hands were cold, and they clutched at Paulo's cheeks. Then they held his chest as he was told to sing. Sing he did, and the maestro seemed suitably satisfied. He called forth a colleague sitting to the side, who, once summonsed, went to the basin and rinsed his hands with vinegar. The fumes flowing from the man's hands were strong as he searched Paulo's ears and mouth and inspected his hands. The smell sent Paulo's heart back to the day he had helped Lorenzo and had his cuts drenched in vinegar. It was not a pleasant memory and made no better by being told to undress. Conti quickly explained the chaffing on his legs, caused by the boy insufficiently being broken into the saddle. Taking off the bandages, the inspector confirmed there was no sign of infection and would be easily treated. Paulo saw his guardian give a sigh of relief. The sour hands continued scouring over every inch of his spine and skin, including his genitals and between his toes. With one nod to the maestro, Paulo was told to dress and sit. He did with head bowed, beginning to trace the tiles on this floor as well.

"Conti, you have done well with this one. He seems to have strong potential. And your others are all progressing through the program and showing great talent. I am sure you have a handsome profit ahead of you."

"Thank you, Your Excellency."

"Here is the contract for you to sign over guardianship to the college, and your finder's fee. At the bottom of the contract, you will see the tuition required to be paid annually if you wish to reclaim rights to this child when he completes his time at the college."

"Thank you, Your Excellency."

The Signore read the terms placed in front of him and signed the bottom of the paper. Placing the quill back into the ink, he used one hand to take the pouch of coins atop the table and the other to pull a similar pouch from his pocket.

"I have the first year's tuition here, Maestro."

"Wonderful Conti. Take this contract and the payment to the secretary and they will record the transaction. That will be all. I wish you a safe journey home."

Both men stood back, and the Signore waved for Paulo to come. Back out at the chairs, another man and boy were waiting alongside the four boys they began with. Signore Conti walked him to the seat beside boy number four and ordered him to sit.

"Boy, I wish you well for your time here. When you are ready, I will take you to sing for the world. So, work hard boy. Work hard for the honour of your family and glory of God."

With that the man who Paulo had only known for two days departed. And then there were five.

Over the next hours, Paulo learnt well every bump, crack and crevice in the wall. He also saw how many lines there were on his hands and how they would split, converge and cross. He remembered Francesca telling him how each line on his palm showed one part of his future. As he traced each one with his finger, he wondered which one had predicted this place. And did the boys beside him have the same marks of fate?

Other pairs of men and boys came. Most ended with another small body sitting silently in the row. Twice, the men left tormented, furious, one dragging the child away, the other walking far too fast for it to follow. What would happen to these rejections? What would happen next for him? All Paulo knew was that he was so hungry, and that then there were twelve.

With the call of "No more," the bearded guard moved to stand in front of the door. And with this conclusion came another commencement. Another man arrived hastily and in a harsh voice announced himself as their dean. They were told to follow, which they did in single file, down the stairs, through the corridor, out the doors, across the courtyard and into a building much less bright. This time, the stairs went downwards, and Paulo did all he could to keep up without wincing. They arrived in a hall lit with lamps and layered with long tables. Told to sit on the stools, they were served with tepid legume gruel and stale bread. Paulo did not care for the taste; of that, there was very little, but its weightiness was welcome within an empty stomach. Some boys, in better clothes than his, showed their disdain, which was met by the strong hand of the dean across their faces. Their preferences were soon forgotten, and they forced the meal down.

Time was not provided for all to finish, for there was more to be done before dark. With stern words and a wave of the dean's arms, they filed to the front, piling their plates and then proceeded down the corridor to the cleaning room; solid ground was replaced by grates. Baths were laced with boiling water. The boys undressed, and their garments gathered into a sack. Some other boys were also adorned with aromatic amulets, but all of these were pulled from their necks and thrown into the pile of potentially disease-ridden clothes. Now, with these gifts gone, Paulo felt truly naked.

Turns were taken to enter the bath, and all were supervised to scrub with tallow soap, even the parts that were bruised and chaffed from the journey. One boy's back was riddled with blue and purple patches, and his thighs showed bruises in the shape of large hands. On others, backs were lined with scarlet strips. However, no one cared, and vinegar was applied to all wounds, with bandages only where necessary. There again, Paulo was sucked into the sacristy, feeling the sting of the slashes that were given to save his own soul. He thought he may be sick and battled to stand, breathing deeply to stop the buzzing in his head. Another boy fell but was promptly pulled up by the dean. Strength was a virtue, and those without it simply needed more practice.

Those who did not have the fortitude to withhold their tears were struck until they understood no such indulgence was permitted. Then, all were provided with stiff gowns and thin socks and shown upstairs to the dormitory. There were two dozen beds, a few already filled with boys wearing the same simple sack. They were too slow in ceasing their chatter, the dean marching in and giving each a clip over the ears.

"Let this be a lesson for all of you newcomers. Talking is forbidden outside of lessons. Your voice belongs to God and it must be saved for the song. You will speak only when spoken to by myself or another tutor. These boys were already aware of the rules, and so will be appropriately punished. There will be no breakfast for you tomorrow. I will see to it. Now, new boys, take a bed and straight to sleep. I will come and wake you tomorrow with your uniform."

The dean blew out all but one of the candles, carrying the remainder with him as he sped out the door, leaving an attendant at the entrance for ongoing observation.

Paulo shuffled his way to a free bed and climbed to the top bunk. The boy with the bruises lay down below. The sheets were scratchy, and now lying in the dark, Paulo wanted to cry. But he did not. He did not feel safe. Even though he was surrounded by boys just like him, he felt alone.

Exhaustion sent him to sleep, but sometime during the night, he was awoken in a breathless panic. He could not remember where he was. He reached out, but there was no cat, no Luca, and no sound of Antonio snoring. He could not hear movement outside. Had he died and arrived in purgatory or hell? Then he heard some boys whispering and the one below him whimpering, with the distinct smell of urine rising. He wanted to help but was worried he would be caught. And he was so very weary, his eyes were weighty, and so he simply shifted position and slept.

Paulo

Paulo was awake well before the first birds, relying on their sight and song to let him know that the sun was on the rise. He rolled over to allow the breeze from the window to cool his face and dry his tears and was glad for the delay between dark and dawn to prepare for the day.

The dean and his attendants arrived as the sky was lightening and lit the lamps to provide what the sun could not. It was a face shadowed in disgust that Paulo saw first as the dean searched for and found the source of the smell. The boy was pulled from his bed, his face rubbed in the wet putrid patch. Then he was shoved into the corridor, the attendants hauling his mattress out after him, ordering him to carry it down to the cleaning room. Paulo could hear taunts as the boy struggled down the stairs carrying this cross made of his own weakness.

The boys on the bottom bunks were ordered to pick up the pots and begin the parade. Soon, the rest of the boys were also on their way. Those deemed too slow to join the line were awoken with a slap. As they washed with warm water, they watched the boy scrubbing his bed while intermittently being beaten. He also bathed, but at the back of the line, when the water was well used.

As the boys dried with small cloth squares, the attendants applied vinegar, salves and strapping to any wounds and then supplied the boys with satchels. This would be their uniform until they began their formal training. Each donned their drawers, covered them with the light-brown linen tunic, and tied them in with the leather strap to stop them shifting. Over their belt was draped a handkerchief to be used to cover all that was deemed uncouth. And in it was tucked their prayer book, with the proclamation that this was now their most prized possession.

Long woollen socks covered their bare bottom legs, and leather shoes protected the socks from being soiled. Paulo's shoes were too big, and he saw another boy wincing with ones that were far too tight. But talking was not permitted. Paulo crunched his feet to hold the shoes as he walked towards the dining hall, trying not to clomp or scuff the shoes along the stones. But he had managed to slip in behind the boy with the bigger feet. Seated beside him at breakfast, a simple tap under the table, a glance downwards, and a shuffle led to a swop and stifled smiles.

The boys punished for talking sat and watched while those permitted to eat received and consumed their sloppy porridge. If any was spilt, smacks would result and the breakfast would be taken, making each child lean closer to their bowls. The dean had no tolerance for idle time, and so within minutes, they had been summonsed back into their lines and led to the cleaning room. Teeth were rubbed with a paste made from chalk and salt and inspected; they must be kept pristine for performances. The boys had learned the price of carelessness, using towels to protect their garments and leaning well over the basins to prevent any mess. Those who had sullied their clothes were made to scrub them, and wear them wet to show the shame. Paulo went behind one screen to release the pain in his bladder and bowels. He was so embarrassed, but no more so he believed if it were to come out later in his pants.

When they were again rallied into their parade, an attendant rubbed rosemary oil onto their chests. The dean announced that they would be expected to show the highest standards of decency. Body odour, he made clear, was also on the list of things that were banned.

Once clean, they were deemed acceptable to Christ and proceeded to the chapel. Pews were already full of other students, and the new boys were instructed to take their place on their knees and to pray. A priest arrived at the pulpit and delivered the morning's sermon, after which heads were bowed. Each boy was left to converse with whatever voice was wandering in their heads and wanting attention. Paulo wished he could hear his mother, or Francesca, but instead his head was filled with Antonio's tirade. Paulo had seen this decision to come here so clearly, but Antonio had cast him away like some abhorrent creature, and being surrounded by so many on the same pathway did not diminish the seeds of distress that Antonio had planted in his heart.

From the chapel, they were convoyed past crowded classrooms to one of their own, where they were given lectures on the sacraments, the role of confirmation and their duties as confirmed Christians. After permission to use the pots and the provision of water, there was singing practice. Here was when Paulo first heard the other boys' names, with the scales tutor asking them so that he could customise their condemnation. Paulo's name was spoken once, which pierced his heart and set forth a promise to himself that it would not be heard again with dishonour.

A brief moment in the courtyard allowed for enjoyment of the sun and some fruit before being shuffled into class again to cover the history of the glorious Mother Church and its doctrines. The aim they were told was to deepen their faith, ready for confirmation. The only thing Paulo felt he learnt was just how much effort one has to expend to prevent sleep. One poor boy learnt the lesson of taking every chance to use the pots the hard way. He sought permission during the class, which was denied, and resulted in great distress, a beating and being dragged to the cleaning room for bathing. Paulo saw that evening, as they slipped into their nightgowns, that this boy's body was now covered in black and deep purple patches.

Lunch was a light offering of cured meats, cheeses and bread, after which they were again made to brush their teeth, oiled and then marched to more vocal practice. This time, they were formed into a choir and taught the hymns for the confirmation mass. Then, there was a rehearsal of the confirmation ceremony. The heavy hands of the attendants shifted those bodies that were too slow and slapped the faces from which responses were too tardy.

The classroom was next on the agenda, and each child was given time to contemplate their spiritual journey. One by one, they were called into the room opposite to meet with a priest, who heard their confession and provided guidance on whatever he thought was needed for this offspring of original sin.

The break in the courtyard came as a blessing. It was then Paulo realised how little he had touched the ground since his arrival. It was as if he had been excised from the earth and now expected to rise above the dust from which he was born. A squeeze ensued on their way back in, with a line of bigger boys commandeering the space in the corridor. Paulo and a few boys behind him were bounced against the wall, with no dean noticing. Their guardians certainly did not see the sneer that was shared by the stronger ones or the anger on the face of one who looked just like Antonio.

Paulo's promise to himself was broken several times during the afternoon vocal training. Although he was not alone. All students were deemed useless, with no leniency given for the fact that this was their first time learning such complex techniques or that they were still too small to produce the strength of sound expected. By the end, Paulo's throat and head hurt, and his body was exhausted. However, this was not the end of the day.

Before supper, they were taken to different areas to complete their chores. Paulo was relieved to get garden duty and not be tasked with cleaning the pots, soiled undergarments or floors. He gave thanks as he picked, pruned and plucked out weeds and hauled the cache to the kitchen. The sun was still hot, and soon he was laced with sweat, using the chance to also release some tears; for digging in this dirt, he was suddenly struck by just how much he missed his home and the fact that he would never return.

He met back with some boys from his dormitory scrubbing hands and then joined the rest of the group in the dining hall for supper. There numbers were now expanded with another six shown in by an attendant and seated with them. A sparse stew and pasta were presented, and all ate quickly, quietly, and without waste. They were all learning well. Although some did fall asleep during vespers and were given a violent awakening. Paulo only prevented such a fate by biting his tongue and the inside of his cheeks, a trick he had learnt at school. He did not know how he was able to get up from the pews, but he did, disguising his grogginess somehow and allowing himself to be guided to the cleaning room. Here, Paulo prayed again, a more sedate and silent round of thanksgiving prayers for the water, fresh underwear, and even for the taste of chalk and salt that signalled he was closer to sleep.

Forty-four tired little legs tramped up the stairs, some tripping, one tumbling and being thumped for his incompetence.

Twenty-two tired little bodies knelt beside their beds, delivering their thanks to the God that had called them to be there.

Twenty-two tired little heads landed on the pillows and had the pleasure of laying down, for a moment, to take the place of their pain.

One little Paulo fell asleep instantly, too weary to worry about anyone around him. Tomorrow would be the same regime, and to survive it, he would need rest.

Paulo

The next three days went by almost exactly the same way, varying only in the content of the lessons, the saltiness of the stews and how sick Paulo felt after the chores. Sometimes, shoves from the older boys were replaced with spit, and sometimes, the sun felt more sinister, but the path was the same. Blessings did come, though. His legs stung less, and so did the dean's discipline and the teachers' attacks. His body was healing, his mind was becoming hardened, but his heart was breaking open.

Each day that he passed away from his family was not getting any easier. In fact, his longing grew greater. When there were free moments, he would imagine playing with Maria and Isabella and making them laugh. That was the most angelic melody he had ever heard. He realised that he had not smiled since his meal with Signore Conti and wondered if he would ever again. Sitting in the sun, Paulo pretended to be back in front of the fire beside his mother. He would place his own hand upon his shoulder and imagine it was hers. She would be praying for him, and that thought did help. As did the memory of Francesca's calmness and her care. Paulo carried this with him everywhere and longed for this memento of his previous life to never leave him. There was even the sporadic wishing to see, once again, Antonio's sneering face and to witness the wars between his brothers.

While this aggression caused everyone anxiety, within it, he never felt alone.

No animals were allowed on the campus for fear of spreading disease. Even the chickens arrived dead and dismembered. There were no dogs to talk to and give him the gift of genuine understanding like only Nero could. There were no cats to cuddle, scratch, and lean in for his love. And there was no chance to talk with the others. Their friendships were founded merely on a shared presence, generous glances and wherever possible, midnight whispers.

This was not a happy place. Here, Paulo was not a child. He was being prepared to become a castrato, woven and wrapped as a gift to others. A gift from God.

On Saturday afternoon, the rehearsals for confirmation were more rigorous, and the punishments for errors were far more severe. Slaps were replaced with straps, and claps to the ears were replaced with cuts to the thighs. Paulo was petrified that his wounds would be reopened and so relieved when the rehearsal ended without hands or tools of harm being used upon him. By vespers, a nervous energy had visited and would wait with them throughout the night.

As Paulo lay awake, filling his fraught mind with images from the farm, he heard unusual sneaking and shuffles. In the morning there were two less boys to be awoken. The dean announced they had absconded during the night, but his response showed little concern. These boys were simply not worthy. They had failed the test of fortitude, and so had no place there or in Heaven. They were in the devil's hands now and best forgotten.

An uncomfortable feeling arose in Paulo, one of jealousy, and one for which he judged himself harshly. Because part of him wished he was one of those who had escaped. But he also knew there would be no freedom, for guilt and shame would haunt him forever. He would do this for God and his mother. Paulo would make them both proud. He just so deeply wished his mother could be here to see him confirmed. Paulo knew how much it meant to her. All he could do was hang on to this thought and allow the meaning it gave her to move him forward.

They would eat first this morning to be perfectly clean for confirmation. Porridge sat uneasily in excited stomachs, with a few boys having to force it down. They had made it to the cleaning room before one boy began retching, with the reek of vomit invading the air not long afterwards. He and the pot of puke were hauled outside before it could contaminate others and cause sympathetic distress. The boy returned and joined them in being scrubbed and oiled, his face remaining ghostly white throughout. Their teeth were chalked, and when each passed inspection, they were provided with their fresh clothes and led to the final rehearsal.

The rehearsal was completed without error, and Paulo wondered whether the dean and his attendants were proud of the punishments they had doled out over the past few days. Gathered into a small room, the group prayed with a priest and then were lined up for the procession.

Paulo was not at the front for this parade and was honestly happy to be hidden in the crowd. He sang well, for there was no other way and held his head high as was expected.

Come, Holy Ghost, Creator, come,
from thy bright heavenly throne,
come, take possession of our souls,
and make them all thine own.

In the space between the words, Paulo could hear the clink of the censer and smell the sweet smoke that swirled around him. This settled him slightly until they stood in the front rows waiting to be received. Then he could feel his insides shaking and his breath becoming shallow. He moved through the mass as if a puppet with no power of his own. He was called forward, gave his assertion that he was ready and received the sacrament. It all happened as if to someone else. Not even the cross of chrism on his forehead made it feel any more real. It was only when he was bordered in with other boys, and all were reciting the renewal of their baptismal vows, did he begin to hear his own voice again.

By the time they were weaving towards communion, Paulo felt more centred and confident. Another choir was singing, reminding him of how much he loved the music. These were not students he had seen before, but their voices were beyond beautiful. As Paulo took the body and blood of Christ, he was fortified by their song.

Hail, true body, born of the Virgin Mary,
Who truly suffered, sacrificed on the cross for man,
Whose side was pierced, whence flowed water and blood,
Be for us a foretaste of Heaven, in the trial of death.

Kneeling, praying, feeling the Body of Christ dissolve in his mouth, and hearing of his Lord's sacrifice strengthened Paulo and restored some peace. With a final blessing from the bishop, the boys resumed their line for the recessional. The organ carried them to a crescendo and Paulo raised his voice with a mix of relief and rejoicing.

We praise thee, O God: we acknowledge thee to be the Lord.
All the Earth doth worship thee, the Father everlasting.

Paulo had been to confirmation masses previously, and there was always a generous gathering afterwards. The community would come together to give their congratulations and celebrate the reaffirmed commitment to the Church. There was no such reception here; no one but the clergy cared, and they were bound by austerity. And so, the boys simply went back to the sacristy and returned their robes. Sundays were scheduled for rest, but there was something that they must do first. The dean directed them back to their classroom, where they were briefed on what would occur the following morning.

Any cheer or comfort Paulo gained from completing his confirmation was quickly washed away. The dean seemed to delight in describing how they would be woken early to pray. Then, they would be cleaned thoroughly and purified for the castration procedure. No breakfast was to be had; the body was not to be sullied for the surgery. They would wait within their room to be called and, afterwards, awaken in a new area. Paulo could hear the humming of the dean's speech in his head; how he would work through weeks of recovery and, when he was strong enough, begin the intensive training only worthy of a castrato. Paulo acknowledged the glory he was giving to God with the sign of the cross. And then he heard the happy news; the boys would be given the afternoon to enjoy the sun and to offer silent prayers and private praise for the blessing they had been given. Still, nothing the dean said stopped the fear from rising. Once dismissed and partway to the courtyard, the retching began again, but this time, the boy made it outside to spew beside the building. No one was there to supervise, so it was covered up, and the boy collapsed onto the grass.

Paulo joined him, not speaking but touching his back. And then both lay, others joining them for surreptitious strokes, pats and clasping of palms. The quiet companionship tried to bolster their courage but was overshadowed by the older boys yelling from the upstairs windows, wishing them luck for the morrow and sending condolences for their loss. Their sarcasm was cruel and made more than one boy cry, covering it by cowering into the grass.

Some turned away from the windows, others feigned naps. Paulo placed his mind back to spending the afternoon at home on a Sunday before Pentecost when Father was alive and Mother was well. For the time before chores when he would cuddle with Nero, chase Maria and rock Isabella to sleep. He was held by his Father, who laughed loudly and sang to Mother as she stirred the stew. This time in the sun was filled with the happiest times of his life. Paulo wondered how Heaven could possibly be any better and whether, when he finally met God, the reward for his sacrifice could be a return to this time. Paulo would do this all again if that could be his fate.

By bedtime, one more boy was missing. It was the boy whose legs had been marked by heavy hands. Paulo became so confused. The path for him was clear, but for those who ran, it was completely uncertain. Did this mean that those who fled had more courage? So why were they condemned? Staying here and going through with what was expected seemed far less heroic than heading into an unknown future. He could not reconcile this in his own mind.

Yes, he was about to sacrifice so much, but those boys had surrendered security. They would be out there at the whims of others, relying upon the generosity of strangers. Did they feel that the people they had met on the passage here were more trustworthy than those within these walls? Paulo's world was becoming shadowy again. His clarity was becoming clouded. It was convenient then that the dean descended upon them with a priest for more prayers and that attendants were posted at the doors for extra security. Anyone who remained had lost their chance to make any other choice.

Throughout the night, sobbing occurred from several beds, which not even the attendants admonished. In the morning, there was a heavy silence, the joyousness of the dean not shared by the boys. Today, their glorious new future began. So why did Paulo feel such fear?

The morning progressed as the dean had promised. They marched down to the cleaning room and were supervised while they scrubbed their bodies, with instructions given to pay particular attention to their genitals and inspections made thereof. There was retching and more vomiting, followed by crying and flogging. Finally, all were ready, and they were placed back into their nightgowns. There were to be no drawers today, but socks and shoes were required to keep their bodies as clean as possible.

The dean led the procession back to their dormitory to wait and to pray.

Paulo

Six were called before Paulo, two at a time, one attendant for each boy, hands on backs and heads bowed. Inside Paulo was churning a sinister mix of starvation and terror. He hung onto the hunger. It was something he could understand, something fixable, something that would be solved after the surgery. This resolve to make it to a meal kept his mind in place and assuaged panic. Each prayer muttered was said in the presence of his mother to make it meaningful and in the hope that God may hear it.

"Paulo Contadino. Giovanni Bianchi."

Paulo rose and went with the other boy and his attendant. With food replaced by fear, he felt lightheaded and was glad to be moving so that he would not faint. As they walked across the campus, he could sense eyes upon him, but he would not look up at the windows. No good would come of that.

The men led the boys to an unknown quarter, one which the sun had still not hit. Down shady steps, they entered a room with a few chairs and a distinct chill. Paulo saw a boy being carried into an inner chamber; the door closed behind him with a bang. Paulo was seated, provided with a mug of sweet-smelling liquid, and told to drink. The smell was soothing; aniseed, cinnamon and honey, just like the tonics Francesca made to balance the biles. Whether he liked it or not, he was not given a choice to drink, the attendant standing over him to supervise its consumption. Paulo could not help but wince with the bitter aftertaste and felt uneasy with how the fluid sat in his empty stomach.

Something strange happened then. The men sat with the boys and began to talk. They asked Paulo and Giovanni where they were from, who they travelled there with, and what they would buy with their first earnings. It had almost been a week since Paulo had talked to any person, apart from the tutors, and he wondered if this was some kind of test to catch them unawares and deem them unworthy. And yet he answered, for it was right to respect your elders, even with the prospect of punishment. Giovanni told of the journey from Rome, of rain and bandits and his choirmaster's courage after an attack. Giovanni would buy his own writing implements, paper and quill so that he could draw. Paulo recounted his time with Signore Conti, the mountains, shrines, fragrant shrubs and fords. His choice of purchase was easy. He would buy a dog.

As Paulo began to describe what kind of dog, he began to feel dizzy. He looked at Giovanni and saw the other boy's eyelids lagging. When Giovanni sang his favourite him, it came out in a slur. Waiting for his turn to respond, Paulo's body became weighty, but his mind lightened. He had no option but to lie down. Veni Sancte Spiritus came out clumsily, and he smiled, hearing his own silly voice. So did the attendant beside him, patting him on the back and leaving him to his makeshift bed and the blur in his eyes. Whatever this was, it was wondrous to Paulo. He had come to a place of no fear, just joy, and he laughed. When there was no retribution, he did it again, more loudly this time, to be joined by Giovanni. Then he closed his eyes, listened to the choir in his head and waved at his mother, who had come to sit beside him, holding him gently. He hardly noticed the sound of the door opening and strong arms transporting him to a table. His father was floating above him, his scent heavy with the smell of his Sunday afternoon alcohol, and the cat had come to lay across his throat. It was wrapping around hard, but Paulo was too happy to care.

Over the next few hours, Paulo swung in and out of consciousness between severe pain and sedation. Awareness and agony were assisted with more medicine and more hours of hazy hurt. He knew people were attending to his genitals and could smell the consistent acrid smell of alcohol. His scrotum was searing and throbbing but cordoned off so he could not see it nor touch it. There were moments when he was desperate to, when out of panic, he needed to feel what remained. But there was no strength in his arms to take any action. His body was medicated to maintain stillness, but his head constantly moved between Heaven and hell. He could not be sure whether the shrieks he heard were those of the other boys beside him or hauntings from his own heart. And he was uncertain whether the murmurings of reassurance were from unknown nurses or really were from his mother.

Paulo did not know how many days had passed before the pain eased enough for him to do without opium, and he was assisted to sit slightly. He still needed help to go to the toilet, and the whole process was nothing short of traumatic. The stitches in his scrotum felt so tight he was afraid they would tear, and every movement was done with trepidation. But his stomach was screaming for sustenance, and so he took in stodgy porridge. The fullness was a wonderful feeling and, for a moment, took his mind off the continual throbbing below. It also created a convenient distraction from a boy down the row who would yell randomly and rudely for more opium. He said he needed it and demanded it in a voice that sounded possessed. They would give him no more as it was time to move on to the next stage of recovery. But his mania persisted, and so he was taken to a different area where his hostility could no longer be heard.

Beside Paulo was the boy who would always puke. He was not sitting yet, and his skin looked the colour of ash long after a fire had died. Between sleep and sweating, he would stare at Paulo. Men would come and inspect his wound with worried looks and sometimes bring boiling water. The boy would howl and bawl, but when it was done, go back to being still. Paulo watched as his cheeks changed from patches of pale to blue and then as his nose and lips progressed to purple. All the while, his eyes pleaded for Paulo, to do what, he did not know. Paulo could only return the stare, hoping the boy knew it was sending support.

When the boy's eyes reflected yellow, Paulo knew he was near the end. The leeches came too late to calm the chaotic breathing and confused mutterings. The boy died like a madman, convulsing like Viggo and Lorenzo, with blood leaking from between his legs. Like his father with the ailing animals, the dottore did not wait for the sickness to take its course. He called an attendant, one much stronger than himself, to choke the boy until the battle ceased. Then the boy was simply wrapped in the sheet and carried away, the mattress taken to be cleaned.

Paulo could not cry. He thought he should, but it would not come. All he felt was empty like part of him had been taken away with that boy's body. He tried to sleep but could not find comfort in doing this either. He tried to hum but had no heart for it. He tried to read the prayer book that had been provided but was well past believing in promises. He merely watched all the other boys, with some watching him in return. He winced when the dottore applied the ice, ate when the nurses supplied the food and tried to forgive them all for what they had done.

Days and days progressed in this same way until several of the boy's wounds were deemed healed enough for the sutures to be removed. Still covered, the sites were inspected, doused in alcohol, stitches snipped, and shrieks turned to sobs and then silence, except for one boy whose wound was misjudged. Bandages were applied before another attendant carried him away, only to return several hours later in an opium-induced haze to begin the healing process again.

With the stitches gone the boys were aided to stand and bear their own weight. They would walk a little way between beds, with each few days the length of their wandering being widened. Within a week they were standing and singing for short periods, their groins inspected closely afterwards for any signs of severance or redness around the scar. Giovanni struggled through all of this, his form had become crumpled and his face cramped. His pain had become chronic, and it had made him cruel. Giovanni would scowl as he passed Paulo and shower those who came too close with scorn and spit. This was when Paulo realised that they had not just been castrated. They had all been changed.

In the darkness, when all was still and silent, Paulo would tempt the Lord's wrath and feel what was left between his legs. The skin was soft and lax. Where there was substance, there was now only slack. The scar was severe. But it was done. And now he only had death to fear.

Paulo

The next week, teachers began visiting the recuperation room more frequently, and the lessons became lengthier and more formal. As the boys became stronger, so did the demand for perfection and the punishment for anything less. Giovanni joined them, now belted around his groin to provide support for the growing bulge. But it was evident for all that the pain was coming from within, and every deep breath was breaking him. He could not force out strength when he was battling to hold so much in. His song was inferior, and he was instructed to return to bed. Between being poked, prodded, belted, iced, leeched and lanced, he bit at all those around him with a venomous voice, until sedation was the only solution. Decisions would be made later by the doctors about his fate.

On Saturday, those who showed no signs of weakness were washed and given new clothes to wear. Dark blue tunics replaced the brown and were adorned with a white collar. Hose hid and held what should not be seen, and their shoes were shiny. And then, with Giovanni yelling at them to get out, they did.

It took some time for Paulo to adjust to the light. It was mid-afternoon and the sun was strong, causing him to shield his eyes. The day felt harsher than he had remembered. Before his surgery he had soaked in this light. Now, he felt he needed to hide from it. They travelled in the shade between the buildings, past a group of younger boys dressed in brown, seated on the grass, supervised by their old overlord. Those sitting were instructed not to look. Paulo wondered whether it was out of respect for the newly-made castrati, or whether the sight of their suffering may cause the boys in brown to flee.

They travelled up several flights of stairs, causing stress to some who were not yet feeling that strong. Paulo broke a sweat and felt shaky but wiped it all away with his handkerchief. Here, they chose their beds, each with its own box, already filled with nightgowns and evening socks. Paulo chose a top bunk again as his own little space. And there were windows. With this, Paulo could breathe. He was back in the world and could again find solace in the sky. After a moment to maintain composure, they were taken downstairs to a classroom, past one already full of fellow students, also dressed in blue. This was the choir that sang at their confirmation, and this gave Paulo courage. They seemed to be well, which meant that Paulo may be too. Their hair was longer, making Paulo hopeful that he may be given the chance to grow his again.

Hours were spent on scales; pianissimo, forte, staccato, legato, crescendo, semplice, solo, as a duo, dolce and with drama. Every way a scale could be done was done, repeatedly. The master would stand with his ear close to each boy's mouth and become mad when a pitch was missed. Then, he would focus on their faces, pushing their cheeks and jaws into the correct placement. To the side, one boy collapsed. He was hauled onto a chair until he could regain composure and then spent the rest of the lesson learning from his seat, pale but persevering. Paulo did not feel well but was determined not to let these people hurt him further. He breathed in big, using the air around him and within him as his ally, and let his song release all that he could not contain.

Their dinner was taken in a different place, beside the boys with the longer hair, but was still done in silence. Vespers were held in a chapel that contained only castrati, and they also had their own cleaning room. Their sacrifice was not to be seen by others, and they should not be reminded of what had been removed from them. The mood within their dormitory was one of resignation. There was no honour here; only healing wounds, the realisation that they would be here for years and that their worth would be decided by others.

As he watched the world turn dark and a distant star appeared, Paulo found the only thing that he could cling to; the wish to make his mother proud. He would show Antonio that he was right to choose this path and regain his favour through the wealth he would lavish upon him. Yes, Paulo could see the way forward. Through his success, he would provide for his family, and through his song, he would keep them safe.

The night was warm, and it was difficult to sleep. So, Paulo had much time to imagine his future. He would sing for Kings and go back to his family on holidays to tell them all he had seen. He would bring Mama and Francesca fine fabrics and foreign oils. And he would shower Maria and Isabella with pretty ribbons, and precious toys, allowing them to feel royal. He would give Antonio money to get more manpower for the farm, relieving his aching bodies and giving him time to rest. He would bring the best dottore for his mother, making her well. For Luca, he would secure a place in the most prestigious academies, and provide lodgings and attire suitable for his new station. In this imagination, Paulo found his intent and inspiration.

The next day, Sunday, was their special day, their one and only day of rest. They were awoken for breakfast but had no duties at mass until cleared by the choirmaster. They were seated on the side of the church, away from the boys yet to be cut and those older, brutish ones from the mainstream school who were not afforded such an opportunity. After lunch, they saw the afternoon out in their own yard. There was no supervision, for escape now would just be stupid. No one would take a castrati whose voice was incomplete. It would be years before they had anything to offer, and so it was wiser to remain here where they were at least fed regularly. The rule of sparing their voices for singing still applied, although, with no one around, cloistered enquiries were made as to whether each was feeling well, and predictions cast on what their week would bring.

After dinner, in their dormitory, their curiosities were assuaged with the new dean informing them directly as to what they should expect. Tonight, they should rest, but of that they did not need to be told. The reason given though was new. Tomorrow they would begin the training that would take them to glory.

It took months for the training to feel less like torture and more like a test. Two boys were too weak to withstand the rigour and were removed. Where they went, no one knew. All Paulo saw was the same boy collapse periodically, and so he was taken outside by an attendant. When the lesson was finished, the boy was gone and did not return to their room.

Another, slapped to encourage greater precision, burst out in anger. The boy only stood as high the master's ribs but hit them with all that he had. Then he kicked, the sturdy black shoes becoming a weapon. Fingernails became knives and scratched at the master's face. This boy's fury was such a shock, delaying the master's reaction and having him cower in defence. Finally, the master called for help, and an attendant hauled the boy away, still thrashing, into the hall. With one hit, he was silenced.

Only on Sunday did the routine vary. Every other day was spent warming up with hours of scales, followed by practice of difficult pieces, many of which made Paulo feel like a dunce. Sometimes, though, there would be a breakthrough, and these little moments of victory were held onto with fervour. Their voices were given some rest during lessons on libretti and liturgical text, but this theory Paulo found far more difficult. He was almost relieved to head into the trill practice. He was determined to master the rapid movement between notes and found the energy exciting. He also began to enjoy feeling the flow of sound through the different parts of his body. Paulo's voice was becoming fully embodied within him, and with this came a sense of power he had never before experienced.

This sense of confidence was quickly stripped away when they began practising in front of a mirror. Paulo hated seeing himself, so he pretended the face looking back at him was another boy; one who had already found his place in the world. He watched as this boy in the mirror became taller, his posture more graceful and his expression full of pride.

He called upon this boy in the mirror to help him with the long afternoons of musical theory, composition and counterpoint, which, after months, he still found confusing. He far more enjoyed the game of transcribing the music played by the master, his ears far more adept than his academic ability. After dinner, everyone was tired, but this did not lessen the expectations of excellence. Hours of harpsichord and composition came next. It was so hard to sit up straight after standing all day and with a full stomach. To remedy this situation, Paulo, along with several other boys, had their arms strapped to their sides and their backs slapped until their muscles memorised what dignity looked like. When his perfect posture had become a habit, then he could concentrate on the superb sound that came from this instrument and begin to string sequences he would love to hear. Paulo would scribble them down in the corner of the room, and then, when it was his turn at the instrument, experiment with and refine his first ideas. Paulo's heart knew what he liked to hear, but his mind also knew what would be accepted by the master. Paulo soon learnt the places and spaces where his music could be free, and those where he must force it into an acceptable form.

By the time winter came, there were fewer horrible surprises being found in their dormitory. In the warmer months it was a regular occurrence to find dead animals and the contents of chamber pots in their beds. Then they would spend hours cleaning instead of sleeping. Everyone knew it was the boys from the other side of the college, the non-castrati. But no-one knew how they were able to get past the guards. The first few times such disgusting objects appeared there was shock. Now it was no longer a surprise. Every time though was a reminder of the threat these boys posed to those on the other side.

While it was hard to find warmth in their room, for it had no fire, the cold at least seemed to prevent sneaking around, so their beds remained clean. For this blessing, Paulo was thankful. He cuddled into the small sack of now cooling coals, pulled earlier from the downstairs furnace, trying to satisfy his complaining stomach by swallowing some of his own spit. Over the past few months, the boys had grown, but their meals had not, meaning each night was spent trying to ignore the growling going on inside, placating it with a pretend meal or dreaming of the gruel that the dawn would bring.

Paulo completed the prayers for his family and tried not to panic when details of his mother and siblings would evade him. He would simply concentrate harder to see their features and hear their voices. Then he would try to conjure the smell of the citrus fruits he would peel for Maria and Isabella by the fire and wonder if it had been cold enough for a frost. Each night, he fell asleep on the farm beside Francesca, figuring out the crescendo to their next famous composition.

CRUCIFIXUS

Francesca

When Paulo left, Francesca felt a light go out. Despite her best attempts at distraction, for months, Maria would keep asking when her brother was coming back. When, during quiet moments, Maria would snuggle into her mother's arms and ask, Francesca could see the momentary flash of despair shoot across her mother's face. This was quickly buried beneath frustration and the demand that the child not ask again. And slowly, she did stop asking. And slowly, Isabella grew enough to stand on the stool upon which Paulo once sat.

There was no singing, though, no hymns of an evening to sustain her mother's strength. Francesca wondered whether this was the reason that her monthly pain became more profound. The remedies, once effective at providing some sense of ease, did little now to reduce the excruciating symptoms. Mother would be bedridden for days, huddled over hot coals and humming through the night. Still, she would exit her room eventually, wash, eat and take stock of what had happened in her absence. She would restore her place and begin giving orders, and with this came a great sense of relief for Francesca.

However, she also knew her mother's recovery annoyed Antonio greatly. During her mother's incapacity, he was the one who was in charge. Francesca could see him expand with a sense of importance and revel in instructing the hired hand. For those few days, his voice got louder, more certain, more commanding. With his mother's return to the table, Francesca could see him shrink back again and heard the uncomfortable silence that separated them.

Mother was unwell on the day that Antonio was confirmed, an undertaking he initiated in consultation with the priest. Permission was granted from his mother, with her unable to deny her son the right to receive the strength of the Holy Spirit. And with the additional labourer, Antonio could take the time required to attend the preparations. Francesca could see the victory he took from this, and the bravado that came from winning this spiritual battle. While his mother was not there to see him become a man in the eyes in the eyes of the Church, when they did meet again, Francesca saw a settling of the tension. Her mother seemed to take a step back, allowing Antonio to speak. And she took his suggestions, agreeing that seventeen would be a good age for him to marry. Then, she asked his permission to speak further with the priest about his intentions. There was no talk of Francesca marrying yet. The children were still too young, and Rosa was still too unwell to allow her to move away and become a mother herself. She was still needed here, and that made Francesca happy.

Yes, there was very little fire left in her mother, and with each month that passed, Francesca could feel her slipping further away. Her body, her vigour and her voice were weakening, and she became less welcoming of Francesca's suggestions for herbal treatments. Her mother had become dispirited. But when Isabella died, she became broken.

Maria became ill first, coming home from school with a sore throat. Francesca was quick to respond with mallow root tea, garlic and thyme, the administration of which tested both girls' patience. Maria would winge and cry, hurting her throat even more and making Francesca mad. So, Francesca made the medicine acceptable with honey, which became a bribe required before the others would be taken. A fever did come, though, bringing with it much fear. The child just wanted to be held constantly, a need to which her mother gladly obliged. Several times, Francesca entered her mother's room to find her rocking Maria in her arms and humming. The song was silenced when Francesca came, but hearing it, even once, warmed her heart and gave her hope. After two days of elderflower tea, Maria's fever subsided, and she began to brighten. The tension Francesca had been holding all over her body eased, and she became excited to think that she had helped cure her little sister.

When Isabella got grizzly, and her throat began to swell, Francesca felt confident that the same system, the same medicine, the same attention and the same prayers would work for this little one. But while her fever broke after a few days, Francesca could see Isabella was not fully well. She would play but become fatigued so easily. She would have some fun or some food but then fall asleep straight afterwards. Guilia came and showed Francesca how to make a nettle infusion, how to cover her hands to avoid the sting, and how to soak it to extract its energising essence. Even laden with honey, getting it down Isabella's throat was still a battle. It did seem to help though, allowing her to start learning the alphabet from Maria and some mathematics from Luca.

That was until the fever returned. This time, it brought with it pain in Isabella's chest and hot, swollen ankles and wrists. The little one would wince and pull away when Francesca tried to feel them or to inspect the ragged rash that was becoming apparent over her arms. Elderflower did little, but willow bark worked to lessen her temperature and made her more comfortable. When the swelling continued, Guilia came again and prepared comfrey compresses for the child, who was now too fatigued to put up a fight. Her mother ran Isabella warm baths, and washed her lovingly, seeing how it made the child calmer. Francesca filled the air with lavender so that all may have their anxiety eased. For it was almost becoming unbearable.

Antonio decreed that the dottore must be sent for, and Francesca did not argue. All was now beyond her capability, and they were getting desperate to see this little girl get well. Antonio also called upon a priest, for obviously, the power of their prayers was insufficient to shift the illness.

Isabella shrieked with fear the first few times the dottore brought the leeches. Her mother had to create a shield so that the child could not see what was being done, and Francesca had to hold her down. Francesca felt ill watching their sleek black bodies swell with her sister's blood, holding back her own urge to vomit. It was with disgust that she watched their fat bodies being burnt until they released and fell into the jar, leaving red rings and a fear for their return. Three times, they were used with the belief that their expansion would lessen Isabella's swelling extremities. They did not. Isabella only weakened, and the oedema travelled to her abdomen and eyes.

Emetics were administered under duress. Francesca and her mother took turns to hold the little girl's head over a bucket while she retched and regurgitated whatever little she had been able to eat that day. What was meant to balance the humours only ended up bringing greater distress. If any harmful toxins were released, there must have been many more that remained, for Isabella continued to fade.

The priest came every few days, and the nuns in between to sprinkle her with holy water and channel the blessings of the Lord. But these tonics did little to strengthen Isabella's breath. Guilia could only suggest that whatever the illness was had gone to her heart, and so motherwort tea was made, and sleepless nights were had in supervision, propping her little body up when she slipped off the pillows, making sure that she could breathe easier. This battle was so sad, and in the dead of night, Francesca would shed so many tears. She thought she had used them all up when Paulo left. But it seemed she had found a whole new reservoir from which her despair could draw.

Francesca wept when she felt her sister's cold hands and feet. She had layered them well to provide warmth, but Isabella's body would not take it in. The iciness crept to Isabella's lips and fingernails and, over the following weeks, to her mind, and she became so confused. Throughout the night, Isabella would become agitated and angry and call out for Paulo. Her mother would take her into her room and settle the little girl, but sometimes, in a wild state, she would even scratch at these loving arms.

Francesca understood when Antonio announced that the priests and nuns would no longer come, and that the neighbours were not to enter the house. If they saw this behaviour, it would not bode well for what was already considered a family compromised.

And so, what was left of the Contadino family began their vigil. Francesca, Maria and their mother would take turns during the day, each only leaving to prepare meals and tend to the fire. Luca would lay with little Isabella before he left for school and as soon as he returned. Antonio would spend some time beside her after dinner to give the women time to do the dishes. With every exhale Isabella made, Francesca would be frozen with fear until another breath would come in. The space in between breaths was becoming more random, and the air Isabella would suck in was becoming more shallow. Francesca watched as each day Isabella's skin became more grey, and the periods in which she was unaware of those around her became longer.

Three days before Christmas, while the rest of the world was preparing to celebrate the birth of the Lord, Francesca was steadying herself for the loss of her sister. While a thunderstorm shook the walls, they all watched as the chest of this little child stopped moving. Her mother wailed, and Antonio walked away. Francesca and Maria waited beside the body, sobbing and witnessing the continued lack of life. Luca cuddled those that remained, tears also flowing down his face. Through the searing pain in her chest, Francesca asked Luca to summon Giulia and the priest. Preparations for the burial would need to be made before Christmas was upon them.

Luca

The storm had passed when Luca left the farm. Still, it left a grey pall and sodden earth in its wake. He wanted to go fast but feared Antonio's wrath if the horses were too tired to work. Instead, Luca jogged for as long as he could before the cool air claimed his breath and a short rest was needed to regain it. He did not feel the cold around him or the heat within. His body did not seem to belong to him. It moved of its own accord, allowing his mind to sit in the haze of anguish.

The dark, heavy fog of sadness and tension that arrived when Paulo left had only begun to lift from the family when Maria became ill. Her recovery had seemed to bring them closer in hope. Now, Isabella's passing would, again, tear them all apart. The mud he ran through that morning made sense to him and Luca sought out the sludge, stomping through it. The muck caked Luca's shoes and stained his socks. And as he passed the piles of drenched mule dung along the road he realised that this too was his path. There was no joy along this journey.

He made it to Guilia's cottage, harrowed, and found no one home. Luca's fugue was cast aside, replaced by frantic knocking, falling and an overwhelming sense of failure. He felt the hands upon him, helping him up, and saw the face of the man next to his. Luca heard the questions and gave the answers. He received the assurance that the man would relay his message and this subtly restored his strength. A woman came with water, which he drank and settled within him. With thanks, he turned towards the town to find the father, followed by the couple's frowns.

It was some way along this winding path that Luca met Guilia. He recognised her from a distance and ran to her, relaying the message rapidly, with many tears but also with great relief. Guilia said she would come shortly with supplies, and with that, Luca took a shortcut through the paddocks. He did not have the energy to watch for nettles, needing all of his concentration to remain upright with the weariness and the weightiness. There was little sleep the night before or the night before that. As Isabella's breath and consciousness became more fleeting, so did their ability to rest. The whole family were days into sleep deprivation.

And so, a tired, tormented Luca entered the church, dirty and drained. When he saw the choir practising on the podium, his heart broke wide open sending a searing pain through his chest. He wished Paulo was standing there and that he could come home with him. He would know just what to do to soothe the women and support the men. But he would return alone and as a scant substitute for Paulo's peace.

With a deep bow and through broken words, Luca explained that Isabella had passed. There were no expressions of sympathy from the priest, and nothing could hide the annoyance on this father's face. The priest said he would first finish this practice and then come to the farm. But between the threat of storms and Christmas preparations, the priest would not stay long. Luca was sent to the cemetery to speak to the gravedigger. Here, in this shanty, he was given a shot of spirits and made to sit down by the fire. When the gravedigger's wife declared Luca was warm enough, she sent her husband off with the mule and wagon to take the boy home. There was no talking on this trip, but in the gravedigger's stoic silence, Luca felt understood. As Luca hopped down off the wagon at the entrance to the farm, this mean-looking man wished Luca and his family well and advised that the grave would be ready the next morning.

Luca felt stronger returning than when he had left and had the generosity of strangers to thank for this. As he passed the barn, he could see their neighbours, the father and eldest son, were with Antonio. They were working the wood, once kept for the fences, now being sawed and shaped into a simple casket. Arriving back within, one of their womenfolk was beside his mother while the other held Maria. Francesca was preparing the waters with which Isabella would be washed and the pouch of herbs she would hold under her little hands.

Luca watched his mother, his sisters, and his brother, all with such a sense of purpose, all with such a clear place. He saw Guilia guide Francesca as a mentor and as a friend, fortifying her as she went to wash her little sister's body. The door was closed to him, which was right and proper, but it opened again when little Isabella was clean, scented, and dressed in white.

Luca kept watch for the priest, chopping wood while he waited. When the priest finally arrived, Luca showed him in, offered him warm wine, and sat at the side while his sister was anointed with oil on her forehead, hands and feet. The priest said the prayers swiftly, sharply, that helped secure Isabella a seat in heaven. He gave the instructions for the family to be at the church mid-morning the next day for the funeral. And then he left, leaving the women to continue their vigil, the candles burning, the tears flowing, and the prayers pleading for this little girl's care in the arms of their Lord.

As night fell and the neighbours returned to their home, Francesca tried to feed them all, but none were hungry. Luca held Maria beside the fire while she nibbled on some bread and cheese, but nothing would sit right in his body. Luca preferred to feel hungry. At least it was some earthly distraction from this overwhelming despair. When Maria went to bed, Luca was left alone. Francesca and his mother maintained their vigil, falling asleep on the floor beside the little girl's body. Antonio was still in the barn, and so Luca went to the one place that brought him peace. He sat under the sky, the clouds shifting to show some stars, the moon waxing, lightening the land below. Luca felt like he belonged, right there, in the dense blackness between the little flashes of light, and he looked upon this scene as a constant he could cling to. Any changes that happened up there were miraculous. Down here, lives were lived in the mud. The heavens were a source of magic, of mystery, whereas Luca already understood the ultimate nature of their mundane human lives.

The next morning, after some porridge was forced into fragile bodies, Antonio called on Luca to help him clear the table for the casket and carry it in from the barn. The place where the family once gathered to share meals and tales of the day was now to hold the dead. As Antonio stood by, Luca was sent to inform the women that it was ready. Their mother came out first, carrying Isabella's little body, wrapped tightly in a white sheet, holding her with a hope that never wanted to let her go. It tore at Luca to see his mother shaking as she put her daughter's body in the wooden box. She did not seem to notice the carved flowers that adorned the sides or the cross that had been carefully placed on the lid. But Luca did, and in that moment, Luca felt love for his brother.

While Antonio hammered in the nails, Luca felt useless. While Antonio instructed him on how to carry the casket to the cart, Luca felt inadequate. Luca felt the same throughout the ceremony: alone and insufficient, and his prayers felt meaningless. The only thing he could offer was a handful of dirt to send Isabella on her way. The gravedigger's wife provided him with a pat on the shoulder, but this was given generously to all in attendance.

He wanted to argue with his mother; they should not attend Christmas mass for they were still in mourning. But it would have been a useless attempt to maintain Isabella's memory and only inflamed the situation further. This was mother's chance to pray in a place of sanctity, and she would not sacrifice this despite her declining health or her daughter's death. Rosa had not slept or eaten since Isabella's death. Francesca, in her wisdom, had convinced their mother to eat and rest on Christmas Eve, as the Lord would not want a waif disrupting his majestic birthday celebrations. Rosa needed to be strong to celebrate the arrival of the Son of God and show the Lord she was worthy. With this in her mind, Luca saw his mother begin again to go through the daily motions, dampened and morose, but at least moving.

The day after Christmas, as the congregation was still glorified by Christ's coming, Luca and his family were beginning their mourning prayers. One month later, they were still praying and making offerings to hasten Isabella's journey through purgatory, and still, Luca had not found a way to help. With school on holidays, he had leant his hands to Antonio and worked alongside the hired labour to feed the animals and till the land. But when Antonio would come and inspect Luca's work it was never good enough. There was always too much or too little feed, the fences were never strong enough, nor were the holes sufficiently deep. He was so relieved when school resumed, and Antonio sent him back. Antonio announced one night over supper that Luca was a burden here, not obviously born for farming, but may benefit the family from his education. His mother conceded this point. And so, each day he would accompany Maria to and from school, and each night continue his studies by candlelight.

The walks with Maria were the best times of his day. They would talk the whole way to school and the whole way home. Every so often, there would be a pang in his heart when he remembered that Paulo was around the same age when he was taken. Luca would share his concern that Francesca was blaming herself for Isabella's illness and how she had seemed to forget how to care for herself. Maria would agree, saying that her elder sister had become even more protective than her mother. This would lead them to their latest observations about the matriarch and her malaise and see them develop plans to support her more. Maria would ask for advice about Antonio's anger and how to avoid it, for she was finding out the same thing Luca had known much longer, that nothing could assuage it. Sometimes, they would talk about what Maria had learnt in school, and sometimes, Maria would suggest they pray. Luca did not really want to. He would have preferred to talk about his ideas for finding a patron and leaving to pursue his studies. But he knew that it may only cause Maria more pain, and so pray he did.

Luca did share his love of astronomy, though, with his teacher, Signore Battista. After school, they would spend time discussing what extraterrestrial events were forthcoming. On special occasions, Signore would allow Luca to take his spyglass home while his teacher joined the scientists at the Accademia or at the private telescope of Count Alessandro. Signore would entertain Luca with tales of the great minds he had met and the power of the telescopes he had used. When Signore was invited to the count's public observation of the upcoming eclipse, plans were put in place to ensure Luca could attend.

Signore Battista received permission from Antonio and the local priest to take Luca to the event. Maria was excited for him and Francesca was supportive. But from Antonio and his mother, nothing was said. Mother gave him money to buy a new shirt and socks before the event. Signore Battista bought him breeches. Francesca came to collect Maria after school that day while Signore took Luca to stay overnight in Naples.

Luca had never felt so excited. Even still mourning Isabella, his stomach was churning with expectation. As the carriage made it closer to the city, Luca had the strange feeling of coming home. The before unseen activity along the streets felt familiar. It made him feel secure. The conversations held in the tavern where they took rest were crass and yet so enticing. Here was a world that he wanted to explore. And as they saw scholars and students pass by, Luca knew he had found his place.

Well-fed and with clean faces, they made their way outside the city and, with the sun starting to sink, scaled the slope upon which the count's court was built. They passed grand estates and giant houses, with Luca feeling overjoyed and overwhelmed. The pathway they progressed through was lined with marble statues and tall cypress trees. The teacher and student arrived at an entrance adorned with carvings and columns and overseen by ornate balconies. While the horse was taken, the two strode up the wide steps to an imposing and yet open wooden door. They were shown inside by an attendant dressed in beautiful blues with white frills and sent to wash, yet again, in a room just off the foyer. When fully clean they were shown through the hall, Luca arching his neck to view the high ceilings and looking all around at the tapestries and paintings. This was a place that Luca was not even able to imagine or to dream of, and yet here he was, discovering all of it.

They walked around the footmen lighting the candles of the chandelier. The reflections through the crystals sent rainbows all along the marble floor, and out onto the public balcony. Signore Battista and Luca followed the light where they were met with servants carrying trays of wine, savoury tartlets, cured meats and candied almonds. Luca was seated on the side with some other older students. They were given smaller cups with diluted wine, which Luca drank slowly, not wanting to compromise this incredible event.

More men arrived, and a few women, all dressed in finery. Luca did not have to wonder which one was Count Alessandro. He came onto the balcony surrounded by men wearing bold colours and conversing excitedly. The count was simply smiling and walking, then raising his hand as a signal for his company to cease their chatter so that he could meet his guests. Bows and curtsies were shared amongst the adults. Pleasantries and praise were proffered and received with gratitude. Luca watched as the count spoke with the Signore and saw his teacher signal over to him. The count returned whatever information was shared with an interested nod and then moved on to the next man.

When all the grown-up guests had been attended to, the count turned to the now six students seated in the shadows. He sauntered over, and they all stood and bowed, with Luca trying to be brave while his stomach was a swarm of bees. The count spoke with each one generously, announcing he was glad to see them and so impressed by their interest in astronomy. And then he came to Luca.

"How old are you, boy?"

Luca replied that he was almost twelve. It was a bit of a lie, given that he was closer to eleven, but it sounded much more impressive.

"Ah, wonderful. Well, your teacher tells me that you seek to undertake further study. After the eclipse, let's go to my study and we shall see what we may be able to arrange."

With that, the count returned to the adult guests, where there was much wine drunk and many animated discussions. The telescope was revealed, and all took their turn; the students only allowed to approach once the curiosity of the elders had been satiated. While waiting, Luca pulled out his spyglass and shared it with those beside him, who were all delighted, even with their inferior views and immature debates.

Over the next hours, the voices and laughter of the guests got louder. A professor retired to a room upstairs, ordering Luca's companions to join him, while the. The Signore and the count came back over to Luca, with both looking a little crooked. Was it that Luca had indulged in too much wine, or had they? Regardless, all were in good spirits, even if their steps were a little unsteady.

"Luca, the count would like to speak to you now. I am retiring for the evening, and his attendant will show you to our room when he has finished with you."

Luca bowed to both and saw the Signore sway through the great hall and up the stairs, past the chandelier that was now being put out. He followed the count and his gold-trimmed coat. The Count's greying frizzy hair fell far down his back, and his black shoes clapped across the floor.

Luca was shown to a seat in the study, a room that had the boy scanning the walls in awe.

"Ah, yes, I can see you are a passionate student. Let me show you some things from my days as a navigator."

The count pointed to the pictures on the walls, providing details of the ships that he had sailed on. He pulled instruments off his desk and taught Luca what they were and how they were used. The count fielded some of Luca's questions with laughter, others with frowns.

"You do ask very good questions, boy. I can see that you will be a superior student. Luca, I would be willing to find you a place at the Accademia, and pay your way, for I feel that your enthusiasm and intellect will be of great benefit to science. I am willing to be of service to you, Luca."

Luca leapt from his seat and gave a low bow, holding it as long as he could before he felt his heart might burst. When he rose, his mouth spurted out profuse thanks and assurances of his academic success. These pronouncements ceased when the count raised his hand.

"Firstly though, Luca, before I prepare the papers, I must know that you are also willing to be of service to me."

Luca thought the count must have been uncomfortable, undoing his sash and unbuttoning his vest to bring about a greater sense of relaxation. As Luca submitted his assurances happily, the count undid his breeches. Now Luca was confused. The count was naked from the waist, with his breeches around his ankles, and he was waddling closer. He was showing off the parts that should never be made public, picking it up and putting it near Luca's mouth.

"I also need to know that you can keep secrets, Luca."

Laying beside the snoring Signore, Luca was not sure what he had just done. All he knew was that he felt sick. Still, there was a promise from the count to start the paperwork the next day and that, within the month, Luca would start a new life.

CRUCIFIXUS

Rosa

Rosa could tell Luca had changed when he stepped down from the carriage with Signore Battista. He stood straighter, and he smiled. That was when she knew that she would lose him, too. Luca stood patiently beside the table as Signore Battista told Rosa of the count's offer and outlined the terms that were displayed in front of her. She could not understand them but trusted Signore Battista. Still, Luca was soon to be a man and should be treated as such. Rosa called him over to review the papers, and asked him if all proposed was acceptable to him. His enthusiastic assent was the assurance she needed, and Rosa, once again, placed a cross that would dramatically change her child's future.

That evening, as Antonio retired early, Luca regaled the girls with descriptions of the majestic home, the marble statues, crystal chandelier, the fabrics, and the food. Francesca asked about his future master, and Luca told of the count's great experience, his adventures on the seas and all of the instruments that he kept in his study. This is when Rosa noticed the stunted smile, the shadow that appeared. Luca shifted and sat differently when he spoke about the count. Like there was something he was hiding. And his words came out a little differently, too. There was a hesitation. Like there was a piece of information he was holding on to.

Rosa was glad for Francesca, asking what she was unwilling to, putting to Luca whether this patron would treat him properly. Luca responded simply; there had never been any complaints from the students under his sponsorship. Rosa wanted Francesca to inquire further, to dig for details about how the count had treated him. But Francesca moved on to start the conversation about how much he would be missed.

Rosa made it to Luca's confirmation on Candlemas. Just as Jesus was presented at the temple, Luca was put forward for the Church to receive. But soon he would also be taken away.

On a Saturday before Lent, Signore Battista came to collect Luca and his few belongings. He would board with the count over Easter and enter the Accademia thereafter. The Signore assured her that the count would clothe him in suitable attire for his position as a student of the sciences and provide updates on Luca's progress where possible. And then they departed to the sounds of Francesca and Maria's distress. Antonio was nowhere to be seen, and Rosa was not sure whether his absence was due to motives sinister or sad. All she knew was that she was burning inside, and her heart felt like it was about to break open, but she would hold it in and let it keep hurting. For that is what she deserved.

Now, both her little boys were gone. She had sent them away. While she understood that the decision was for their benefit, this justification did not soothe the seething self-hate that was sitting within her. Antonio's words stung her, for he was right. She did rue her decision to send Paulo away, but now it was too late.

CRUCIFIXUS

Lent came conveniently to enable Rosa to hurt herself under the ruse of abstinence and repentance. Her monthly torment came again soon, giving her another excuse to reject food and to spend her days in recitations. Her sinfulness, she decided, required that she would not take meat until Easter. Francesca told her she was being extreme. Rosa responded directly, telling her daughter that this was her gift to the Lord and to stop being a dramatic little girl.

With the loss of blood, though, and the poor intake of nutrition, Rosa became pale. It was not long before she was dizzy, weak and a danger out on the farm. Antonio angrily sent her inside and instructed her to stay within the walls. Rosa resented Antonio, for he had acted too quickly. She had a plan and was progressing toward it when Antonio intervened. It would not be her fault if she was fatigued and fell into the river. The Lord would surely forgive her. Rosa just wanted to sink, to stop breathing, to sleep. But Antonio had barred this solution.

Rosa could not hold the heavy pans or stand for any substantial period, so Francesca forbade her to be anywhere but bed. Now, she had become the burden she believed herself to be, and now she would be justified for fading away. She would be doing her family a service, and as such, her passing would not be a sin. Francesca kept coming in with meals and tonics, and Rosa would continue to refuse them. She was fasting for the Lord and for the forgiveness of her sins. She became so tired and simply slept while Maria lay beside her and prayed. She did not join in the invocations. Her energy was invested in looking for signs that each breath may be her last.

Until one day, about a week before Easter, Francesca came charging into the room, flustered and furious. Rosa was looking at the wall and waiting to die when her daughter grabbed her, hoisted her upright, and stared into her mother's eyes with anger flashing fiercely. Francesca told Rosa that Maria had cried all the way to school that morning, asking if her Mama was going to die. And then, Francesca demanded that Rosa stop being so selfish. Through desperate tears, Francesca said they were all hurting, but Rosa's actions were causing more of it, and for that, she should be ashamed. Any other time, Rosa would have slapped her daughter, but she was too weak, and Francesca was right. This had gone too far. She could punish herself, but not her family, not more than what they had already endured.

Francesca did not ask; she told Rosa that she would eat. If she refused, Antonio had decided that she would be sent to an infirmary where she would never see her family again. She would forgo the right to oversee their marriages and make any more decisions. As Francesca said, they were done. They were willing to help with the illness that was thrust upon her but did not support her suicide. After the frantic rant, Francesca left Rosa shaken and in silence to listen to her own heart.

When her daughter returned sometime later both had settled, but Francesca's voice was still serious and sombre. She came with a tray of broth and bread and nettle tea. As she sat it upon Rosa's lap she told of how Lent was not only a time of repenting, but also receiving the Lord's love. He would want her to be strong for her children, to show them the way, to guide them to His glory. And then Francesca began to feed her mother. One mouthful at a time. Rosa did not resist. She looked at her daughter with a glance that begged forgiveness, and Francesca returned it with pardon generously given. On Maria's return from school, Francesca sent her in to pray with her mother, and this time, Rosa held the little one's hand and joined in, mumbling in parts but keeping pace.

By Easter, Rosa was still weak but well enough to attend the celebration at the church. While she wore a stoic face, Rosa's heart was filled with gratitude for Francesca. For she doubted whether she would have survived the guilt that would have smothered her if she had missed Easter mass. Instead, here, her role and her mission were strengthened.

Queen of Heaven, rejoice, alleluia
For He whom you were worthy to bear, alleluia
Has risen, as He said, alleluia
Pray for us to God, alleluia.

Rosa prayed to the Queen of Heaven, her mother, Mary, to help her bear the suffering of her children. Rosa imagined herself standing at the tomb, waiting to embalm the tortured bodies of her children, Isabella, Paulo and Luca, but instead being met with their radiant glory. Mary faced the fate that God had decreed with faith, and her child ascended into Heaven and received everlasting life. This gave Rosa hope that her lost children would do the same. The alleluia from the angelic voices in the choir strengthened her spirit, and the chant from the bishop confirmed her resolve.

Christ conquers, Christ reigns, Christ commands.
Christ conquers, Christ reigns, Christ commands.

Christ conquers, Christ reigns, Christ commands.

Rosa stood for as long as she could without falling but succumbed to sitting to save a collapse. When her body was steadied, she let her heart sing the words that her voice could not.

Christ is risen today,
For the comfort of all people.
He who suffered death the day before,
For the miserable human being.

She was miserable, weak, and unworthy, but she would do God's will.

After the mass had concluded, Francesca found a stool so that Rosa could join in the conversations with neighbours and friends. But Rosa did not stay there long, preferring to wander with her cane to the cemetery. There she sat with Isabella who gave her guidance from Heaven, which Rosa heard clearly. She would follow these instructions; let her oldest children take the reins, give them the responsibility that will help them grow, and focus on finding them suitable partners. The message came that Maria was a pious little one and so may have a place in the Church. This made her heart sink, for Maria was such a blessing. And yet, as Francesca had said, she can no longer be selfish. Rosa was to eat, pray, sleep and praise the Lord, for she too had risen from the dead, and now she must do God's work. As she saw the rain appear on the horizon, Rosa wandered slowly towards the sacristy to find the priest.

Antonio

Antonio did not want to marry, and yet there was no choice. His mother was becoming unreliable, at times requiring more care than she was able to give. Now that Maria was old enough to fend for herself, Francesca would soon be found a husband, and so another pair of female hands would be required around the house. He did not want them, though; having to deal with another woman, all of her frailties and ailments, made him angry. There was something inherently within them that he did not trust.

But now he had come of a suitable age, confirmed, and expected to fulfil his heavenly duty to procreate and fill the world with God's people. At Easter, his mother had petitioned the priest to propose a suitable match, and when all were seeking shelter from the sun months later, Father called them inside to announce he had found Antonio a fitting wife. Isabella Ferrara would be the ideal match. Antonio's heart sank when he heard the name. How could he marry someone with the same name as the gorgeous little girl he had buried? His stomach churned with a bitter bile. How could the priest be so heartless towards his family? His mother displayed a solemn acceptance and expressed her thanks. So did Antonio, although adding this to his ever-expanding pile of grudges.

They knew of the Ferrara family. They were merchants in the town and not farming families with whom they usually mixed. Now, their families were to be melded. The reasons Father gave for choosing Isabella were practical ones. She was a dutiful daughter and had proven her worth within the family home. She had not yet been required to undertake labours on the land, but she was healthy so there was no doubt that she could work hard, and all of her reproductive routines were normal. As one of several girls, her dowry would be small, which was fitting for their station as a farming family. Yes, Isabella would add just the amount of value the Contadino family deserved.

Arrangements were made to meet with her family the following Sunday after mass. Antonio was agitated the whole week but refused the herbal teas Francesca made for him. He would deal with this in his own way and show his sister he did not need her assistance. During the mass, Antonio looked around and found the Ferrara family. When his head was not bowed, he watched Isabella's father. He stood straight, moved with confidence and stepped forward for the Eucharist with a solid energy. The other men he observed over the next hour held the same stature. Antonio would be the same. He would stride forward and be the man that his own father would have been proud of.

When the two families gathered in the small room at the back of the church, Antonio had become one of the brave men he had studied during the mass. He bowed low, his face remained serious, and he sat steadfast, with his hands upon his thighs. He caught glances at the girl in front of him, but extended eye contact was not polite, so for much of the time, he looked at the floor. From what he did see, this Isabella appeared acceptable. She was not pretty like the girls his friends would talk about after mass and hanker after marrying. But she was also not one of the ugly ones they made up names for. She had some breasts and was carrying some weight, which gave her a solid shape and Antonio confidence that she could bear the burdens of the farm. Yes, even though Antonio hated her for being called Isabella, this girl was acceptable.

Antonio answered Father's questions in short statements and did not smile. He was agreeable to beginning the courtship and its planned cessation in the following spring. Then, a decision would be made as to whether bands would be exchanged, the dowry negotiations would be complete, and if all was well, the couple would become betrothed.

From then on, after every mass, the families would sit together for an hour, supervising the pair, whose time next to each other involved much silence. There were intermittent questions about Isabella's studies and the role she played in her home, to which Isabella would reply quietly and quickly. Isabella would ask Antonio about the animals on his farm and the status of the crops, and Antonio would respond simply. And so, it continued. As the winter came, the conferences began to be held within Isabella's home, and they started to feel a little less awkward. Antonio was always relieved when they ended, though aggravated that he had missed time with his friends. He hardly got to see them anymore, moving between the farm, mass and supervised sessions with his possible future wife. Even at festivals, the couple was expected to attend together, always flanked by their families. It was wearing away the Sunday afternoons he had to rest for the following week, and as each day passed, he was seeing his freedom slipping away. Apart from the farm labourer, he was surrounded by females and felt ever more trapped.

When the winds became warmer, Antonio became more worried, but Francesca got the message and stopped offering the teas and tonics. He subdued his fears and frustrations and set about being strong. He made more decisions about the farm, organised the sales and went personally to inspect the seeds for the next season's crops. When the scent of spring flowers was in the air, there were light showers of rain, and there was hope for a good season. It was with this air of optimism that Antonio strode into the decisive conference. There had been little talk with his mother about what they would do. She had simply asked him whether he would move forward with Isabella, to which he replied that he would. She appeared to be a good woman. He said this with an intonation that implied he knew there was much more to women than they showed, and he was now the one who would cast judgment.

The priest asked both parties the same question and there was a common assent, but no smiles. Such displays of excess were not suitable for the house of the Lord. Plans were put in place for the betrothal to occur in four weeks. The wedding would be held on the Feast of Saint Anthony of Padua, a fitting day for celebration. For this day, a feast was already being planned, and it would relieve pressure on the families to provide for the party afterwards. Other couples would join them to also be wed on this day, making it a marvellous event for the community. For this, Antonio was relieved. There would be less focus on him.

As the couple sat outside and watched the wind through the trees and the birds fly between them, Antonio resigned himself to the way forward. The next few weeks he distracted himself with making the betrothal gift, selecting a piece of walnut wood he had left from his sister's casket. He had run out of time to do another ring of flowers before the funeral, and so this block had sat, staring at him, taunting, ever since. It seemed fitting now to be using this piece on a gift that was to see the end of his liberty. Would this new Isabella consider it cruel if she knew the original intent of this piece? Perhaps. But then that was her problem. He would make it nice so she would have no right to complain.

In the evenings, as the sun held its light for longer, Antonio would chisel the shapes to his satisfaction, his mind focused on finishing this offering. Here, he found beauty in the rich colour of the wood and the graceful grain. He took his time planning out the patterns that would adorn this trinket box and received much satisfaction in scraping away just the right amount. The roses revealed themselves well, and his work gave him pleasure. The pumice stone made it perfectly smooth, the linseed oil enhanced the grain, and the beeswax made it gleam with a soft, warm lustre. He knew that he loved this process of creating and wondered whether he would ever feel the same passion towards his future wife. For at the moment, all he felt was annoyed and nervous.

In exchange for his box, Antonio received an embroidered handkerchief inlaid with their initials. The priest blessed two small medals of Saint Joseph and placed them around their necks, a symbol of their commitment to each other and their shared faith. And then the dowry discussions began. There was no negotiation, simply an offering and an acceptance. Both families had neither the resources nor energy to engage in a show. Isabella would come with furniture for the married couple, a small amount of cash to assist with the rearing of any children, a suit for Antonio and she would also supply the rings. All was satisfactory, and once scribed by the priests and signed by the parties, they were free to begin the betrothal celebrations. Isabella's brothers and father took him away from the women and supplied him with wine. He found their company challenging and was glad to hear the thunder that concluded the event and had his family hurtling home. His head was weary, his heart was confused, and he just wanted to sleep.

The next Sunday afternoon, Antonio was called upon by the men from the neighbour's farm. They knew of his impending nuptials, and as he was without a father, wanted to share with him what his role as a husband would entail. Antonio wondered whether his mother had put them up to it, and the thought made him irate. He was a man and did not need her help. But he also could not be rude to those who had been so generous in the past and whom he may require again in the future. Antonio stood in the barn with them as they drew images in the dirt. Honestly, he was disgusted with the description they gave of the consummation process and the aids he might need to make it work. He knew his own member; he had touched it before, and since Luca and Paulo left, he had been able to investigate it further. He had not stroked it, though; to do so would be a sin. There would be times, though, when he would wake in a sticky mess and then spend the day in prayers of penance in case he had been sinful while he slept. Now, he was to insert this into Isabella; it was his privilege, his right and his holy duty. He may need to use some force, and she may feel some pain. But his job was to procreate, and Isabella was his possession. His woman would get used to it, and she must yield to his authority. That is what it meant to be a man, and that is what he would also teach his children.

The day before the wedding, the Ferrara family came to deliver the dowry. A bed was constructed in the boy's room, and a chest of Isabella's clothes was placed at its base. Antonio's suit was hung on the door, and a pair of shiny leather shoes was put beneath. Signore Ferrara placed a bag of coins in Antonio's palm and gave him a warm embrace. The men sat out in the sun, drank and talked while the women were inside frantic with the food preparations for the feast the next day. Isabella's father spoke of his delight with the thought of grandchildren, hinting at what would come the following night. After a simple supper, the Ferrara's said their goodbyes. Seeing Isabella working with his mother, Maria and Francesca, he changed his mind. It was good that there were other women in the household. They would be there to comfort and guide Isabella and care for her so he would not have to.

The couples arrived well before the feast day mass, presenting the priest with their rings to receive God's blessing. Then Isabella sat with her family, and Antonio with his, separate for the last time. The church service was spectacular, rivalling the arrival of the baby Jesus. There were flowers and magnificent music, and then, after the procession, the bishop returned for the marriages.

Five couples stood before the congregation and made their claim upon each other. In the eyes of God, they were joined forever more, and rings were placed on fingers to seal the sanctity of their union. With pledges made, they all walked down the aisle to applause. Outside they were overcome with well-wishers, each couple showered with flower petals and placed on a carriage where a procession led them to the town square for the communal feast. Antonio spent the next several hours beside Isabella, only parting ways when each needed to relieve themselves, but then returning to each other promptly. Isabella was provided with a little wine, carefully supervised by her mother to prevent anything from compromising her wifely duty. The men gave Antonio grappa, whose warmth aided his relaxation and reduced his anxiety for the trip home.

Antonio stumbled a little as he carried Isabella across the threshold, although not enough for anyone to notice and not enough for him to feel any shame. There were cheers behind them as he continued carrying her into the bedroom and closed the door. Antonio placed Isabella gently on the bed and sat beside her. For a moment they just shared the space and observations about the decorations; garlic, lavender, wheat and rosemary hung from the walls, and small bowls of salt had been placed in each corner. The bedposts were adorned with red ribbons and a crucifix was centred above them.

Antonio knew that Isabella was waiting for his command. He did just as his neighbours suggested, telling her to take off her dress but to leave the slip on. Then, he told Isabella to remove her undergarments and to lay on the bed. She did all of this while Antonio turned his back. When she was ready, he removed his trousers and lay beside her, telling her to make him hard. It seemed Isabella had received suitable instruction, and it was only a short while before he was trying to get inside her. There were moments of feeling, but these were swamped with frustration. As suggested by the men, spittle was employed to provide some ease. Even still, Isabella had to hold in some small yelps of pain. Antonio forced much harder than he thought it would be possible, and yet, once her insides were wet, it gave him so much pleasure. He could feel the surge coming and pushed forward, looking away so he did not have to see Isabella frown, and so she would not be scared by his frightening face as it contorted beyond his control. In the final few moments, he was in ecstasy, and nothing would intervene. She was his. He would have her whenever again he wanted. He was the master in this marriage and as he held in his growl, he knew then that God was good to give men the gift of women.

CRUCIFIXUS

Paulo

It was approaching Paulo's sixth Christmas at the college. As he cuddled into the warm coals in the bed that was becoming too small, he tried to conjure forth the faces of his family. As much as he tried to hold on, the memories continued to fade, now commandeered by the compositions he was working on and the mixed praise and punishments of his masters. Less and less did he have time to wonder about the health and happiness of his mother and siblings. Any spare space in his mind was becoming filled with music and the maestro's suggestion that he had the makings of a great castrato.

At the end of each semester, the students would be tested and graded based on the potential the teachers saw within them. Paulo had remained as a primo throughout the years and this gave him a great sense of pride. Signore Conti visited once and promised to provide an update when he passed the farm, so that Paulo's mother could share in his achievement. But the Signore had not returned, and Paulo could not be sure that the message had been received by his mother. However, he had already learned to cede control and so continued to concentrate on his studies.

While Signore Conti provided little obvious support, at least he still kept paying the tuition. Dante was taken away when his patron stopped providing for him. Dante had been called to the maestro one morning and whispered to Paulo about his predicament that afternoon as they were washing the windows. The next morning, after breakfast, Dante was taken away. It had only been a few months since Dante had been designated a terzo. His patron would have been advised that fame would be unlikely for this boy, and thus his personal tutoring would be terminated. From the talk Paulo overheard between the masters, there was always some money to be made from postings to positions in local parishes or private choirs, but given that he had not completed his training, this did not appear to be an option for Dante. Or perhaps Dante's patron had died and there was no one left to continue his legacy.

Paulo knew Dante could have continued if he was graded higher. The Church was willing to fund positions for those designated as primo, seeing a future fortune in the making. But in Dante, they could see nothing but cost. Where Dante went, no one knew. Paulo hoped it was back to his home but could not be sure, so he prayed heavily for him. Paulo could not help but think that the secrecy surrounding Dante's move served as a dire warning for those who would also let themselves slip to a low standard.

Paulo did not know Dante well, not like he knew Leonardo. Leonardo had been his bed buddy since the beginning, sleeping below Paulo. They did not speak at the start for fear of the dean's wrath. With each year, though, the dean's strictures had eased, and they were given more space without supervision. That's when Paulo began receiving requests from Leo to peek his head over the bunk and chat. It was clear that Leo was feeling shaky and looking for some reinforcement. He had recently slipped into being a secondo and was scared that he, too, may be cast aside.

When whispers across the space between did not meet with any discipline, after the candles went out each night, Paulo moved to sit at Leo's feet. The boys talked about their lives before college, their longing for the future, but also their loneliness now. There was something about Leo that made Paulo feel so comfortable and so he shared things with Leo he would not trust to anyone else.

Leo talked about how he was becoming short of breath, which made it hard to hold the notes. Leo was so worried there was something wrong with him. Paulo tried to provide reassurance, but sometimes, when Leo was particularly sad, Paulo would stay the night and sleep on his chest. They were not the only boys who found comfort in the caress of another. There was much movement between the beds as the boys did their best to find the support they needed to survive.

Paulo was so hopeful that with his care, Leo would get more strength in his lungs and return to the primos. He wanted Leo to succeed and for them to be stars together, travelling the world as famous and fast friends. But when, in the cool of the night, Leo's cough became consistent, they both knew that whatever condition he had was worsening. Leo was sent to the infirmary and cleared of being contagious. It was a great relief to many but not to Leo and Paulo, who were still unsure what it meant. Over the months, Leo kept trying but was getting weaker and unable to keep up with training. Leo was tested, declared a terzo and sent to the dottore.

Leo returned to their room in an inconsolable state. The dottore had seen his rounded fingertips before and told him that he would be dead within months. In the morning, he would be taken to an institution to be cared for until his condition took him. There was no comforting the couple that night. Tears were withheld through dinner and vespers, but the sadness was let loose once the attendants had extinguished the lights. Other boys came and sat on the floor beside Leo's bed and held his hands. They would keep a vigil, for that is all they could do. When Leo's coughing ceased for a moment, he turned to Paulo. In breathless and broken sentences, Leo stated his wish; if he could not stay here with Paulo, then he would rather be dead. The moan that came from Paulo's mouth was a noise he had never heard before. It came from a place deeper than the darkness surrounding him and tore at his heart, creating new wounds within.

After breakfast, eaten through red and puffy eyes, Leo was led away by an attendant. Paulo wanted desperately to run after him, pull Leo from the attendant's clutches and hold him close. He would declare that Leo would remain, under his protection and care. For a moment, he believed it was possible and that he had such power. In reality, a simple touch of their hands across the table and a goodbye glance was all they could achieve.

Without Leo there, Paulo's wounds festered. The infection did not show forth in obvious and overt ways but in subtle sabotage. He allowed his mind to become scattered and his song undisciplined. His distraction was met with slaps and a designation as a secondo. He did not care. How could he be in this place and around these people who simply sent Leo off to die? Paulo had seen much cruelty, but this crossed a line, and now he would let go and let the hate consume him. He would protest against the system in his own personal way. While, he had been hanging on to do his family honour, they felt too far away to provide any sustenance.

Paulo was pulled from this destructive pathway, not by punishment, but by a triad of tenderness.

As Paulo was actively resisting his future, his friend Gabriele was becoming frozen with fear. Over the few months since Leo was taken, Paulo could see it progress. Gabriele slumped, slept and did not even wince when he was slapped. Paulo could permit his own suffering but could not stand by and see Gabriele succumb. Paulo snuck in and spoke to the kitchenhand, asking for her assistance to make a tonic like the one he had seen Francesca prepare for his mother. She was happy to help, and the medicine was smuggled into the room awaiting a chance to administer it by moonlight. But Gabriele refused to take the tonic. Paulo begged the boy to not let this place take him. Sometime through this pleading, Paulo's words were heard by his own heart. While Gabriele worsened, unable to get out of bed, even when he was beaten, Paulo became more determined; he would not give up, not like this. And when Gabriele's folded form and vacant eyes were removed from the room, Paulo's determination to succeed was restored. It was only through his triumph that retribution against this evil would be possible.

The second source of generosity came from the gardener. He was an old man and only spoke to give the boys instructions, until a few days after Paulo had sourced the tonic from the kitchenhand. Perhaps the cook had told the gardener of Paulo's predicament when she came to collect ingredients for the potion. Or perhaps this grandfather had seen enough of the goings on in this place to know when someone needed words of support. Sitting beside Paulo, pulling the weeds, he reminded the boy that these people had taken his past but he still had power over his future. Looking into Paulo's eyes, he provided sage advice; show everyone how strong he is and stop with the sinful self-pity. With a pat on Paulo's back, the discussion ended and the man walked away, leave Paulo suitable scolded but substantially wiser.

The third act of kindness came through song. The secondos were assigned the Dies Irae in preparation for a requiem mass. As Paulo sang the words, they seemed to bring a message from the Heavens directly into Paulo's heart.

Day of wrath and doom impending,
David's word, with Sibyl's blending,
Heaven and earth in ashes ending.

O what fear man's bosom rendeth,
When from heaven the Judge descendeth,
On whose sentence all dependeth.

Wondrous sound the trumpet flingeth,
Through earth's sepulchers it ringeth,
All before the throne it bringeth.

Death is struck, and nature quaking,
All creation is awaking,
To its Judge an answer making.

Lo! the book exactly worded,

*Wherein all hath been recorded,
Thence shall judgment be awarded.*

*When the Judge his seat attaineth,
And each hidden deed arraigneth,
Nothing unavenged remaineth.*

Paulo knew what he was being told through song; that all the evil treatment, towards the boy with the yellow eyes, Giovanni, Dante and Leo, would one day be punished. It was not his place to do so, but to protect his own integrity. Over and over, Paulo imagined kneeling before the Lord and being judged. He would not be found wanting. Prayers in the dark were resumed, and Paulo felt assured that his friends, one day, would be avenged.

CRUCIFIXUS

Francesca

Francesca was married within a year of Antonio, taking her mother to live with the newlyweds in her husband's home. She was not pleased to be wed and answerable to another, but she was glad to be free of Antonio. She had seen her brother change when Isabella came. His ability to have complete control over his wife made him callous and even more commanding. He would bully his wife and use the Bible to justify his behaviour. Antonio never hit Isabella, well, not where it could be seen, but pushing her of the way was commonplace. Isabella accepted it without question, just like she was taught to do and just like Francesca was now forced to.

Although Francesca had fared well in a match. Her husband was the son of a farmer from the other side of the mountain. Their farm was prosperous, and they had plenty of brothers and labourers nearby, which all helped to ease the burden. Every now and then, her husband would get tired and throw a tantrum, but with wine and a woman's attention, it would blow over, and by morning, he was his calm and constructive self once again. She could sing as she did her chores, well out of the earshot of her mother, who increasingly spent her days inside. It was obvious that her mother felt cumbersome here in the marital home of her daughter, but it was more comfortable than being with her son. Francesca was grateful to her husband's family that they conceded to the request, but also proud of herself that she had put it forward.

For Isabella would not know how to handle her mother's monthly condition, and it would place another pressure onto Antonio's wife that she surely did not need. Here, Francesca could protect this ageing woman from anger and abandonment and support her faith, even if Francesca did not share it. There was also a selfish motive that Francesca was willing to attest to. She did not want to be alone with these people, who felt very much like strangers. Because of the distance between the families, the normal rules of betrothal did not apply. There was a single meeting where decisions were made and the dowry confirmed, and then two months later the deed was done. The marriage had meant a move to a different parish, a new chapel, new priests, merchants and networks. It eased Francesca immensely to have her mother help her navigate all this uncertainty. Rosa, too, had experienced it when she married, moving away from family and friends, and was a great source of support through the isolation and loneliness of the early days.

Her mother was also there to provide care and comfort when Francesca lost her first child. There was no warning when it happened; nothing Francesca could have prepared to prevent it. Her mother made teas and heat packs to ease the pain and swiftly set about cleaning the mess. Her mother stayed close during the following days of distress, bringing her chamomile tea to help her rest and broth to regain her strength. When Francesca had regained a sense of solidity, there were conversations about what she could have done to deserve such divine retribution. Francesca dared not mention the singing to her mother. She could not bear to hear criticism from one so close, or to feel her mother's condemnation if now she were to fail in her earthly duty to deliver heirs. Had her disobedience of the Church's orders resulted in the death of her child? Would her wilfulness leave her without any legacy? These were the questions that churned in her stomach as she tried to sleep.

When Francesca was well enough, her mother accompanied her to confession. The priest was shielded from sight, nothing but a shadow on the other side of the screen. Still, his voice was harsh as he handed down the judgement that would cleanse her soul. Given Francesca's weakened state, fasting, vigils and pilgrimages were ruled out as possible penances. And due to the fact that the prohibition was not broken in public or in a sanctified space, there would be some leniency shown. To be forgiven, for the next month, Francesca would need to recite the rosary three times a day, to be followed by the seven penitential psalms. Her mother was overjoyed with this outcome, eager to join her in the daily prayers. But despite her persistent pushing, Francesca would not divulge to her mother the nature of her sin.

Before penance, both women would provide for the man of the house, feeding him breakfast, lunch and dinner. When he was full, the women would attend the shrine in the corner, kneel under the cross and before the small statue of Mary. Moving through their wooden beads, they would complete the sign of the cross, the Apostles Creed, an Our Father, three Hail Mary's and the Glory Be. Their words were well-rehearsed and rhythmic. By the time they were into the ten

Hail Mary's in each decade, the monotonous mumbling sent Francesca's mind wandering into the mysteries.

When this daily duty began, Francesca was seething. Each time she said "the fruit of thy womb" was like torture. It was as Mary's being with child was paraded in front of her, a cruel reminder that now she was barren. It brought up much bile and bitterness. By the end of the month, though, Francesca felt a shift. She began to believe there may be hope. Each day, as she looked up to Mary she began to understand more why this woman meant so much to her mother. Even in statue form, Mary's eyes exuded compassion, and her hands, held outwards, were ready to lift her up and hold her tight. Her mother did this after every session, embracing her daughter and lifting her to her feet. Through this, a very special closeness came to be.

The penitential psalms, though, perturbed her. She found all the groaning, pleading, panting, blood guiltiness, brokenness and withering pathetic. She read them repeatedly, their descriptions full of everything she despised. They were a foul display of vulgar victimhood. She wondered about who wrote them and what he would look like. Such words would not have come from a farmer, who would have brushed the dust off and simply gotten back to work. No, a farmer would not have time to rant about how bad they felt or what their enemies deserved. Such indulgence would not plant the grains or get the sheep to market. Francesca decided they were written by someone with far too much time on their hands and a severe case of self-righteousness. These psalms definitely felt like a punishment, as did the message she received from her hometown. Next month, Maria would be sent to a convent.

Francesca and her mother packed for the journey and parted warmly with her husband. His sister would stay with him over the next week to care for him while his wife was away. Francesca was thankful that he allowed her to leave and see her sister, and for that, she could almost say she loved him. They left after mother recovered from her latest illness; Francesca frustrated that they had to delay their departure by days. But when they were finally on the road, her mood eased, and she could enjoy seeing more of the countryside. Setting off at sunrise, they had made it to their old home by sunset, and Maria came running out to greet them.

Maria was delighted by the future Antonio had chosen for her. There was little money left for a dowry meaning it was unlikely to find her a suitable match. And her little sister was graced with such a spiritual nature. It was as if she was attuned to the angels themselves. It was fitting for her to join the convent, and because of this, there was an air of festivity. That is until Antonio appeared. The women's presence was obviously a source of annoyance to him. For once Francesca did not care. She had her own husband to answer to now and she was there for Maria, not for him. In a way, Francesca was also there for Isabella, to offer the support she suspected Antonio's wife needed. Isabella seemed to have shrunken in stature since they last met, and passed the fussing child on her hip over eagerly. Rosa was so excited to hold the child, stroking its cheek and checking it had all the required parts for a boy that one day would become as important as his father.

Over the few days Francesca and her mother stayed in the spare room, softly talking about their concerns for Isabella and their intention to do what they could to help while they were there. They took the child whenever possible, seeing Isabella brighten without the constant burden of her boy. It also became apparent that Isabella was bearing another child. Many congratulations were given from the visitors but they received a very reserved acceptance from Isabella. Playing with her nephew strengthened Francesca's resolve to do all she could to become pregnant, and she decided to continue the rosary each day, and to ask for Mary's aid in this endeavour.

They women went for an outing, with the guests taking Isabella and Maria to the markets. They brought Isabella a new sling so that she could carry her child with ease. And for Maria, they purchased a special set of rosary beads, taking them to the church and getting them blessed. There were tears as they were given and received, but also a reassurance that they would be used every day to pray for these other wonderful women.

The day before their departure, the Contadino women went to the cemetery and sat with the memory of little Isabella. After some time, Francesca's mother asked to be alone, and so the two girls went into the town to purchase some candles. On the way, Maria asked her sister how she was progressing in her aim to become pregnant, which made Francesca unexpectedly weep. There was something about her sister that made her feel safe enough to let the emotions out. Maria held her hand and put her arm around her shoulders. Maria promised that she would speak to God and petition for Francesca's pregnancy. There was no need to fear; she felt that it would come soon. Francesca just needed to have faith.

After collecting their mother back at the cemetery, they passed the school and, since classes had ceased, went in to see

Signore Battista. He was still there and was able to assure them that Luca had settled well into the Accademia and was excelling in his studies. He was doing his family proud. However, there was no news of Paulo.

CRUCIFIXUS

College Officials

The cloaks rustled and chairs were filled with God's representatives, alongside men of finance, medicine, law and music, all ready to review and regulate. The mood was buoyant, and heads were bowed while the Chairman commenced the proceedings.

"Dear Lord, we gather here to give you praise, for it is right and just. It is our honour to serve you and these students, who have made their sacrifice in your name.

Guide our hearts to make decisions that will bring glory to you and to the Holy Mother Church. And we beseech the Holy Spirit to be with us as we build your kingdom here on Earth.

Amen."

Bodies were crossed, and eyes raised towards the Chairman.

"Let us begin.

Maestro, it has been a few months since you took over the reins of the college, and we thank you for your seamless transition. What would you like to report or request?"

The new maestro stood, much smaller than the last and far less flamboyant. He was, however, sturdy and solid, and his voice came with more seriousness than song.

"Thank you, Monsignore. My brothers, I can confirm that the previous maestro has now taken his place at the private opera of one of our greatest patrons, Count Alessandro.

I had the privilege of witnessing a performance there last week and the popularity of this opera is hard to fathom. I saw one of our former students send the audience into what can only be described as an enchantment. The crowds crave the angelic voice of the castrati, and it does truly lift their hearts to the heavens. At one stage, they even appeared hypnotised, as if the Holy Spirit itself had landed upon them.

The love of the castrati in the opera is also fortuitous for our college. It creates a very profitable pathway for our primos. I met with the maestro a few days after the performance, and he advised that several other patrons are eager to contract our castrati for their own private arts programs. Each is willing to buy out the contracts of the finders that brought them here. Moreover, will pay us handsomely for the skill we have invested in our students, including offering an ongoing portion of their profits."

The maestro had to mute his emotion when he said:

"It is foreseeable that one or even more of our students may even end up in the court of the King."

There was no applause, for that would be hedonistic in a room dedicated to the holy. Instead, wide-eyed glances and satisfied smirks were shared in silence.

"With the help of the Consigliere we will facilitate these discussions for those in the graduating class that show such potential."

At this, the Monsignore asked,

"And how many may we be speaking of? How many may offer such a financial opportunity for our school and the Holy Mother Church?"

"There are three identified, Your Eminence."

Referring to the piece of paper on the table, he read out their names.

"Paulo Contadino, Matteo Moretti and Fabio de Luca."

"May they all be blessed and you too maestro for your superb oversight. And what of the others who are soon to leave us?"

"Thank you, Your Eminence. It is my honour to do God's work here on Earth. The remaining primos will be provided to St Peter's and the Pope's own choir. The secondos have been secured places in the parishes and are to receive stipends for roles in the choir or as music teachers. Two have been placed in patrons' homes as music tutors. With regard to the terzos, there are very few of these, thanks to the hard work of the masters. Two have been placed in a theatre troupe, securing at least a small payment towards their tuition. The remaining two would, unfortunately, despite all of our efforts, only reduce the standard of our work if they were to perform in public. We have secured them places at a monastery, a fitting place where they can continue their service in seclusion."

"All sounds well, maestro. Wonderful."

"Monsignore, if I may?"

"Of course, Father Farelli."

The priest that stood represented the parish in which the college was contained. He looked hesitant to address such a gathering and yet adamant that there was something he needed to say.

"Please excuse my ignorance regarding the financial necessities of the college. However, are we not veering away from our original spiritual purpose, now supporting private programs and negotiating profits?"

The maestro seemed unruffled by the enquiry, perhaps already prepared for such a challenge.

"Monsignore, may I present the case of the college?"

"Of course, maestro, continue."

"Brother Farelli, I do understand your concerns. Of course, opera was not the original intent, and yet let us praise the Lord, for God has found new ways to stir his people. Our student's popularity is unsurpassed, and through them, people's hearts are being lifted. I have no doubt that each person listening to their voice is also reflecting on the bodily sacrifice these men have made and, in turn, the blood spilt by Jesus to save us from our sins. These castrati are a doorway for these people back to Christ.

Yes, money is changing hands, but this is not a case of traders in the temple. What we are offering is in God's name, and all the money made goes back into His service.

My brother, I believe we cannot keep these gifts only for the use of the Church; that would be selfish. The Lord has shown us new ways to reach his people, and I believe we must humbly accept His Guidance."

"Thank you, maestro. Are there any other questions to be raised at this time?"

Father Farelli stood again.

"Yes, please, Monsignore. I thank the maestro for his clarification and now better understand why this path is being taken. I do, however, worry that we are putting our students in places where they will be tempted by sexual perversions. I, too, have heard of their popularity, particularly with women, some who are willing to pay for the pleasure of laying with them, and men too, who are willing to hand over money to marvel at their holy bodies. Should we not play some role in protecting the souls of our students from corruption? Can we not make stipulations in their contracts that they will not be misused for immorality?"

The Monsignore's hand was held up to the maestro, indicating that he would provide the reply.

"Father, I thank you for your concern for the souls of our students. I share your solicitude. However, God, in his wisdom, has given us all free will. And we have given our students the grounding they need to live in God's glory. It is not our place to intervene if they now choose to sin. With the signing of each contract, they are no longer our students. They are now in charge of their own souls. Let us pray each day that God protects and guides them with His grace.

Speaking of which, maestro, how many students have been taken by God this month?"

"Only two, Your Eminence. Their bodies were too weak to sustain the sacrifice. There may be one more to report next month as the infection appears becoming impossible to rectify."

"May God bless them all. And tell me, how many new students can we expect to come?"

"Monsignore, our college continues to expand. With thanks to the investment made by the Holy Mother Church, we are creating more space on this campus and an additional two facilities across the region. We will be in a position to receive over one hundred this month, and even more over the coming year."

"Let us give thanks to the Lord. And Consigliere, any news of unsanctioned surgeries?"

"Your Eminence, on a tip off from a loyal parishioner, we did find evidence of a place where castrations were being conducted without consent from the Church. We are working with the police to find the perpetrators, but with no resolution as yet. We have our people undertaking continual surveillance and pray that they will not be swayed and bribed to turn their backs on such brutality."

"Ah, brother, that is always the risk. Where there is money to be made, it will always draw those with malicious intent."

Paulo

Paulo awaited the Feast of the Epiphany with both desire and dread. This was the day of revelation. Just as Jesus was made known to the Magi on this day, the maestro would declare Paulo's place in the world. Paulo had worked hard and channelled all of the chaos in his heart to be the best castrato possible. He had regained his place as a primo, and now Paulo would find out what others had chosen as his fate. As he sang the hymns in the choir with the other castrati, Paulo sought fortitude for whatever his future may be and faith that it was what God wanted. He prayed fervently that the decision made was not driven solely by mortal motivations.

> *As with gladness men of old*
> *Did the guiding star behold*
> *As with joy, they hailed its light*
> *Leading onward, beaming bright*
> *So, most gracious Lord*
> *May we Evermore be led to Thee.*

In the afternoon, Paulo was called away from his compositions. He was sitting in the shade, feeling the solid earth, and sketching out a new piece, this time, a prayer. He was playing with a descension in notes and determining what words would fit with this grounding energy. Other castrati were clumped into groups around the grounds, and he could have joined them. But Paulo was done with forging friendships. They would end, and likely in excruciating ways. He could see no purpose to inviting in pain. Paulo would observe and assist from afar, but he would not, and could not, risk any more injury, for it may just flatten him for good.

Paulo joined two other primos he regularly practised with inside the maestro's office. This new maestro was largely unknown, which made Paulo nervous. But with deep breaths, he calmed his heart, so that he could hear where he would be sent.

The new maestro smiled at what were now three men who stood before him and seemed to be subduing excitement. He declared that their hard work had paid off handsomely, and they had secured positions in a private opera. Count Alessandro would become their patron, a generous supporter of the arts and sciences, and owner of the best opera house in Italy. They were reassured that this would only be the beginning. The count also had contacts in many courts, both domestic and foreign, and so there was no doubt they would travel far beyond these shores.

No reaction from the primos was required, for they were trained to be still and stoic. They had been taught severely over the past years that showing emotions was an excess which would not be tolerated. Neither was any response requested. The maestro continued, telling them of what he had witnessed when he attended the opera and how they would be adored. He informed them that much work would be required to acclimate to the intense attention that would be placed upon them. However, the count had assured him that they would also be protected. Fame, the maestro said seriously, would require that they fortify their souls for the temptations ahead. The maestro concluded with the mention of the composers who were now writing music specifically for their voices, and how this was a great honour. The three men were dismissed with a reminder that their sacrifice was a blessing from God.

Paulo resumed his spot in the shade and started to process the news. He watched as the other two castrati whispered and smiled, slapping each other on the arm and throwing their hands in the air with excitement. But Paulo could not make any clear sense of what he was feeling. He knew that fame would bring honour to his family, that such a position amongst those of power would make them proud. Yet, a posting in the opera seemed so far away from what he fought Antonio for. Paulo had wanted to be the voice of hope, to bring people to God. He wanted to lift them beyond the brutality of this life and take them to a place of joy and peace. Now, it appeared that instead of being an angel, he was to become an attraction.

From that point on, the training for these three primos changed significantly. They were separated from the rest of the coterie and made to practice secular songs and operatic pieces. Hymns were sung with the others for feast day celebrations, but they spent most of their time with a whole new range of composers. Time was subtracted from scripture studies and placed into tutelage on fashion and royal etiquette, lessons overseen by the maestro himself.

In addition to singing, the trio were also instructed on how to speak. The primos were made to practice humble and polite replies to requests. They were taught how to use their words to inform and inspire and not to insult. For they would have a fine line to tread to secure their fame. Paulo could see how the elevation in their status was accompanied by an increase in vulnerability. The higher they rose, the further they would have to fall, and the more diligent they would need to be about their grip. Paulo was used to stepping around the sensitivities of his masters, but this new world was unknown and unnerving.

As Paulo lay on the top bunk, on a mattress clearly not made for a man, he watched the moon cast its light on the cross. He beheld the blood flowing from the crown and wept. Then, he prayed for all those who had been cast into the tomb with no further thought. Lorenzo, Leo, Gabriele, Dante, and the many boys who, for him, still had no name. Including the one who had died the night of The Epiphany. He was a terzo, and the rumours told afterwards were that he was chosen to join a theatre group. Out of shame, he had scampered onto the roof of the dormitory building and thrown himself off. They all knew the fall did not kill him, for at the first call of the guard the students watched through the windows as the body below wriggled, then was hauled into a wheelbarrow and hurried away. Cleaners were summonsed to wash away the blood, and the next morning lessons began again with no mention of the previous night's misery. They were told days later that the boy had deceased, but there would be no funeral, not for one so selfish to take his own life; a life owned by the Lord.

Tonight, Paulo tried desperately to conjure clear views of his mother, but even as he sang Ave Maria in his mind and petitioned Mary's help, there was only a mist.

Hail Mary, full of grace,
Mary, full of grace,
Mary, full of grace,
Hail, Hail, the Lord
The Lord is with thee.
Blessed art thou among women, and blessed,
Blessed is the fruit of thy womb,
Thy womb, Jesus. Hail Mary!

Holy Mary,
Mother of God,
Pray for us sinners,
Pray, pray for us;
Pray for us sinners,
Now, and at the hour of our death,
The hour of our death.
The hour, the hour of our death,
The hour of our death.
Hail Mary!

Paulo was planted in the scene, on the farm, by the fire, seated beneath his mother and beside his sisters. But he could not see the faces of his family. They remained fuzzy and faint but still not forgotten. He wondered whether they were all still alive or whether any had seen the hour of their death pass. Paulo calculated their ages on his fingers and guessed Antonio and Francesca would likely be married. If he were to return, would there be nieces and nephews to dote upon and shower with gifts? If Paulo did see Antonio again, would his brother even acknowledge him, let alone accept him? Perhaps Antonio would declare him an abomination and forbid him from seeing his offspring. As much as Paulo replayed a reunion in his mind, he knew in reality it would be almost impossible. He was a castrato now, and would be confined to churches, courts and concert halls.

The Feast of All Saints passed, and Paulo had another birthday. It was not recognised, regarded or celebrated, just covered over with routine. The initial interest in the new lessons had subsided, and now the practice of perfecting their person had become normal. This was Paulo's seventeenth year on Earth, and in two months, he would be leaving this place, his residence for the last ten years. Surprisingly, the thought of departing the college brought no sense of sadness. It did not bring many feelings at all, which, Paulo thought, the maestro would consider a sign of a successful education.

During the celebrations, Paulo joined the other castrati in proclaiming the unity of God's Kingdom.

Let saints on Earth in concert sing
With those whose work is done;
For all the servants of our King
In heav'n and Earth are one.
One family, we dwell in Him,
One Church, above, beneath;
Though now divided by the stream,
The narrow stream of death.

But Paulo knew that like any family, the Church had its fractures. He saw these clearly when the serving lady had wished Signore Conti to hell, and when the boys on the other side of the college left dead animals in their bed. The family of the Church was just like his own; a mix of generous souls, and threatened tyrants. Pretending it was perfect was paramount to insanity. And as Paulo sang about the narrow stream of death, he decided that this is not how he would describe it at all. From his experience, death was no silvery, calm flow but a gutter full of grime, with guards to make sure you could not get out. Death was not a source of cool sustenance but a foul drain; one to be feared, one you do not slip into peacefully but one into which you are forced.

More and more, the psalms Paulo sang started to feel like propaganda. Faith and devotion were becoming increasingly difficult. From what he had seen, he could no longer buy into them blindly. He knew they were not the truth. What was real was the torture and callous lack of care condoned and encouraged by those supposedly chosen by God.

The past decade had seen certainty replaced with conflicting priorities, and Paulo spent more time composing to help him unwind the chaos. In his works, he would explore the soft and the strong and make both swirl together. His master was greatly impressed and called upon Paulo to present his work to a local conductor. After much praise, the piece was happily purchased for the orchestra, and then it too, was no longer Paulo's. The only things they could not take from him was the process of creation and he would cling to this with a passion.

It was then that Paulo began to consider the benefit of being at the opera. Here, in this hedonistic life, things may be far less murky. There would be far less confusion when you removed the expectation of care.

What worried Paulo the most about his upcoming appointment was his appearance. He would, wherever possible, watch other normal men. Whether it was the gardeners, attendants, the maestro or the other boys in mass, Paulo would inspect the shapes of their faces, the spread of their jaws and the clump in their throats. As they walked, he would examine the tightness of the shirts around their chests, the shape of their muscles, and what it looked like to be a man. He was not one, and this was becoming increasingly clear.

As he washed, he would take stock of his scars. Where once there was a solid scrotum, there was now a sagging sac that served no purpose except to remind him of who he was and what he had lost. It would hang, causing rashes in the heat and having to be bound if the breeches were tight to prevent bulges causing embarrassment. Instead of the strength he saw in other men's chests, Paulo had begun to develop wilting women's breasts, which were also bandaged when making public appearances. Paulo also had fat hanging on his hips and thighs, creating a strange shape and requiring specialist tailoring of his uniform. His bone structure was not bold like other boys but delicate; his limbs were not energetic but elongated, and his shirts were always too short. He was told his height brought him closer to the heavens, but he could not help thinking it merely made him eccentric, and this he was finding difficult to embrace.

Count Alessandro

Willow bark tea and oxymel were what the count ordered from his majordomo that morning, brusquely from bed. He would repose here for the next few hours while his headache shifted, and he again became strong and sensible. The past few nights had been full of entertaining and excesses, and now, this time would be spent restoring his equilibrium. For he would need all the energy, intelligence and nous he could muster for the next few months.

Just like his country, the count was wedged between the wills of the French and the Spanish. The Spanish owned the south but were nudging north. The French had claimed the north but were spying on lands in the south. Each monarchy sought to dominate the riches across the region, and both were finding ways to possess power. In the middle sat a number of strong republics, all walking a fine wire with allegiance on one side and autonomy on the other. And in this space sat the count. He had watched from the sidelines and seen many reputable players fall prey to politics. They had involved themselves in intrigues and indecencies and, in doing so, lost their independence and their integrity. They had taken sides, showed their hand and were cast away when the winds changed.

The count was smarter than this. He would not partake in politics, well, not directly. No, the count was a patron of the arts and sciences, seemingly above the pettiness of these power struggles. He catered for common humanity and was there to serve the enlightened pursuits of all people, well, all those who could afford its artefacts.

He would entertain the emissaries from the Hapsburgs, happy to show them around his academic facilities and delight them with his dramas. Likewise, he would feast with the French consuls, regaling them with his alchemy and operatic troupes. He met these men where they were at, with what mattered to them the most; knowledge and hedonistic pleasure. Of course, each event was tailored to the strict sensibilities of the Holy Mother Church. However, the count also respected free will. At the right price, the count would happily veer from virtue, show his vetted guests to the secret rooms, and, with loyal witnesses in attendance, facilitate their deepest desires.

Some craved inclusion in ceremonies, where they could gain the second sight and be initiated to the eternal wisdom. Here, pride was the prize. These guests returned to their roles with a new sense of superiority. Others sought more somatic pleasures. The count saw to the provision of mistresses or of men. There were those who wished to be gifted young girls and some who wanted to be brought boys. It was not for the count to judge what gave these men satisfaction, for he knew the specific thrills of them all. He smiled remembering the act of bastardry a few weeks earlier when he aided the French and Spanish to share an act of sodomy. Yes, he was smart. Through service the count had secured his place.

In the community within which the count lived, those willing to offer their bodies for entertainment were easy to come by. It took very little to secure loyalty from those who were suffering. Many were happy to hand over their children for bread; it was better than begging on the streets. For superior specimens, the stakes sometimes needed to be raised. Then, the count's men would offer a more sinister bribe. In exchange for the use of the man's wife, daughter or son, the count vowed not to pass on the compromising information he had about their family to the Church. Over the years, the count had built up a long list of resources from which he could draw. He sent his people out regularly to check the health of his assets, remove those who were no longer deemed decent and to secure replacements where required. The count did not have to play the risky game of politics. The game of pleasure was so much easier.

Of course, the Church did make some things difficult. The echoes of the Roman Inquisition were still evident, and heresy was still a reason for hanging. While several decades had passed since Galileo's death, the Pope would provide no leeway for any teachings that did not support the scriptures. And there were spies. So, the count led a double life. He spent a significant amount of his time showing his support for the religious orders and officials so his absolute devotion to the Church could not be questioned. His Sundays were spent in worship, and a portion of his profits ploughed into Church projects. His masterstroke came with the patronage of the castrato program.

The count could not have prayed for a more perfect way to get everything he wanted. He could see the rising popularity of the castrati, and this was confirmed when he had hired some for his opera. The Church was reluctant at the time to let their castrati go for such a purpose, but the count had assured them this was an inventive way to do God's work. Besides, they could hardly pass up the generous donation he was willing to give in return. The new maestro was easy to manipulate, and when showered with wine and women, the count readily won. He had then secured the first bids for the next bunch of graduating boys. His cleverness had made him the proud patron of three exceptional castrati, all of which he could use in whatever way he wanted. The count wondered how much his guests may pay to see their scars.

And with the willow bark doing its work, he could grin as he reflected on his guile. For the count had used the greed of the Church for his own gain. He had positioned himself not just to control some heavenly voices, but through the arts and sciences he was slowly usurping the Church's spiritual supremacy. The count was determined not to be stuck behind with those unwilling to change. More than this, he wanted to lead the charge, be ahead of his time, and be first to the treasure. Now, with the castrati, all of the pieces of his triumph were in place.

The count called for the curtains to be opened and for bone broth and bread. With a few more sips of tea, he ordered that his writing instruments be brought to him, and that his opera master join him promptly. For he had a Christmas pageant to prepare, and this year, thanks to the Glory of God, there would be castrato to draw the crowd.

Luca

Luca cherished being at the Accademia and counted his blessings every day for finding a way in. His masters were firm and fastidious but fair. They demanded discipline, dedication and meticulous attention to detail, all of which came easily to Luca. Each teacher was more concerned with the pursuit of tangible, incontestable truth than playing ephemeral politics. This latter concern was left to the patrons. It was the place of those in power to placate the Church and carefully censor publications, keeping the more controversial for their private consumption. Everyone at the Accademia knew of the necessity not to threaten the supremacy of the spiritual fathers or the scriptures. There had been too many intellectuals whose work had been interpreted as denying the presence of God and who had died in imprisonment. As a result, the work of Luca's peers was framed very carefully, in line with the Church's creed, and to celebrate the glory of God's creations. Count Alessandro was a master at this, although all of the faculty saw through the façade.

With all Luca was learning, committing to the Nicene creed, a compulsory part of each mass, was becoming more challenging.

I believe in one God, the Father almighty, maker of heaven and earth, of all things visible and invisible.

And in one Lord Jesus Christ, the only-begotten Son of God, born of the Father before all ages.
God from God, Light from Light, true God from true God, begotten, not made, consubstantial with the Father; through Him all things were made.
For us men and for our salvation He came down from heaven, and by the Holy Spirit was incarnate of the Virgin Mary, and became man.
For our sake He was crucified under Pontius Pilate, He suffered death and was buried, and rose again on the third day in accordance with the Scriptures.
He ascended into heaven and is seated at the right hand of the Father.
He will come again in glory to judge the living and the dead, and His kingdom will have no end.
I believe in the Holy Spirit, the Lord, the giver of life, who proceeds from the Father and the Son, who with the Father and the Son is adored and glorified, who has spoken through the prophets.
I believe in one, holy, catholic and apostolic Church.
I confess one baptism for the forgiveness of sins, and I look forward to the resurrection of the dead and the life of the world to come.
Amen.

Luca may have believed such things with the simplistic view of a child. But now he was seeing things were much more complicated. Luca had held Galileo's Starry Messenger and seen the drawings of the moon, mountains, and craters. It was far from a perfect sphere, the "eternal pearl", as the priests described it. Even the sun, the shining example of God's greatness, was pocked with spots. It was not immaculate or apparently meticulously manufactured. And we were not the only planet with moons. Luca had seen the ones of Venus, so could there be life there too? And why was that not written about in the Bible?

Luca knew that light did not come from light. It was not that simple. He had created it from heat, bent it with lenses and broken it down into its colours. He had seen it arise from the abdomens of fireflies and now Luca was working with theories that it actually travelled, not in lines, but in waves.

From what Luca could discern, the Earth was far more interesting religion would have them believe. There was no pure black or white, just many shades of grey. And eternal was an erroneous proposition. Everything was shifting and changing and challenging all they thought was right. As Luca wrestled with the words he was required to speak, he also wondered where he should place the praise. Perhaps he should give God much more credit for the complexity He created. Or maybe the Church should be congratulated for their ability to cling to crude and convenient perspectives.

Although Luca did not waste too much time with this worry. He knew with his work, it would all become clearer to him, or so he hoped. So far, with each discovery, even more questions arose, and that truly made his heart sing. He never felt this way with his family; he never felt at home. Here, he felt like he belonged. Here, he felt like he was among a band of brothers. They were not bound by the routines of day and night. Time was irrelevant, and energy was endless. They did what was needed, and when, to satisfy their enquiries, and did so with passion. Yes, they suffered for their science with long hours of study and observation. Conversations and calculations continued well into the night. Yet, he was surrounded by clusters of companions, shared projects and goals with his peers, and revelled in friendly competition and respectful rivalry. He learnt from the great Cassini and Viviani and was encouraged to express his own ideas about how telescopes and lenses could continue to be advanced.

Here, Luca was heard. Here, he was challenged. Here, he could question. And where there were no answers, he was encouraged to explore and to find ones for himself. This was a whole new world from the one he knew on the farm. He was handed answers to repeat, but was permitted to pursue his own understanding. No wonder, he thought, that the Church was feeling so threatened.

From what he had witnessed over the past few years, he could clearly see the flow of fear. It washed its way down from the Church to the count, his servants, and the children under his care. Everyone was tainted with insecurity. The only thing that differed was how many others you could usurp and use to give yourself a sense of solidity. Those at the bottom had to simply bear the brunt until they could stake a claim over another. This had surely been Luca's experience. In the early days at the Accademia, he had been called on regularly by Count Alessandro and made to lay with the man. But as his studies continued, and he was now overseeing other students, his place was confirmed, his future more certain, and he was called on less. He had proven himself and, as such, had been substituted with new students.

Still, every time Luca attended an event at the count's estate, or happened upon the count at the college, Luca would feel ill. His stomach would turn, remembering his body rejecting what the count had forced into him. Luca's cheeks would flush like they did when he would choke, sending him into shame. Luca could say honestly that he hated this man, because unlike those who stood at the periphery, Luca had seen behind Alessandro's mask. And unlike those who had simply benefited from his benevolence, Luca also knew of the man's brutality. This loathing, though, would help Luca make his legacy. It drove him to learn, to become a reputable power in his own right. With each experiment, he moved further away from the count and towards a position where he may be believed if, one day, he decided to reveal what was behind the count's bookshelves.

Luca had entered the Accademia to learn astronomy. However, lately, he had been drawn to discover more about light. He had been taken under Bianchini's tutelage, and they were following the great work of Grimaldi to understand the true source of this spirit. Bianchini was becoming a star, but Luca just admired him as a scientist and a friend. Luca was ready to decline the invitation to Alessandro's Christmas concert, but with Bianchini was beside him he knew there would be great conversation and much comedy. Likely, he would have to carry Bianchini to the carriage afterwards, but then his friend always returned the favour.

The night of the concert, there was a great deal of curiosity circling around the crowd. Like so many others, Luca had only seen castrati in church, or from far back at the opera. He had never seen one close up, and certainly not in a place where their song could be intimately appreciated. From what he had heard, he would describe their voice as divine. Still,

Luca could not fathom the surgery or anatomical adjustments that created them, or the significant shift that this would have on the core of their being. And he could not imagine his brother being one, which always led to wondering whether little Paulo was still alive.

And then the question was answered.

The castrato was announced as Alessio, so named in deference to his dedicated and generous patron. But Luca knew it was Paulo. His brother's body was no longer that of a boy and certainly could not be called beautiful. It was long and lanky, with fat in feminine places. He was not of this world anymore but was a merging between man and woman. And yet his eyes were the same, just far more serious.

> *Alleluia. Praise ye the Lord in his holy places: praise ye him in the firmament of his power.*
> *Praise ye him for his mighty acts: praise ye him according to the multitude of his greatness.*
> *Praise him with the sound of trumpet: praise him with psaltery and harp.*
> *Praise him with timbrel and choir: praise him with strings and organs.*
> *Praise him on high sounding cymbals: praise him on cymbals of joy:*
> *Let every spirit praise the Lord.*
> *Alleluia.*

Luca's heart raced when he saw him, and it beat harder when he heard him. Paulo's voice floated across the crowd with passion and purity; it was both technically excellent and ethereal. As Alessio accepted the audience ovation with grace and generosity, their eyes met. Luca smiled; Paulo could not, and yet there was a recognition and a softening of the singer's solemnity. While the spectators were still standing, Luca's sibling was whisked away, allowing the count to take the stage and receive the remaining acclaim.

With excitement and optimism, Luca confided in Bianchini and begged him to ask the count if he could have counsel with the castrato. Luca suggested that his friend feign interest purely for scientific purposes, thinking that the count may be more conducive to this approach. Bianchini was happy to be of assistance, but the frown he wore when he returned, from what was a very short conversation, crushed Luca's hope. The count had advised that the castrati were not for mere mortals such as them; they were spiritual creatures, not to be sullied by science. Unless, of course, you were willing to pay for the privilege. The price the count proposed was far out of reach for people of their station.

During the rest of the evening, Luca was distracted by a deep pull to be with Paulo. He began scheming about how he could evade the security that surrounded this castrato and get close to the brother that he once knew.

CRUCIFIXUS

Paulo

On his first pass exploring the audience, Paulo was not sure. He recognised the excitement in one man's eyes, but it took several more scans to realise that man was Luca. Paulo could sense Luca was not just appreciating the song but wanted to advance. And the little boy buried inside Paulo had wanted to run to his brother too, to hold him and pummel him with questions about his life over the last ten years. Paulo had almost forgotten his family, and now there was nothing more he craved than to have this connection. However, castrati were not to be subsumed by such earthy concerns. So instead, Paulo took generous glimpses, assessing Luca's clothes and companions and concluding that Luca was secure, supported and successful. It was only at the conclusion of his performance that Paulo could afford a shared glance, and he wished he could also smile and wave. But these actions were unworthy of a castrato and would wreck the visage of the divine that it was his duty to uphold. He could not be both a castrato and a commoner. He had made his choice.

Paulo asked the maestro permission for his brother to be brought to him, so the siblings may sit in Paulo's dressing room and talk away from the curious eyes of the crowd. But that was forbidden. Only those dedicated enough to deepen their spiritual journey were permitted to be in the castrato's presence. This, the count had explained, was evidenced by how much they were willing to pay. The count would decide who was worthy of this castrato's company.

The maestro had described the count during his proclamation on The Epiphany, but Paulo had only met him the day before he was due to perform. Two months out from the concert, the count's opera master came to the college and gave the trio the pieces they would perform individually and in trio. He stayed three days to listen to them practice and then left, satisfied that they had taken on his specific instructions.

A few weeks earlier, they were visited again, this time by the count's tailor, and were fitted for their concert costumes. They were shown sketches of the tunics and headpieces they would wear, all encrusted with crystals and feathers, fearless and flamboyant, and far from the austere robes they wore in the church choir. This was when the flutters began for Paulo. He could not discern if they were born of excitement or fear; all he knew was that they felt like anxiety. It was then Paulo began picking at his fingers, pulling at the cuticles until they tore. Sometimes, he did not even realise he was doing it until he received a slap. His fingers became so unsightly, ripped and red, that the maestro made him wear gloves all day and all night.

On the eve of the concert, the three castrati, who were soon to be the count's, were whisked away before dawn, loaded into a carriage and taken across the countryside. It had been ten years since Paulo left the college, and he was curious to see how the outside world had changed. Not long into the day, he began to feel scared, for this world was so different, and so was he. Paulo sought relief by rubbing at the fingertips of the gloves. It was not as good as being able to make himself bleed, but it was better than nothing to calm his nerves.

Paulo tried to remember the journey that brought him to the college so that he could compare what he saw now with what he once knew. But it was a different time and different place and back then, he had the naivete of a child. Now, as he looked around, he was in awe. Everything looked like it had multiplied. There were more people, more markets, more merchandise and everyone appeared busy. The grand buildings and bustling streets Paulo saw outside the carriage windows spoke of prosperity and opportunity. He wondered what it would feel like to be amongst all this energy and whether he would get lost within it.

Between the buildings and around the corners of the church, there were shadows. In these darker spaces, Paulo could see people sitting and people begging. Poor people, people barely dressed, dirty, diseased, bent, broken. Parents with children, children alone, with some being pushed back by the police, so they could not be seen. They were far too lowly to deserve light. Every city and town they passed through was the same, and soon, Paulo found himself seeking out the shadows to understand the true essence of each place.

The maestro travelled with them, playing the dual role of chaperone to the castrati and the count's guest. He was there to ensure they maintained their enigma and did not engage in any excesses that would put the college or the castrato program into disrepute. This was considered a danger given the confinement from whence they came, and so the risk was lowered by ensuring their ongoing custody, disguised as care. The maestro also now considered himself part of the count's circle, and Paulo could see a new air of confidence in this man as they made their way closer to the patron's estate.

They travelled most of the day, stopping only briefly at a monastery to take on refreshments. By mid-afternoon, they approached the gates of the count's estate, and immediately Paulo was enchanted. He had heard the maestro speak of such places, preparing them for their new life outside the college. But Paulo could never have imagined how grand one person's home could be. The guards let them into the gate and closed them behind, and for the first time, Paulo felt like he could breathe. While he still did not know what was ahead of him, at least the outside world was shut out, and here, he was relatively safe.

The carriage moved slowly along the road between the gate and what Paulo could only describe as a palace. It gave him time to view the manicured lawns, the fountains and sculptures and to determine the count was certainly a man of culture and means. Inside the foyer, fear was replaced with awe and wonder. He wanted to reach out and touch the marble columns, the crystal chandeliers, and the hands on the statue that offered knowledge of ancient times. Outwardly, though, he presented the composure and grace he had practised for a decade.

The attendant informed them that the count was out for the afternoon, but they would be shown to their rooms, with baths to be drawn and refreshments to be provided. They would dine with the count in the evening; until then, they had time to recover from the journey and explore the grounds. They were guided along a lengthy corridor and to a wing at the rear, then up two flights of stairs to where they would reside for the next two days. A sense of disbelief struck Paulo as he entered his room. One whole room was for him alone, and it was fit for what he considered a king or at least the king's children. The furnishings were rich, and the fabrics were plush. The bed was four-posted and was bigger than he had ever seen. He could not wait until he was alone so that he could spread out on the massive mattress and smile. For now, though attendants were there, drawing his bath with buckets of boiling water, bringing in breads, cheeses and wine, and placing it by the window.

Just before the attendants left, the maestro stepped in, instructing Paulo to wash and eat and then he would be collected for a tour around the grounds. They would not be left to their own devices this afternoon or at all why they were here. The maestro explained it was for their own safety, but Paulo was not sure how or why it was required. Although without understanding the society in which he was now placed, he was at this man's mercy.

There was not a time that Paulo could remember himself laughing, and so what escaped from his mouth felt so foreign. Still, it felt good, as did the bath. It was wonderful and warm, with a hint of heat that went through his skin into his flesh. It brought a sense of relaxation that was so far removed from what he had ever known, except maybe in a faint memory of being held by Francesca.

Paulo lathered with scented soaps and scrubbed with beautiful brushes. He soaked in silence, sensing how much this space felt strange. He spent time splashing, moving his hands across the water and hearing it from above and below. When the water became cool, he arose and wrapped in soft cloaks. He had never felt so clean and never felt this comfortable. When he was dry, he indulged in the oils, smoothing his skin with jasmine and rose and combing it through his hair.

He did not have long to laze on the bed, bemused as to why it would need to be so big, before the attendant came to collect him for the tour. The walk was wonderous, not just because of the shapes of the shrubs, the grand gazebos, the ponds of colourful fish and the presence of deer and dogs. But because of the time. The time to wander and to watch. The time to appreciate and the time to think. It was such a strange experience, both enjoyable and unnerving. He was somewhat relieved to be told on their return that they would be spending the rest of the afternoon in practice with the opera master.

It was the count that came to them, entering the music room, introducing himself and hearing the end of their rehearsal. His delight was evident and the concert was discussed over dinner, where they were joined by other performers – a master harpsichordist, harpist and wind trio. While the others were allowed several goblets of wine, the maestro instructed that the castrati would only have one. Straight afterwards, the count summonsed the castrati and the maestro to his office and ordered digestives to be brought.

They were seated in front of a desk full of scientific instruments and surrounded by pictures of the sea.

The count reiterated how happy he was with what he had heard, expressed his hope that they were comfortable, and his honour to have them as part of his legacy. Then, he presented the rules of their partnership. Firstly, they would receive a new name, as was common, to honour the generosity of the patron. Paulo would now be Alessio – the voice of an angel. Paulo thought it sounded nice and bowed his head in thanks. Then they were reminded that as castrati, they were special, and so, under his supervision, would be treated as such. They would not mingle with the public but be contained within private rooms near the hall. Guarded, of course. Guests will be allowed into these rooms, but only those approved by the count and only for those acts that the count would condone. The castrati were reminded that anyone who joined them were also guests of the count, and thus must be treated with the same respect. No detail was provided on what acts the count considered appropriate, and so each person there made their own assumptions.

The one digestive permitted by the maestro had made Paulo feel a little dizzy, and now he understood why their consumption was monitored. They were not used to normal life and needed to be protected. Paulo had no problem with that. The count dismissed them, ordering that they get a good rest for the performance and meet the opera master tomorrow morning for the final practice. The maestro saw them to their rooms and instructed them to sleep. And Paulo did, at first, spread out across the bed and then snuggled into one sliver on the side. He would awake intermittently, afraid, until he remembered where he was. Then, he would sneak his feet along the sheets to feel their softness and wrap his hands around the spare pillows to comfort himself with a cuddle.

CRUCIFIXUS

Paulo

The new year saw Paulo settling into his new home in the musical manor on Count Alessandro's estate. The manor was far from the main villa, so the castrati never saw the count. They were overseen by the opera master who was almost mad with desire to make the count's opera truly magnificent. The first few months were intense, although no different from the discipline that Paulo was used to. It was difficult, though, to get used to his new name; he had to keep saying it to himself to help it sink in.

The manor was provided with its own dedicated guards, the purpose of which the master explained was twofold. The count did not want any spies stealing his ideas or eroding the enigma of his castrati. The competition in the opera was escalating, with other patrons creating their own, so the count had to be very careful. Also, there had been recent incidents of some unsupervised castrati being attacked by Catholic extremists. It would seem there were those in the community who did not see the castrati as a spiritual asset but as a sin. While the majority of the population enjoyed their magnificence, security was necessary to protect the count's property from the minority. This news made Paulo a little nervous, as did the shadowing by the guard when he went for his strolls.

The master advised that the castrati were not permitted to leave the grounds unless it was under direct instruction from him or the count and would always require the accompaniment of a guard. And there were to be only guests sanctioned by the count. Paulo was happy with this simplicity, comfortable in the confinement and with time to focus on his compositions. But he could sense the other couple was getting restless. They seemed less content to be cooped up, let out only for performances, and then to immediately return. They spoke over dinner of the adoration they had received from the crowds and how they wished to receive some in private. They desired no longer just to be puppets, but to talk with other people and potentially even to touch some. Yes, they were spiritual beings, but they were also human and, as such, should have access to appropriate pleasures. They petitioned the master to present their requests to the count. The response – they would go on tour.

The count understood their need for greater excitement and exploration. He would give them this, introduce them to the nobility across the surrounding nations, and let everyone know their name. At the same time, this tour would allow him to seek out collaborators for the expansion of his programs. He would get in before his rivals, securing the most strategic spots and the most advantageous relationships. The count thanked them for encouraging him to be proactive in his pursuits and gave them one month to prepare.

Honestly, Paulo did not want to go. He was happy here in this home, with his music, without the complexities of other men or of women. He did not want to be with others but to be left alone with his music. He was working on a new piece, one which he was hoping the opera master would let him perform. It was a secular piece, celebrating the beauty of the sky, the one that existed, untouched behind the weather. Yet, within the words he had woven spiritual undertones, just enough to assuage his guilt at veering off the virtuous path. Still, Alessio was bound to the patron that provided his name, his home and the privilege to spend his days with music. Reluctantly, he packed his costumes and boarded the carriage with the other castrati, the one in which the opera master sat and which followed the count and his artistic adviser.

They began in the south, in the Spanish territories, serenading within the personal salons of the powerful and gaining great acclaim with foreign dignitaries. He also regaled those citizens blessed with sufficient means, performing in private halls and theatres. The joy that Paulo felt when he saw the eyes of his audience look upwards to the heavens, or close to succumb to his song, never decreased. He was distracted sometimes by the pain in his back, but he could bear it long enough to bring people to this state of being. When he sang, Paulo's body and mind were one, and he felt whole; he felt worthy; he even felt thankful for all that he had been through, for he could see what his gifts gave to people. It made them peaceful, happy, and hopeful, and that was his honour.

Paulo hoped each night that he may see his family, for some performances were held in travelling distance from the farm. He was certainly not allowed to visit them. He thought that perhaps Francesca might come, although even if she had secured an advantageous marriage it was hard to imagine how she could have surplus funds to spend on such exuberant entertainment. And there would be no way in which Antonio would attend. He looked for Luca whenever he could, but it was always too dark to see any specific face. Still, he yearned to make contact once more. He had held onto that night before Christmas as special, clinging to it closely as confirmation that there was more to him than this; that there were people still out there who loved him. But he had not yet been able to build upon it. It was still only a notion.

Regardless, if Francesca was there, he must present a face that would fortify her faith and ensure he would not be a source of disappointment. For that would break her heart. So, Paulo tried as much as possible to sway his repertoire towards sacred and reverent pieces but was sometimes usurped, told to perform what was popular.

Paulo could see this shift escalating, away from the holy and to the hedonistic. This change was deepening his conflict and his confusion as to his place and to his purpose. It did not help also that the strictures around his supervision were slipping. Many were very willing to pay for private audiences. Paulo explained to the count the pain he was bearing and his need to rest after each performance. However, the count would not permit any pause, allowing a consistent stream of people through to meet what he now called "stars".

The count would bring the guests to Alessio's chamber, where the castrato would be informed of what the visitor had paid for. Initially, it had always just been allowing the guest to sit with and see the castrato up close. Paulo bore through the cramps in his back to give the show that the count expected. There would be no speaking, no questions; they paid merely to be in this special creature's presence. Paulo had become comfortable with being observed and capable of being calm through the challenges being presented by his body.

But then, this did not seem to be enough for some guests who the count considered strategic and essential to the program's expansion. Then, he would instruct Alessio to provide a private performance, of just one piece. Not to be outdone, others were allowed to converse with the castrato, to ask questions and receive answers, with an attendant closely monitoring that the right responses were provided by the count's prodigy.

It was on the last night of the tour in the north when all decency was disregarded. The Count, obviously bibulous, ordered Paulo to show the Duke of Savoy his scar. Paulo paused, thinking that he was merely overtaken with revelry and if given time to rethink would rescind the order. Instead, the count stayed during the process and gained great satisfaction from the sight, and from the duke's questions that followed.

"Was there much blood?"

Paulo could not satisfy their curiosity, for he was unconscious.

"Was there much pain?"

Paulo could only nod and put up the walls in his mind to stop him from remembering.

"Can you still get it up?"

Another nod.

By then the count was getting bored.

"Well, that's enough Alessio. Come Duke, let us enjoy the other entertainment."

That was the moment that Paulo lost all trust in the count. There had been incidents causing Paulo to feel insecure in the past, but he had continued to give the count the benefit of the doubt, just like his mother would have counselled him to do. Now, he knew that under this man, he was no longer a heavenly voice. He was purely a product, a profit maker. Now, with this realisation, so many other concerns made sense. He thought about the request he placed with the count to provide some of his wage back to his family. There was very little of each payment, for the count took most to cover the costs of providing for him and his career. Regardless, Paulo was desperate to send even the smallest amount back, to let them know he was alive, and to provide what he could. But Paulo's request was denied. The count told Paulo that any surplus would be placed in a bank to provide a financial base for his future. The banker came regularly to receive their cash, provide them with statements and explain the necessary deductions for his administration. The banker would also be there beside the count, consuming fine wine in his rich fabrics, funded by what Paulo suspected was his fees.

Each day, gratitude for his situation, and thankfulness for the count's support, was becoming harder to muster. Feeling bitter at being used erupted far more easily. Especially as the pain in his back was extending to his neck and knees and growing greater with each passing month. He put his whole life into his work, processing everything he felt, playing out the paradox of being swept up in the spirit and then used for sensual satisfaction. He was always writing new pieces, becoming a prolific composer, but none yet seemed good enough to be put on stage. Instead, Paulo would simply hand his works over to the opera master to do with them what he would.

There was so very little Paulo could control about his life, and it was starting to feel like he was going crazy. He needed more agency, something of his own to hang on to, something uniquely his. Then, he realised he could control what he consumed.

While the others enjoyed every morsel on their plates, Paulo would regulate. It began as a game, starting with identifying what would be eaten and what would be left. The time at the table became a test, one at which he was getting more proficient at passing. No one seemed to care that he ate very little or was becoming significantly thinner. He was not surprised. It merely confirmed the complete lack of care they had for him, and so he continued.

At the same time, he found that wine filled the well and helped ease the pain plaguing his bones. After the tour, the relaxed regulation at the manor meant he could easily request a bottle be brought to his room – purely for creative and medicinal purposes. For the first few months after he had shown his scars, the bottle would last for four days, one glass enjoyed as a comforting night ritual and an aide to slip him into sleep. Then two glasses replaced the one, and then a bottle disappeared into his empty belly before bed. Sometimes, it would slosh around in the grumbling space, and he would have to spew it back up, the liquid pouring into his bedchamber, looking like blood.

That was when the dottore was called. The count was assured there was no need for concern. This castrato was in good health. The pain could be treated with poultices and a good dose of amaro before bed to balance the humours. With that prescription, Paulo had the dottore to thank for his progression from wine to spirits. The liqueur was bitter, but it went down warmly, settled his stomach and reduced his rampant thoughts. It would be administered by an attendant each night, and became a routine that Paulo came to enjoy. One night, due to an oversight, a half bottle of amaro was left in Paulo's room. It went down far too quickly, easing his mind. But there was still an edge to his pain, which the poultices were no longer lifting. Paulo knew more amaro would help, just like more wine did before the dottore interfered. But he did not wish to wake anyone, and knew his request would likely be denied, so he snuck out. The hallway was hazy. The stairs were slippery. And Paulo could not help but scream when he hurtled downwards, and his wrist snapped.

Francesca

Francesca was living each day balancing between fortitude and fear. Most of the time was spent in the former, with her spirit stoic. However, in some moments she realised just how much she had to worry about, and then she was sent reeling. Her husband was almost ready to begin the harvest, and it was not unheard of for the yields to be taken by fire or floods before they could be sold. Their future hung on what happened over the next few weeks, and she was conscious of creating an air of calm. Francesca could feel him becoming more restless, continually checking and reassessing when would be the right time to pull the plants from the ground. There was no way of knowing what would come the next day or what the weather would be the next week. Francesca covered his anxiety with optimism, warm meals and sedating spirits. And while he slept and snored, it was she who lay awake, anxious at every roll of thunder or scent of distant smoke.

Most of the day, she was too busy with domestic chores to have time for other concerns. However, in the small spaces between tasks, thoughts would erupt that would tease and torment. What if she was never able to bear a child? What would become of her if she could not produce an heir for her husband? What if the penance was not enough? And with the first cramps that signalled her monthly menses came the concern as to whether the discomfort would escalate to the same excruciating affliction as her mother. There was no relief when they did not, for the mere fact that her menses was upon her confirmed that, again, Francesca was not with child.

Then, there was also the despair about Paulo. She knew it rattled her mother when there was no news from Signore Battista and a lack of contact from Signore Conti. Every time Francesca sang softly in the safe places outside, Francesca thought of her little brother, and her heart would sink. She did not know if he even survived the surgery. Each night, Paulo was included in their prayers, with her mother adamant that he was still alive. She could feel it, she said. A mother knows these things, she said. Francesca was not so sure; until the letter arrived from Luca.

The message had made its way to them via Antonio, appearing to be unread, simply redirected. It arrived in the late afternoon while Francesca was feeding the smaller animals before nightfall. When she arrived back in, her mother was holding it, with a look of trepidation across her face. It took Francesca a few deep breaths before she was ready to open it, and as much as she could, read the news it told. Luca had been kind enough to keep the content very simple, using words she easily understood. Luca was well. And he had seen Paulo performing. He stated that Mother should be very proud, for her son truly shone. His name was now Alessio, but there was no doubt it was her son. He was an angel and Luca would try and see him again. Her little boy was now a man and looked healthy, although a little lanky. Luca would write again when there was more news and signed off with his love.

Francesca wished she could bottle her feelings and the look on her mother's face. For such relief would be a welcome respite on other days when the worries wrung at her. They lived in the light of this news for days. Both boys were well; that was all they wanted. Hearing that they were also making their marks on the world was magnificent and a blessing brought upon their family. That Luca had not mentioned he was courting anyone was a source of concern for her mother, which Francesca swept away with the mention of how busy he must be establishing himself in the academic society.

A few weeks after the letter arrived, the last of the harvest left the farm, and their funds had been secured; another burden had been eased. Her youngest brother-in-law's wedding was to be attended, and so their family also indulged in some entertainment. Francesca started to feel like some energy had returned. The caring she did seemed to take less effort, and her faith flowed more freely.

Her menses, though, did not. Her mother noticed, mentioning there were less rags to clean, but did not overact. Her mother had seen the torture of her first loss and did not want to lift her up if this child did not live. The older woman's support was far more subtle this second time. Extra servings were subtly put on Francesca's plate, and suggestions were made that she should reduce rigorous activities. Francesca assented, careful to not let her husband hope for something that could still be taken away. The waiting to see if this pregnancy would hold was painful. She tried to not be afraid, to act like everything was normal. She tried not to cling to the concept of being a mother and yet could not stop the daydreams about what it would be like. Soon after the second bloodless month, the nausea began. Still, Francesca was unsure whether the absence of blood was because of a baby or because of her worry. But it was time to tell her husband. The conversation was constrained, for they both knew how this could end. And despite the herbal tea the husband and wife took before bed, there were hours of sleep missed between them each night. Every little niggle, every small nudge in her abdomen, made her wonder if this would be the start of a miscarriage. Instead of this being a happy time, Francesca became hypervigilant, and her constant frown gave her headaches.

Her mother helped where she could, praying with her to Mary for the Divine Mother's support and strength. Rosa would keep Francesca distracted so there would be less time to think, ensuring she ate well and had plenty of rest. It was dedication to routine that saw the third month come and the pregnancy confirmed. It did feel different from before, but Francesca still did not want to assume it was solid. She started to show but told herself that anything could still happen. Francesca felt movement and a moment of joy to know the child was alive. But there was still fear. She had been with Guilia when a child of this age had come, not fully formed, a fearsome creature. And she had seen the procedures required to cleanse the woman of what was left inside. It could happen to her.

Francesca progressed through the next five months; each day as uncertain as the next. The women at church said she should be so proud. However, honesty, she was petrified. Soon, the worry about whether the baby would survive in her womb was replaced with the anxiety about how long it would live outside of it, or whether she, too, would die during the birth. Nothing about this process was guaranteed; nothing was known, and every scenario gave Francesca knots in her stomach.

She should not have risked it, but the only thing that kept her sane was singing. She justified it to herself, saying that they were songs praising the Glory of God, that they were not heard, and that the music was medicinal. She also knew that if she lost the baby, she would only have herself to blame. Sometimes, when she was too close to the house to chance being heard, she would whisper the hymns. At the very least, she would hear the song in her head, and it would still be her heart.

Francesca was cooking the evening when the cramps came. There was nothing sinister about them, just a soreness. She confided in her mother, who suggested this was the commencement, having had the same beginning to the birth of several of her children. But there was nothing to be done except continue and wait for further evidence. So, under her mother's orders, Francesca stayed in bed, feeling every little shift in her body. Then, with no warning, there was a gush of liquid between her legs and a panic to light the candles to see if it was blood. Francesca thought she was going to be sick until she saw there was no stain. Whatever had escaped her was clear. Holding between her thighs, she woke her mother, who told her husband that Francesca would now remain in her mother's room and instructed the man, in the morning, to send for the midwife. For at the moment, there was no sign of furtherance but it may not be far. Both women knew, though, that everything needed to be kept clean and calm, so the water was boiled, brews of chamomile and willow bark were made, and warm packs were prepared. Francesca tried to be still, attempting to match her mother's composure. She could not help but shake and wished desperately she could sing through this. She did in her mind, imagining herself in the fields, her voice arising from her depths and flowing out to meet the daylight. Her mother made her pray, and then when both were sure there was no more progression, the mother slept, suggesting Francesca do the same, for, in the morrow, she would need strength. Francesca closed her eyes, but sleep would not come. Instead, there were continual checks for signs of motion and close monitoring of every little change.

By sunrise, the cramps were turning into contractions, shifting from a dull ache to directed stabs, strong enough to make her wince but far enough apart to allow some rest. The midwife came and listened for life, which was confirmed, along with the belief that this would be a long labour. A firstborn often was, and Francesca knew this for a fact. With Guilia she had seen a first-time mother labour for days, so she steadied herself for this possibility. However, nothing, not even seeing others endure the same, could have prepared her for the excruciating pain that came.

In the early evening, the jarring jabs became all-consuming. The contractions were coming faster, rolling through her like thunder and torturing her like lightning. What was once confined to her womb now made her whole body writhe and wail. Where there was once peace in between, there was nothing but bearing down for the next storm. Her mother and midwife were doing all they could to ease the pain and to maintain her energy, moving her, heating her, feeding her and feeling with her. For they both knew exactly what she was going through, and their tears said what they could not.

All night, this continued. When Francesca could be still, the midwife listened, looked, poked, prodded, adjusted and then waited for the next gap to do it all again. Even with this support, though, Francesca was struggling. She had lost control, and she hated it. She could hear herself moan and cry out, succumb to the suffering, and she felt weak. Francesca heard her mother speak of the pride she held for her daughter, but all Francesca felt was pathetic. Francesca had watched other women in the throes of birth, but she wanted to be better. She wanted to be silent, to be stoic, to be sedate, and yet here she was thrashing and screaming. Her husband would be disgusted.

Towards the dawn, Francesca was broken. She pleaded for God to take her, for she could not bear any more. That's when she seemed to disappear. Francesca could hear her mother berating her, no longer buying into her distress, demanding that she do her duty. She heard the midwife's calls for her to push, and she did and then felt herself slipping away. She did not feel the fire and the ripping; all of the sensations seemed to end, and that's when she thought she was dead. For a while, she was happy with that thought. Even the cry that came from the child could not convince her to come back. But the warm water on her face and the weight of the baby on her breast called her back to consciousness.

The midwife declared she had a daughter, and her arms were folded around the little bundle. Then, a spark stirred her to open her eyes, and seeing this small creature made her smile. The midwife made her do a bit more work to expel the placenta, but while the cuts were cared for, there was peace. Her mother, her dear, dear mother, sat beside her, stroking her hair, and watched with her as this helpless baby wriggled its way to secure its first feed. This brought forth a chuckle from both women, and an overwhelming gratitude from Francesca that she was still alive.

This was Maddalena Rosa, so named in honour of the family's matriarchs and born to the world on the first day of spring.

After suckling for a short while, the baby slept and so did Francesca, deeply. She was awoken by the child's screams and her mother's support, putting the baby back onto Francesca's breast. When its belly was full, it was cleaned, wrapped and taken out to show its father.

The next few weeks were full of wound care, weariness, worry, women and wonder. Francesca could not yet stand, for the stitches in her perineum made movement difficult. They would burn whenever she urinated but were saved from bursting by the laxative tonics to be taken until they had healed. The midwife would come every few days to check them for infection. Then, there were also the wounds on her nipples. Little Maddalena was having trouble attaching, and Francesca's breasts were red and cracked, throbbing and burning. With salves and strict attention to positioning, this problem was solved, but not before several sleepless nights and tears were shed from frustration and a sense of failure. There were many hands to help, though. Maddalena, the elder, travelled to spend time with her newest grandchild and brought her eldest daughter along to provide assistance.

The nuns came too, to see the newborn and offer their blessings. Wives of neighbours had heard of the birth and so came to bring gifts and to bear the child for a while so others could rest. The house was cramped and continuously busy, and there were times that Francesca wished for time alone. But that would come soon enough. For now, she would indulge others and their sense of celebration.

Her husband was careful and caring with little Maddalena. Still, his disappointment that his firstborn was not a boy was evident. He would, in his clumsy way, assert that now her ability to bear a healthy child was proven, they must continue to procreate and pray for a male to continue the lineage. She agreed and petitioned the Lord for a boy, not just to placate her husband, but to deliver a brother for beautiful Maddalena; a brother to be like Paulo and not like Antonio. How hard would it be as a mother or wife to Antonio? Isabella had given birth to another male baby, so was now wedged between two boys and a man. Francesca also secretly prayed that Isabella's next child would be a girl to give this woman some sense of balance.

Yet her concern for Isabella could not detract from Francesca's enjoyment of her baby; the brightness in her child's eyes, charming coos and innocent chuckles. Nor would other people's struggles take away from the sense of strength she gained from enduring the greatest test of her life. Yes, she was still ashamed of some of her behaviour, of her screams, and her submission to the suffering. Still, she had brought forth life and now had a deeper appreciation of all she was capable of. As she kneeled before the Divine Mother on the altar, she felt closer to Mary than ever before.

CRUCIFIXUS

Antonio

Antonio tried not to be angry. He knew he was showered with blessings; a supportive wife and two healthy boys. It had been a plentiful season; there was enough food on the table for all and more to store for leaner times. Some extra funds were also available for another labourer, helping to make Antonio's days lighter and less long. Yes, there were many blessings. So why did they all feel like burdens?

The boys were boisterous, far more than he ever was. They were still too young for school, so Antonio took it upon himself to instil discipline. He would not have wayward children under his roof, and his wife was far too mild to be of much benefit. Any bad behaviour Antonio witnessed in the evenings or on Sundays was met with a beating, either with his own hands or his belt. Of course, the child would bawl, but they had to learn a lesson and this was the Lord's work.

Isabella would try to intervene, to talk him down and away from the boy. She would attempt to justify their naughtiness; they were tired, hungry, or ill. But Antonio knew it was his job to turn his sons into men, not hers. And everything he did was in line with the teachings of the Church. Antonio knew the Proverbs well enough, for the priests and the schoolmasters recited them regularly at school. Now, he shouted them at Isabella as he stomped towards his sons.

"Withhold not correction from the child: for if thou beatest him with the rod, he shall not die. Thou shalt beat him with the rod, and shalt deliver his soul from hell."

This was the tough love he wished his father was here to help with. But he was alone. His wife did not understand, and he increasingly believed she was useless. Isabella's father, whenever they visited, would sing his daughter's praises, pronouncing that she was practically perfect. After too many wines, he would rib Antonio and declare that he was a very lucky man to have made such a marriage. On the surface, Antonio would be polite, but underneath, there was a rage ensuing that he could only reduce by excusing himself and spending time in the stables with his stash of spirits.

Was his father-in-law blind? Isabella was merely of average beauty, and age was beginning to show on her face. Yes, she was kind but clumsy, far too weak to work on the farm and a poor cook. Here was Antonio, providing all manner of produce for her to use, but all that came from the stove was either too salty or simply tasteless. Some nights, Antonio chose bread and cheese over her stew and then would scold her for wasting fine food with her incompetence.

Antonio also hated how much Isabella's family would interfere. Her mother and sisters came to stay when the babies were born. They would butt in to comment on the furnishings of the home, the children's clothing, the food Antonio asked for and the work that his wife was required to do. Antonio would never challenge them when they were there but shared his extreme annoyance with Isabella after they had left. Just like the children, she tried to explain, and then excuse, their candour. They were from a merchant family, where being frank and forthright was expected. In response, Antonio reminded her that this was his home, and Isabella would do well to counsel her family to close their mouths next time they visited, which he added, should not be again until hell froze over.

For they did not need any more helping hands. The only thing required was for Isabella to toughen up. She was not a merchant's daughter anymore. She was a farmer's wife and she should start acting like it. Antonio was furious that she had to teach both his children and his wife what to do. In many ways, he found Isabella just like a child. She would cry far too often, giggle like a little girl, and was just as soft. In so many ways, she brought back memories of his little sister, the one he had made carvings for to put on her coffin. And as he was taken back to this time, the anger returned. From reliving little Isabella's death, he next travelled further back, to the night he was beaten by his little brother, and his own mother had sentenced her son to become a castrato. It would not have happened if he had asserted his place as the head of the family. Antonio had conceded, and his brother had become an abomination. He would not allow himself to be overthrown ever again.

Since the birth of the girls, Antonio had to deal with a woman who was physically compromised. She would waddle when she walked and would often smell like pee. She would also complain that she could not carry the children long distances. He would have to take the carriage to church despite his desire to rest the horses for the week ahead. When he would have sex with her, he tried not to look. Isabella had grown a large bulge beneath her navel that made her appear malformed. He could not watch her face either, for she would wince and frown like he was hurting her. Personally, he had long stopped caring. For she really did have to harden up, and it was his right to have his wife whenever he wanted. By the fire at night, she would tell him she was tired, perhaps to try and dampen his desires. But he would not be denied, and as he skulled the last of his spirits and pulled her to the room, he spat Ephesians in her face.

"Wives, submit yourselves unto your own husbands."

Antonio would not hit her often. Only when she truly deserved it; when she let the children go undisciplined, or did not understand what he wanted, or did not give to him willingly. Besides, he would hear the other men brag about doing such things at the gatherings, so he did not feel guilty. In fact, Antonio thought himself better than most of the men he spoke with, for he never struck Isabella in the face. Not that he hadn't wanted to, and came close few times, but he did not think displaying evidence of her inadequacy was proper.

Antonio could never gain dominion over Francesca; she was far too fierce, but he would not let his boys become second-best behind their mother and sisters.

Isabella

Isabella lived an internal life. She was too afraid to speak when her husband was around, lest she bring his ire. She had tried so many words in the past but had found the only thing that seemed to bring him peace was her silence. She had attempted so many different actions, desperate to find a way to dote on him that would work. But the only thing that would settle him was her distance and spirits. Isabella had not known Antonio to indulge in grappa when they were wed, and it was still a rare indulgence after the birth of their first son. However, sometime after the second child, the incessant crying started, and so did the increase in her husband's consumption.

After supper, Antonio would excuse himself, saying he had work to do in the stables. Then he would come back blurry-eyed and smelling of strong alcohol. There were nights he would sit by the fire and be friendly towards his wife and children. When the latter were asleep, he would take Isabella to the room and have sex with her before falling asleep and then snore his way through the night. Isabella was convinced this was the real Antonio – the good-hearted boy she had wed. But then, there were other nights when he appeared possessed. He would scold, snarl and slap. He would scream Proverbs at her, attesting to the value of the rod and assuring her that his boys would not die from discipline. Isabella was scared that Antonio's body may not withstand the fury that spewed forth from it. There were also times she came close to collapsing with worry.

Isabella never knew what each morning or evening would hold. And that became her weakness.

When her husband left in the morning to join the labourer, she could finally breathe and let her body relax. Then, she had time to tend to any wounds on the children or herself and to ground herself in the day's chores. And of these, there were so many. The boys were no longer young enough to need constant care but were old enough to get into a mess and mischief, meaning she was always having to follow behind them. The twin girls were gorgeous and growing fast, but now that her mother and sister had left, she often felt overwhelmed.

Isabella wanted her sister to stay for a few more weeks to see the girls through the next growth spurt, but Antonio would not have it. This was his house, and he was sick of feeling like an outsider. Isabella would have to cope alone one day, so it may as well be now. Her heart sank when she saw the women off, not only because of the struggle with the babies that she must now bear alone, but with them gone, Isabella knew she was no longer safe. When her family were here, Antonio would not touch her. Now they had left; it was only a matter of time before he would lash out.

Isabella had one simple strategy; to keep moving. This worked most days, with the constant motion preventing her from falling asleep. She had made the mistake once, of sitting for a few moments and must have drifted off quickly. She was roused by Antonio's stern voice, irate that his lunch was not ready. This, he said, was a sign of her utter selfishness. She did not protest.

Now, Isabella kept her eyes and one ear on the children and one ear on the entrance for her husband's return. That way, she could warn the boys and make sure they curtailed their bad behaviour. She could plead with them not to make their father angry and remind them of the consequences. The boys were getting wiser and understood the risks inherent in their father's presence and with this, the episodes of punishment were becoming less frequent. But these boys were also constantly changing, growing and finding new things to explore and experiment with. Inevitably, something different would annoy Antonio, and they would soon learn the hard way that this was not acceptable.

It was the twin girls now that were the main source of Antonio's madness. They were teething and so constantly irritable. The herbal remedies would help, but never to the standard Antonio expected. The second-born girl also had a weak stomach, and each day was spent cleaning up spew, each night battling to get her to sleep. The baby could not lay down without being in pain, so Isabella would sit up by the fire with her strapped to her chest, both sleeping until the episode had passed. Antonio demanded that she always return to their marital bed, for she must not coddle the children and make them weak. However, when the whining began in the middle of the night, he readily pushed his wife out of bed to go and fix the problem.

With the girls, nothing seemed to stop; there was no end to her duties. Isabella could not find a way to get all the children asleep at the same time without her, and the tiredness was building to the point where she could start to feel herself slipping. The neighbouring farmer's wives were wonderful. They would bring things during the day; meals, treats, tonics, and other hands to hold the babies. But they could not stay for the night shifts, and despite their suggestions, she certainly could not sleep. She was far too afraid of what Antonio would say if he unexpectedly returned to find neighbours in the house and his wife indulging in a daytime nap. That would be beyond selfish, given the burden he was bearing on the farm. Instead, she spent her days like a sleepwalker, like a shadow.

Until one night, Isabella had nothing left to give. She could hear the baby girl coughing. It would clear, she told herself. It would go away. And it did when the baby died. Exactly when the coughing ceased, she was not sure. It would have been some time after the wheezing began but before the other baby girl stirred. Isabella stood over the cot the next morning, relieved to have had some rest but horrified when she finally took in the sight. One baby was wriggling and crying, fussing for a feed. The other was stolid and cold, her tiny mouth open like she was still gasping for air.

Isabella was too tired to cry, and too weak to chastise herself for seeing this as a blessing; that there was one less child to care for. She was grateful to her husband for providing the guilt that she could not yet find the strength to muster. Yes, she should have burped the baby again before bed. Yes, she should have sat up with her again as she had done every night before. Yes, she should have taken action when the wheezing began. Yes, she should have checked on her constantly. Antonio confirmed that the baby's death was caused by her incompetence. Although, he said, it was only a girl. And there was one left. With that he went to get a box and to send the labourer for the priest – for the blessing of the child as well as for Isabella's penance.

That evening, as the baby lay dead in the box, ready for the next morning's burial, Isabella asked Antonio for permission to sleep in the same room as the remaining girl. Isabella did not want this child to sleep alone, fearing desperately that this girl, too, may be taken. Antonio simply answered that if God so wanted their child, He would take her anyway. No, Isabella's place was beside him in their bed. She would not be making his children weak and needed to be there if he wanted her.

The baby girl was promptly buried beside little Isabella, with her grown namesake holding the remaining daughter close to her chest. Isabella tried to be sad. She knew she should be, but she was numb, and Antonio only stared as the dirt was cast on top of the tiny coffin. Isabella wondered what the priest must think of these parents, so callous they could not even cry. The boys were sad to lose their sister and could not fully comprehend that she would not be coming back. At home that night, the eldest began to bawl, telling his mother to bring his sister back. Arriving back in from the stables, Antonio grabbed the strap and started striking the boy's thighs. Isabella pleaded for him to stop. The boy was not at fault. She was in the wrong, so she was the only one deserving of such punishment. Isabella grabbed Antonio's hand, looked her husband in the eye and told him to take his anger out on her instead.

Antonio agreed. He grabbed her hand and, even hearing all the children crying, took her to the room and wielded the strap relentlessly around her body. She coughed when he punched her in the stomach, wetting herself and the floor she was standing on. He called her disgusting and told her she should be ashamed. Antonio ordered her to kneel down and rubbed her face in the mess, just like the priests did to any child who dared soil themselves at school. He made her get cloths and clean it up, whipping her all the way as she did.

When the eldest boy caught site of one strike he shouted at his father to stop. Isabella heard her husband's response.

"No son. Your mother needs to be taught a lesson. One day you will need to do this too."

Wiping her urine off the floor and feeling the sting of the strap on her back, she realised her sons must be saved.

And that's when Isabella decided to visit Guilia.

College Officials

The mood of the men who marched into the room that morning was sombre and serious. A seat near the front of the table was saved for the maestro, and as he arrived in place, bows were made, and the men sat. Then, while they waited, the whispers began. What would the next few hours hold for their future? Some suggested that they would be forced to close the college. Others provided contrasting views, stating that they were sure they would all be safe. Refutations were presented; how could they ignore the Pope's instructions? Then, in the midst of all of these mutterings, they were made to be silent and to stand, for the Chairman and Cardinal Bellarmine entered.

The Chairman, usually outstanding in his attire, adorned with embroidery and brocade, was, on this day, usurped by the vivid red form of the Cardinal that flowed beside him. The scarlet silk cassock displayed the wearer's dedication to shed his blood in the defence of his faith. The red cape confirmed his authority and the skull cap, his status. His hands were clenched below the large cross that hung over his chest, and the amethyst on his episcopal ring reminded all of the respect that was to be afforded.

The Chairman showed the Cardinal to the seat at the head of the table and took his own, opposite the maestro. He led the low bow to the Cardinal and then called for all to sit.

"Thank you, brothers, for joining us here at such short notice. And to you, Cardinal Bellarmine, for bringing news from Rome.

Before we begin, Cardinal, we would be honoured if you could lead us in prayer."

The Chairman sat and the Cardinal stood, holding his hands outwards, calling forth the support of the Holy Spirit and the faith of all those present.

"Almighty and Eternal God, we gather here today in Your holy presence, seeking Your divine wisdom and guidance. As we deliberate on the matters before us, we humbly ask that You illuminate our hearts and minds with the light of Your truth.

Heavenly Father, grant us the strength and courage to do what is right and just in Your sight. May the Holy Spirit descend upon us, filling us with the fortitude to uphold the well-being of Your people.

Guide our actions and decisions, O Lord, so that they may reflect Your will and bring honour and glory to Your holy name.

We ask this through Christ our Lord, who lives and reigns with You and the Holy Spirit, one God, forever and ever. Amen."

Heads were raised, eyes opened, chests were crossed, and bodies moved to be made more comfortable. The Cardinal sat and signalled to the Chairman that the space was now his to fill.

"Brothers, I am sure you are aware of why we meet here today. The new Pope has issued an edict against castration. Not only that, but he has condemned it and called it morally unacceptable. Of course, our college is the main provider of castrati to the Church and private artistic and spiritual programs. Therefore, we are right to be nervous about what this statement means for us.

This is why I have asked Cardinal Bellarmine to join us. We are all hearing rumours, some malicious, about what is to become of our program and our positions. His Eminence has always been a strong and much-treasured supporter of our college, so we are right to seek his advice. Also, he understands the subtleties of the situation, and so today, we call on his wisdom to guide us as to how best to respond to this news. Your Eminence, please."

The Cardinal arose, pulling his cape around his shoulders and stroking the silk covering his thighs.

"Thank you, Monsignore."

The Cardinal took in a big breath and released it rapidly.

"Yes, brothers, you do have cause to be concerned. The Pope's edict is clear. He does not support the practice of castration. He is of the view that it goes against the sanctity of our bodies, which belong to God. So, on the surface, if we are to take this statement at its simplest, yes, we should shut down this college."

There was a pause, allowing many of the men to shuffle in their seats, showing their nervousness and concern.

"However, I am here to tell you to bear no mind to this edict and to continue your sacred work. For while the Pope stands alone as the prime source of authority for the Church, the implementation of his decree requires the support of all those beneath him. Let me reassure you that those within the Holy See who agree with him are in the minority. For example, the choirmaster in the Sistine Chapel has stated openly that he will continue to use castrati as the main source of song. The Pope is aware of this and has not moved against him.

There is a reality here, brothers, that you must be aware of, and that is the fragile support that the Pope has. He is a good man, and his intentions are noble. However, we all know the only reason he was selected by the French was because of his promise to restore a surplus and reduce the drain on their own coffers. The Pope is doing this well and holding to his pledge, but his cost reductions are also reducing his allies. He is known as the "Father of the poor", but now he suggests that his own clergy should also live like the common folk. In his ignorance, this Pope is pushing us to exist like paupers, which is not how we can best support our people.

Brothers, to lift our people up, we must first be strong. If we were to follow the Pope's ways, we would be far too weak to hold them up to the Heavens. We must be what they desire and aspire towards, not what they are praying to be free from.

The Pope, unwisely counselled by those close to him, is also blind to the benefit that the castrati bring to his people. It is clear that they serve a substantial spiritual purpose. All those in the pews are brought closer to God, and is that not our divine purpose? If we take castrati from our churches, we will lose our congregation, in body and spirit, and many of us believe this in itself would be a sin on our behalf. We must do all we can to ensure the angelic voices are heard for the sake of our people and their faith.

Besides, what would all these boys do? They have been chosen. They have been called and made their sacrifice accordingly. Should we now simply cast them aside? The Pope is planning to open a shelter for castrati to help those who have supposedly been harmed by the process and are suffering ill health. Many of us believe that this should be his focus; those who were too weak to uphold the gifts of the Holy Spirit, instead of outlawing those who genuinely want to make this offering.

There is one more thing to consider: the expected longevity of this edict and the Pope who has delivered it. As you may know, the Pope has recently removed the French right to asylum and, in doing so, caused the ambassador terrible trouble. This move, I fear, may be one too far for the French, and many will not be surprised if our beloved Pope is assassinated. I know we all pray that he will be protected, but we cannot downplay the wrath of the King.

And, as you may be aware, if the French do not kill the Pope, then there is no doubt the kidney stones will. It must be known that the Pope is not in good health. This is all the more reason to not overreact. There is no need to create distress when none is due.

Please be assured that all those with direct power over musical programs are adamant there will be no disruption. My message to you is to stay the course. Remain strong, for the edict is only words. They hold no weight among those who make the daily decisions.

I am here to offer you my support and that of many others who sit in the Apostolic Palace. Proceed, brothers, and go in peace."

There was little more to be said, and no space provided for questions. The decision was made. The meeting was over.

CRUCIFIXUS

The Cardinal held out his hand, and one by one, the men moved forward, knelt beside the Father, and kissed his ring. This show of respect was right and just.

Rosa

Rosa cuddled into her coat as she joined the end of the procession out of the church. She could feel the chill coming off the sandstone, and the cold made it harder to move. Her hips and knees had grated and groaned when she tried to genuflect, and her bony hands ached as she crossed herself with the holy water. But while her whole body felt sore and weary, her spirit was warm. The scriptures and the songs had stirred her heart, and she was leaving lighter than she had arrived. Now she was eager to get the sun on her skin so that it may match the fire in her heart. The sun was still yet to offer the radiance of summer, but provided some relief until she could make it back to be near the fire. Francesca had gone ahead to feed the child, who was becoming increasingly fussy; a child for which Rosa felt so fondly.

Yes, there were many blessings. Her daughter had been given a child and was gaining more confidence each day. Rosa suspected Francesca could be with child again but would respond carefully, for anything could happen. Instead, she would simply pray for protection from the Divine Mother and leave the rest in God's hands. Rosa gave thanks each day for her reduced affliction. With the cessation of her menses, the monthly pain also seemed to subside. It was not lost all together, but it had ceased crippling her, and for that, she gave the Lord much praise. In its place, though, the aches in joints had gotten worse. The winter was not kind, and kept her housebound, except for Sunday mass when she would bind herself up with warm coals in her coat so that she could make the journey in comfort. Rosa was relentless in her need to be in the church, to hear the choir, and to see the castrati.

Rosa could not read much, barely a few words, but "castrato" was one that she instantly recognised. Its contour was repeatedly referred to, pointed at and even underlined by Signore Conti on the contract, the one she marked with an X, and which gave permission for him to take Paulo away. This word was burned into her memory, as was the day she bade her son goodbye. So, when Rosa saw the same word written on a notice nailed to the church wall, she had to stop. She scanned the rest of the text but could make out very little, nor link the pieces together to comprehend what the note said. She excused herself to a passing Nun and asked for the sister's assistance. When Rosa heard the words "condemned" and "morally unacceptable", her heart sank and her face flushed. She thanked the sister and then stood still in shock. What had she done?

That day, Rosa did not go out to meet the other women and talk about their families, chores and afflictions. Did they, too, know about the edict? They knew that she had sent Paulo to become a castrato. Now, she would bear the shame. She should have listened to Antonio.

But when Rosa sent Paulo away, she was assured that his sacrifice was supported; no more than that, it was praised by the Church. The fathers had told her that her family would be looked on favourably by God and that her son would be a model of martyrdom. Now, this notice had made him a monster, and Rosa was responsible. This decree meant that she had hurt her son far more deeply than she ever thought possible. Had she condemned them both to hell? She knew one thing: her actions were morally unacceptable, which for Rosa was akin to a sin.

So, Rosa did not go out to socialise in the sun, seek support from others or warm her bones. She did not deserve such indulgences. Instead, she would stay inside and pray for forgiveness and her son's soul. Rosa found a priest and pleaded with him to hear her case. She had sent her son to castration. They were both now condemned. Would he hear her confession?

"Vecchia, do not fuss. There is no requirement for forgiveness stipulated in the edict. It is a simple statement, and no specific actions are needed.

I have been assured that castrati will continue to hold a sacred place in our choir, and I am sure it is similar elsewhere. Your son will be fine. There is no need for confession.

Go about your business, Vecchia. There is nothing more to be done."

With that, the father walked quickly away into an area that Rosa could not follow. His speech was filled with reassurances, so why did she not share his certainty?

Rosa was still working her way through yet another round of the rosary when Francesca came to collect her. Maddalena was strapped to her mother's chest, asleep and Rosa was lifted by seeing this angel. Francesca knew there was something awry and gave Rosa a deep frown as she helped her up and out of the church. After another awkward genuflect, Rosa tapped her daughter on the arm and showed her the notice. They travelled home in silence, both women trying to process the implications of what had been posted on the wall.

That afternoon, while the women cooked for the week ahead, Rosa broke her silence and called on her daughter to help her make sense of the Pope's message. Francesca's first concern was why such an important fiat was not announced. Why was there no proclamation during the service? Why was it simply set on a wall with no further formality? Rosa could not provide any answer, reiterating the priest's guidance given to her; continue as normal.

Francesca sounded just as confused as Rosa felt. How could the Church, in one year, sanction something, glorify a boy's suffering as a sacrifice to the Lord, and then in the same child's lifetime say that the decision made was amoral? How could these men actively seek out boys to become castrati and then, after the fact, condemn their choice? How could a decision deemed honourable in one decade now be declared horrific? What about the parents? How could they laud the parents for their sacrifice and selflessness and then turn around years later and suggest they are, in fact, sinners. No answers came from this questioning, just despair from Rosa and anger from her daughter.

Then Francesca came to a conclusion that brought Rosa a small degree of calm. The condemnation, she said, was directed at the church officials, and that is why it was not announced. Those preaching from the pulpit could not stand and declare what they had done was wrong. They were not that strong. It was the choirmaster, the bishop and Signore Conti who conspired to take Paulo away to become a castrato.

It was the fathers who spoke the sermons that supported the scouts and facilitated the boy's future. They would never admit their fault in front of the entire parish. They were too proud. And yet, Francesca assured her mother, it was them that the Pope was condemning. Their family were simply innocent victims of the misuse of power and of corruption.

Rosa would not participate in Francesca's disparagement of the clergy, and yet she knew her decision had been heavily swayed by their authority. She also knew Paulo's path was paved by their promise that this was God's wish. Whether they had lied or simply been wrong, it mattered little. The body of her boy had been horribly altered, and those she had placed her faith in were to blame. Still, she would do her own penance for her participation. Rosa had been the one who signed the contract. She was the one that sent him away to do something amoral. So, Rosa would pray every day for his soul, and hers, that they may be spared from the fires of hell.

Rosa thought this proclamation may not have meant much to the people who, out of duty, placed it up on the wall, nor to most of the people who walked past it. But in truth, this edict meant everything to this mother.

CRUCIFIXUS

Paulo

It had been many months since Paulo's wrist had been wrapped and since he felt the wrath of the count. The count's vitriol came via the opera master, as the count was far too busy to belittle himself by entering a public hospital. The criticism hit hard, ruthlessly piled on top of the pain in his hand and in his head. He was injured and vulnerable, but in the eyes of his supervisors, nothing less than inconsiderate and a villain. Right then, though, Paulo felt like a victim. That was until the opium took effect. First he felt dizzy, then he felt as if he was dreaming. Then came the detachment from his body. He would sail above his bed, but down below was not his adult form lying on the bed. It was the body of a boy who had just been castrated. He floated and watched what before he could not; behind the covers at the cut, the bloody bandages and crude stitches. And he laughed; he laughed so hard at this boy's anguish. And when the laughter had been used up, he cried. He cried for this child who was showing so much courage. He watched as the younger version of him consoled a boy beside him as his last breaths were taken. From the heavens, Paulo watched as his younger self closed his eyes, trying to keep calm as another boy broke down and said the most savage things, yelling brutal insults and having to be restrained. Paulo watched as the bandaged boy started to stand, winced, and the worry spread across his face, the same worry that would stay from that day on.

With the opium, Paulo felt no pain. With the opium, Paulo could sleep. With the opium, Paulo did not have to deal with the echo of the count yelling, "How dare you" after he had made it home. With the opium, he could slip into the role of Alessio with little resistance, donning the gloves that had become his signature accessory. For the wrist had not repaired. It was a malformed mess. Well, that is what the count called it. Alessio was no longer a perfect product. And yet, he was still a performer and his voice was still vibrant. The Count's anger subsided over time as he saw Alessio continue to gain the audience's adoration. Alessio's voice was truly angelic, and with the opium, he even had developed an ethereal presence. Alessio would seem to float onto the stage and fly as he sang. Sometimes, a curse can also bring a blessing. Since the accident, Alessio was more popular than ever.

Paulo was also happy, for now he had an effective prescription for his pain. He could relax and calmly apply himself to the count's after-concert activities. It only took the tiniest amount of the tincture, and his anxiety would be replaced with a warm tingling. He would socialise as required and even enjoy it. However, the night he was introduced to Vittoria Orsini he became very nervous. Paulo had entertained husbands and wives who wanted to view the castrato's holy body. But never a single lady, and certainly not one with such an air of grace.

Contessa Vittoria commanded attention, not from her outlandish dress or overt demeanour, but by what Alessio could only explain as a distinctive combination of elegance and excitement. The count explained, as they all sat politely, that the Contessa was the daughter of one of his great friends. She had come to him asking for some time with Alessio. But not here, not simply for counsel, nor just for song, but to be close to, to lay with. The count informed Alessio that he condoned such an arrangement, for Vittoria was a wilful girl but also wise, and she could be trusted with Alessio's secrets. Also, the count believed it would benefit Alessio, for there was nothing like a woman to inspire great music, and maybe the Contessa could help him find even more magic. It would be done, and with these words, the contessa smiled.

The following afternoon, the Contessa would visit Alessio at his home in the count's estate. All had been arranged. And with that, Paulo felt something stir within him, something that he could not attribute to the opium and something that felt very odd. Perhaps it had something to do with the confidence and curiosity that emanated from this woman. Or was it the way she looked at him like he was a gift? In reality, it was the stark realisation that he was soon to have his first chance to touch a woman.

The nighttime dose of opium let Paulo's thoughts and reservations about the morrow slip away into a restful sleep. There were many vivid dreams in the midnight hours, which Paulo wrote down eagerly the next morning as inspiration for his next compositions. The morning dose of opium made Paulo feel warm all over and encouraged his appetite. Although he was determined not to eat much; enough to sustain, not satisfy. Paulo was still determined to control what he could, and this diet was a discipline that made him feel good. As he walked through the hall to the dining room he assessed himself in the mirror. His elongated limbs were thin and lanky, covered over with the full sleeves of his shirt, his bent wrist protruding from the cloth. If he pulled his shirt tight, he could see his ribs poking through and thought how much like Christ he was actually becoming. Standing back and seeing the whole picture, he changed his mind and decided that, in fact, he was much more like a twig. In many ways, this comparison was much more fitting, for on some days, he, too, felt like he could just snap. His sanity relied on the music, the opium, and now his own curiosity; what would it be like to be with Contessa Vittoria?

At lunch, which Paulo again kept very light, the count came to join him. Paulo was not sure whether it was out of care for him or concern for the Contessa. He came to inspect Paulo's room, and check the castrato had not imbibed too much tincture to compromise Alessio's performance. The Count, in great detail, explained the parts of a woman and how to pleasure them. Although the count was not sure exactly what the contessa was expecting, it was best to be prepared. He allowed Paulo one more dose, enough to see him through the next few hours, and then confiscated the tincture, placing it in his coat pocket to be returned after the contessa had departed.

"She has paid handsomely for this privilege, and extra to ensure her father never finds out. You must do me proud, Alessio, and you will tell no-one, or your days here are done. Are we clear?"

Paulo nodded, trying to hide the resentment that came with the thought of how much profit the count was making from this clandestine communion. The count called for a cleaner, then left, stressing how important this interaction was and shouting down the stairs for Paulo not to "stuff it up."

Paulo chose Alessio's costume for this performance carefully, already feeling his indignation slip into a sense of detachment. Where would he be without opium, he wondered. After fragrances were applied, he was adamant not to waste this feeling, and so as the cleaner concluded, Paulo held a pencil in one hand and played the harpsichord with another, consuming himself in connecting notes when the contessa arrived. She was announced, and Alessio appeared.

The castrato rose from the stool with a smile, and with a low bow, the countess's chaperone closed the door. Together stood two strangers, smiling at each other awkwardly. Alessio admired the simplicity of the countess's apparel, for it was also incredibly stylish. It hugged her form beautifully and was made from superb fabric, shimmering subtly with every movement, reflecting the light in a dance of silver and black. A cascading white scarf was folded softly around her fine neck, and a sweet smile graced her face. The Countess came forward, holding out an elaborately bound book, explaining that she had bought Alessio a gift. As he acknowledged her generosity, the countess removed her buttery leather gloves, revealing slender fingers. It was getting very difficult to view this woman as either a cacodemon or a customer.

Alessio signalled to the contessa to take her seat and requested her favour. Would she have wine, coffee, tea or chocolate? It would be wine, she said, which Alessio would be delighted to join her with. However, he would also request coffee in case stimulation was needed to counter both forms of sedation. Alessio opened the door, gave the attendant the order, and then joined the countess opposite her on another ornate chair. Alessio gave great regard to the book, the

Theatrum Orbis Terrarum, and genuinely and generously delighted in the detailed maps and the craftsmanship of the gilt edging and embossing. The Countessa told Alessio that she hoped to sail to China one day to explore the East. He could see an authentic curiosity coming forth from this women, which he found so appealing.

With wine, the words flowed more freely. Long before the alcohol could have affected her humours, the contessa appeared lighter, and her questions became lengthier, less superficial and more personal. Alessio was the host here, but the Contessa's innocent inquisitiveness had a way of pulling Paulo into the conversation. She wanted to know everything and said as much, apologising for what he was sure to find annoying. Let's start from the beginning, she requested, moving into queries about where he grew up, his brothers and sisters, his schooling, and the day he left for college. Was he scared? Was he sad? Did the surgery hurt? How long did it take to heal? Was the college hard? Did he have friends there? What did they eat? How many hours did they train? What was his favourite song? Had his family seen him perform because she was sure they would be so proud. What was his real name? What did he think of his new one?

Alessio lost track of how long they went back and forth between question and answer. However, her investigations did not feel like an interrogation. The Countessa, who had asked him to please call her Vittoria, was calm in her curiosity, and showed great care. Alessio started dropping his guard and giving Paulo space to sit with this wonderful woman. As she smiled at his successes and looked truly concerned at his college challenges, Paulo came forth more, and she began to sink beneath his skin.

Then, there was a moment of silence. The conversation ceased.

There was no fuss. They simply sat and looked at each other. It was a moment of understanding, of honesty, and of hope. Vittoria stood and slowly moved over to the castrato, asking if she could call him Paulo. He conceded, and then she bent down and kissed him. Her lips tasted of wine and sugary treats, and he had never felt anything so soft. It was like a beautiful combination of cuddling his kittens and singing a sacred hymn. It was moving; it was magical.

But he was confused. What should he do next? He did not have much time to think as Vittoria moved her chair beside him so they could be close. The afternoon flew between conversation and kisses, holding hands and honest gestures, looking at books and looking out of windows. When the sun was headed towards the horizon, the contessa excused herself and bade goodbye. Her father would be furious if she was home after nightfall, even with a chaperone. Before leaving she begged that she may visit again the next week. Both Alessio and Paulo said yes, it would be their pleasure, and then Vittoria, Paulo's first love, departed.

CRUCIFIXUS

Paulo

Paulo knew that he had become dependent on opium by dawn the next day. The count did not come back with his tincture that evening, and despite desperate requests to the attendants, his patron was nowhere to be found. Paulo assured himself he would be fine, and consoled himself with more wine. This substitute sent him to sleep for a short while until he awoke in a sweat. The moisture on his forehead spread to cover his full body, and it was not long before his clothes and sheets were drenched in an acrid, alcohol-scented perspiration. Paulo's muscles ached, and he groaned not only in discomfort but in agitation. Soon after, the shaking began, uncontrollable tremors that jerked his head and his hands and sent shivers along his limbs. Beneath all of this, the pain in his back was becoming ballistic, bearing down on him and bending him into a babbling ball. The cramps in his bowels were cruel, and he was lucky to make it to the pot before the diarrhoea poured out of him. It was a putrid mess. He was a putrid mess.

Sitting in the stink, Paulo sank into deep sadness and shame. What if his mother saw him now? What would she say? He was not worthy of her love and certainly not fit to be friends with Vittoria. Hours later, when there was no more excrement to expel, he crawled off the pot, cleaned himself up the best that he could and then called for an attendant to assist. As he was washed, redressed, and the sickening evidence of his weakness was taken away, anguish turned to anger. A rage welled up from his wound, and it twisted its thorny tendrils around his twig-like limbs, plunging through his protruding ribs into his heart. He could feel it crawling along his throat, squeezing it tight, scratching the flesh, creeping along his cheeks, clawing and cutting. Then, this wrath attacked his eyes, and the pain was excruciating. It thrust through his brain to the back of his head and wrapped around his skull. Now, he had a crown of thorns. Now, he was Christ nailed to the cross. Paulo was helpless. He could not tell whether he was whispering for help or yelling for it. He could not hear anything outside his own world and felt trapped within it. Paulo tried to fight, to free himself from the sinister swords that were piercing every part of him. And then something snapped.

He gave in.

He would die that night.

And he did not care if he went to hell.

He just wanted it to end.

As Paulo retched and spewed in his bed, he tried to remember where he put something sharp.

He fell out of bed, and, covered in the contents of his stomach, he crawled towards his desk. The letter opener would do.

Then the door opened. The dottore was there with men to restrain him and more opium tincture.

It took several days for Paulo to regain his strength, but he knew he would never recover from the shame. Slipping down the stairs drunk was considered a stupid act, and the guilt from his first accident was still raw. But the mess he made this time was simply disgusting. He was disgusting. And he was dependent. Paulo was out of control and felt the chaos in every crevice of his being. The count made things very clear, stomping into his room on the second day while Paulo was still in bed.

"Is this how you repay my kindness? By being too ill to perform? You are a star, so start acting like one. My dottore is at your disposal. Get yourself well, Alessio, or you're out. And don't think you can go elsewhere. I will make sure all of my competitors know what a risk you are. I am giving you a third chance, Alessio. But it is your last."

At that moment, Paulo hated the count so much that it physically hurt. However, after more medicine, he mellowed, and his mind began to chart a path forward.

He called for bread and wine and his writing tools. By the end of the day, he had drafted what he considered his best work yet. It was furious, forceful, and everything he felt when he was wrapped in the violent vines. The words were placed in song, but they were a shout from his heart, the one that he had to hold in. It was deep, it was dark, it was dramatic. As he drifted off to sleep, with sheets of music beside him, he began planning the second part.

Paulo distracted himself with composition and following the dottore's orders. Of course, opium was part of the plan. It had to be. The pain in his back was only getting worse, and he had to perform. But it would be metered by the medical team, with only a small amount kept by the attendants for an emergency. He could cope for the moment. What was prescribed allowed him to cross the threshold from pain to pleasure, from cramping to calm. Most importantly, it allowed him to sing, and to compose, and to entertain Vittoria.

By the time she arrived for her second visit, Paulo had physically recovered. However, there was a dark leech left inside, the one that gnawed at him constantly, telling him he was not good enough to be in the presence of this remarkable lady. He would suppress his shame, adorn himself in the attire of Alessio, and give her what she deserved. He would drown Paulo's nerves with the needed tinctures and other available analgesics, and he would put on a perfect performance for her.

Vittoria fairly skipped into his room, showing a level of excitement considered at the very edge of decorum for a lady of such distinction. Her eyes were bright with a sparkle that made Paulo's smile shine through Alessio's mask. On this day, she did not wear a fancy fontage but a mob cap of fine linen with lace edging. It framed her face so perfectly, allowing Paulo to appreciate her delicate features and flushed cheeks. There were hardly any formal greetings before Vittoria had pushed forward with another present. Icones Plantarum, leather bound, embossed in greens and golds, a truly stunning specimen. She hoped that Paulo liked plants. She had read this already and learnt so much. What was his favourite plant? Hers were the oleander. She also liked the rose but enjoyed the oleander better for its simplicity. She also loved the fluffy little follicles that poked out from the middle. Could she have hot chocolate today? It was quite cool out, and she would benefit from something warm. Would he move her chair beside her again? She was eager to be close. Perhaps they could look through the book together?

With her hands on his arm, they looked down the long list of plants, all provided with Latin names. Then they worked one by one through the delicate drawings, their comments punctuated by kisses. Paulo could feel the pressure change on his arm and knew when she was creeping towards him, turning just in time to meet her lips and then see her lovely smile. Vittoria must have felt him tense, or perhaps she saw him frown as they arrived at lavender. She was of the opinion that everyone loved lavender. Yet, there was obviously something about it Paulo did not like. Again, she was pulling him out from underneath Alessio and asking for his story.

He considered telling her a lie; that lavender gave him a rash. But she was too kind for him to be deceitful. He took a deep breath and explained about the sachet on a string that his mother and sister tied around his neck when he left home, and how the smell now brought such sadness. And of the one the lady at the Inn had given him to wish him well, which made him feel cared for when others were being so cruel. It brought back memories of hard times, hence his desire to keep it at a distance.

Vittoria was still and silent, simply listening. When he had finished, she bent and kissed his hand. Then she kissed his cheek. And she kissed his forehead, finishing with his lips. Then she sat back and looked lovingly in his eyes. She vowed to remember this and never fragrance herself with lavender, for she would never want to cause him discomfort.

Paulo did better at hiding the pause that came when they viewed the bougainvillea. The thorny vine looked so close to the one that had terrorised him during his hysteria. He did not want to explain this experience and so excitedly moved on.

The afternoon had warmed up and there was heat invading through the windows. It seemed like the perfect time for a walk. With the guard going slowly behind them, they exited the building and wove their way around the gardens. Vittoria would stop and smell every flower and fondle the leaves she found lovely. She held his hand and asked about what he was writing at the moment. Had he written a song about roses? There were plenty of poems about them, perhaps he could find some inspiration in these? She would bring a book of poetry next time. Paulo had never thought about composing music for anything as trivial as flowers. Yet, watching this woman show them so much tenderness, and bearing witness to the coming together of these two beauties, he began to think there could be something in her suggestion. And as she returned to him and again took his hand, he realised that he had become her man, and she, his muse.

They re-entered Paulo's apartment and were left alone by the guard. Taking some wine and water, they both became a little giddy. Paulo knew what was coming and tried to act nonchalant, but when she came and stood in front of him, put her hands around his waist and kissed him, he started feeling very nervous. When she asked him to lay with her, Paulo had to call on Alessio's courage and charisma, for he felt as uncertain as a child. At the bedside, she removed her cap, her scarf, and her shirt, calling on him to help her with the corset. They both chuckled as he struggled and when it was off, they faced each other, flesh to flesh. Vittoria's skin was so soft, and he could not stop stroking her arms. They lay beside each other, and she moved his hand to her breast, twitching a little bit as he touched her nipples. Vittoria returned the touch for Paulo, and he felt the spark as she brushed along the bumps, making him smile. Then the game began, of how much they could make the other moan. Paulo found Vittoria's neck and nipples particular places of pleasure, although her fingers, when sucked, were just as fruitful. Vittoria found his vulnerability, too. His ears, it seemed, got him very excited, so much so, he got an erection. Vittoria played with it under his pants but promised she would save this adventure for the next time.

Paulo was dumbfounded. He asked Vittoria where she had learnt how to lay with a man. Her reply – you can learn a lot from books. Then she offered to bring some of those ones next time, too, although she would have to bind them well before bringing them out in public. And so, over the next weeks, except for those when she was on her menses, Paulo gained an extensive education. Vittoria brought the books she spoke of, and Paulo was stunned. They explored each other with no shame. She kissed his scar and stroked his sagging sack. Vittoria showed him in anatomical detail how he differed from other men and what made him so special.

Together, they gently and calmly followed the instructions in the books. He knew he could never be brought to climax but learnt the techniques to make Vittoria ecstatic. He adored seeing her so happy. Then, when both were spent, they would share wine and discuss ideas for songs. Vittoria, it appeared, had her own sketches for an opera, one that would see a battle between an angel and devil and have the humans helpless in the middle. Paulo was awestruck by her idea and told her so. He would love to help her progress it, so plans were made for their next visit. She would come just after breakfast so they could dedicate time to her opera. They would spend all morning working on her project, and after lunch, they would enjoy each other in bed.

As the months passed, there came to be a rhythm to their rendezvous, and both became more confident in each other's presence. Then, Vittoria sometimes brought her puppy, a greyhound called Piccolo. It brought Paulo so much joy to play with it, and pat it, and cuddle it. Holding this precious creature close, Paulo would cry. When he did, Vittoria would wrap him up in her arms and kiss his forehead, calling him gorgeous and her angel on Earth.

Between kisses and touches, talking and giggles, Paulo would explore Vittoria's eyes, trying to discern their exact colour. At one moment, they looked hazel and then grey. There were flecks of green, then blue, then gold. Her eyes were a mystery, one which he never wanted to solve. He was so happy to lay beside her and be embraced by it. Paulo felt no desire other than to touch her, to feel her through his fingers and his lips. He had no yearning to conquer her, just to be in her company. He had no drive to be her lover, just to learn about and from her.

Paulo was still struggling with pain, and wary that the effects of the opium were wearing away quicker. The dottore conceded that he had to up the dose which took days to adjust too, but still it was effective at providing ease. Still, this struggle paled against the pleasure he received from Vittoria's weekly visits. It was clear to all, especially the count, that Vittoria brought a new vitality to Paulo. He missed her desperately when she was on her menses, but dedicated the time to advancing her opera, adamant that he would have something stunning to present to her when next they met. Paulo could not provide everything she needed, but he could do this. And he wanted to do this, and so much more. Paulo had resigned himself to the fact that he cared for her deeply; that he loved Vittoria.

For Vittoria had given him the perfect life. He had his music, his medicine, and he had his muse. He had the excitement of singing under the lights, tonics to ease his pain, and the ecstasy of being with a woman full of spirit. With Vittoria's support he was producing works that were being brought by other producers and which, more importantly, felt true to his own heart.

Paulo tried to ignore the fact that Vittoria's visits were paid for, and every time she came, she was handing over money to the count. He should feel like a prostitute. But it was impossible. Vittoria had such integrity and made him feel safe and invincible. He almost began to think that he should be paying her for lifting him out of a life-threatening hole. Often, he thought about asking her why she chose him. There were many other castrati available that she could enjoy. What did she find particular about him? But he never went ahead with this inquiry, for he feared the answer may be simple; that the other castrati were already taken.

He reconciled himself with the monetary aspect of their relationship by thinking that she was paying not for physical pleasure, but for permission to be herself. It was his honour to do this for her. In return, Vittoria was encouraging Paulo to remember who he truly was and for this he would be eternally indebted to her, and, he conceded, to the count for their introduction.

One visit came with an invitation, for Paulo to join Vittoria at her summer house near the ocean. Her family would be travelling elsewhere, so they would have the entire estate to themselves. The opera would be on holiday, so Paulo could possibly spare the time. The thought of being with Vittoria all day filled him with delight. He could pretend to be her husband for two weeks. If this went well, then perhaps there could be a more permanent arrangement? Yes, he could not marry, but maybe they could find a way to make some sort of union. He accepted the offer, of course, on the condition that it would be approved by the count. Vittoria told him not to worry; she would work her magic on that man. As Paulo watched Vittoria's coach pull away, and heard the clops and crunch turn to silence, Paulo felt hopeful. He felt heavenly.

Isabella

Insomnia was usual for Isabella; she was so tired, yet she could not sink into sleep. She stayed at the surface, unsettled, seeking out sounds that may signal her children required attention, while staying still so as not to stir Antonio's ire. Her nights were not a time of ease but of abeyance. This night, though, she had something to do. She lay in the dark, planning the next day.

As usual for a Wednesday, Isabella would feed Antonio, fix his lunch in advance, and then head to the market with the children. This outing used to be such a source of joy; now, with the children, it was a struggle. There was no one to care for them, so they would accompany her, and between buying the staples for meals and home maintenance, she would deal with their crying, feeding and the fear of them getting lost in the crowd. This day, though, she would have no time for self-pity. Isabella would have to keep control and be efficient. For unless Guilia was at the market, she would need to make an additional stop and hope she would not be seen.

With her husband headed out onto the farm, Isabella tended to the boys and her baby, filled their bellies and covered their bodies for the journey. She strapped the girl to her chest, bustled the boys into the back of the wagon and was on her way. The boys amused themselves by throwing rocks they brought with them, sometimes far too close to passing people, requiring Isabella to shout her apologies to the passerby, stop the cart to administer a reprimand and confiscate the ammunition. Isabella hoped that the youngest boy had not eaten any rocks before she took them away; a strange behaviour she had seen regularly of late.

Isabella hitched the horse and wagon as close as possible to the market so she did not have to haul the supplies too far. She gave the horse a long rope so that it could reach the water and told the boys to go and play down at the river. Behind a tree, she sat, put the baby to her breast and fed it hurriedly. With the little girl satisfied, Isabella grabbed the supplies swiftly, not tempted to talk or to see what might be new. Her eldest boy, Antonio, named after his father, needed new shoes, but it would take far too long to fit them today. His toe was poking through the leather already, but he would survive another week. She was in a rush, and if Antonio the elder asked, then an order had been placed.

With the essentials secured and the baby still asleep at her chest, Isabella carried the basket and sack back to the wagon. Hauling these heavy items hurt her back and belly so much, yet there was no choice but to cope. She shuffled and stopped several times and winced when she lifted them into the tray. It was then she wished for a way to get rid of all her pain, and with this, she remembered that she must get to Guilia.

Isabella found the boys by the bank of the river, with Antonio squishing tadpoles between stones and Matteo pleading with him to stop. Antonio's response, as always, was to push his little brother away. She called them to come, and another ruckus ensued. They wanted to stay. Isabella hated hearing herself, but the only way to get them to move, was to threaten to tell their father about their misbehaviour. Begrudgingly, they followed her, but not before more rocks were slipped into coat pockets. As they came towards the wagon, she saw the youngest, Matteo, put a small one in his mouth and Isabella yelled at him to spit it out. She did not need any broken teeth today. Instead, when both boys were in the wagon, Isabella passed them apples to keep them amused. She should be nervous, she thought, but all she could sense was sadness.

As Isabella was seating the boys on Giulia's veranda, the old woman appeared. Guilia had heard the horse arrive and came to greet them. The medicine woman smiled wide, said it was wonderful that Isabella had brought her a baby and was eager to cast her eyes upon her. But where was the other one, her twin? Isabella attempted to look solid, stern, and in control, yet she could not hold back the flood. It all poured forth as if this was a place where she could finally be free. Guilia simply listened and let her expel all of the blame, all of the shame, all of the sinister thoughts. Isabella admitted she did not know what to do. It had to stop. It was either going to be him or her. To which Guilia asked Isabella to consider, which parent could the children best live without?

Things started to become clear for Isabella. She had family that could care for her and her children. There was her father and the husbands of her sisters, so they would not be left alone. Guilia confirmed whether Isabella really wanted this to end or whether she merely wanted to scare her husband into submission. Isabella's response? The risk of Antonio returning in an even worse form was too great to bear. It must end. It was the only thing she had been certain of for a long time. Guilia told her to wait and went into a separate room, rustling around for quite a while. Isabella looked down at her daughter and felt nothing but numb. This was another sure sign that she was a failure as a mother.

Guilia came back with a small vial and some simple instructions. Only give her husband half. The bitterness needed to be masked by a strong wine or herbed spirit. If there were no symptoms in half a day, provide him with the remainder. If all works well, discard the rest. It should take a day and will affect the heart, making it look like the same affliction as his father.

Isabella asked what it was, but Guilia refused to tell her. The medicine woman suggested they share some tea, but Isabella was adamant that she could not stay, slipping the vial into her pocket and pulling out the payment. Guilia would not accept it, saying that she would come and see Isabella within three days, after things had some time to settle.

There were things that must be done, though, before Guilia would let Isabella go. Guilia got a large bottle of tincture from the shelf, to be taken to help Isabella regain her strength. Then, the baby was unstrapped and inspected, with some balm applied to the speckled rash on its bottom and another gel rubbed into her gums. Guilia wanted also to look at the boys but Isabella said a firm no, for they could not be late.

Isabella felt Guilia's embrace around her arms; it was all-encompassing. Still, it did not stir her heart. On the way back to the farm, she felt nothing but warm. Isabella would reach intermittently into her pocket to check the vial was still there. So much uncertainty floated about in her mind about whether it would be her or her husband who would drink this poison.

She had been pretty clever, allowing Guilia to think that she was firm in her decision to give it to her husband. Isabella knew that Guilia would not have given it to her otherwise. But now, honestly, she was not so sure.

By early evening, though, her original intent had been reaffirmed. Isabella had started to prepare supper when her husband hurried in.

"Get out here, woman. The labourer has already gone, and you need to help me with the stupid goat."

Isabella held the female around the shoulders and watched as Antonio roughly tried to wrench the kid from its mother's body. When this did not work, Antonio brought a knife to extend the opening. The distressed animal started banging its head against Isabella's hip, hurting her too. The baby came out, finally, not breathing and with its front leg bent strangely. Isabella asked Antonio to shake it as there could be a chance it may awaken.

"Don't be stupid. It is useless. I will burn the kid and take an axe to the other one tomorrow. There is no space for a bad breeder here."

Isabella wondered what may have happened to her if she was unable to bear healthy children.

Antonio hauled off the kid, the blood from the birth spilling down his shirt. She was instructed to get ready for marinating goat meat tomorrow. Isabella tried to console the creature, who was now stunned, too scared to scream and shivering from shock. Isabella understood the realities of life and how sometimes cruelty could be kind. But it was the brutality of her husband she could not bear. There was no care for anything that did not live up to his extreme expectations.

For the first time in her life, Isabella felt hate. She let this feeling sink into her heart and help her make the decision.

The poisoned wine was ready for her husband when he walked in for supper. She had chosen a strong wine as Guilia suggested and smelt it closely, comfortable that the aroma was not overtly altered. She did not, however, watch as he slurped it down. Her back was kept to him, stirring and serving the stew. She rallied the children to the table and awaited Antonio to say grace. Isabella prayed silently for whatever would happen to be swift.

Isabella's curiosity fuelled her vigilance that evening, monitoring every little murmur. It was when she was putting the children to bed that Antonio started complaining. She could not show a smile but was satisfied that it had begun. Antonio's voice started strong. He was shouting that he felt uneasy and dizzy and that the idiot labourer must have infected him with his illness. Isabella suggested that he hastened to bed and that she would wait on him. Sometime later, after constant checking, her husband said he could not see. His vision was blurry, and in a weaker voice, he shared his worry that he was going blind. He was babbling like a baby, becoming so scared. At the same time, Isabella was becoming more confident that the potion was working. Antonio slipped into a stupor, for which Isabella was glad, broken only by groans and a clutching at his chest. Well into the night, Antonio became much weaker; the poison was wearing him down.

Towards dawn, he was losing consciousness. She should pray for his soul. His breathing became shallow. She should pray for his soul. His face became pale and clammy. She should pray for his soul. Antonio's body began to convulse. The baby cried. She did not watch the end. Her baby needed her more. Isabella came back to an eerie stillness and a stark silence. The light was shifting, though, with the first shards of daylight providing more illumination than the little candle. It was then that Isabella could regard the exact nature of extinction. She closed her husband's eyes, covered his twisted body and closed the jaw that was wedged open. Then, he looked peaceful. She no longer needed to be afraid.

Isabella prepared herself for the arrival of the labourer. She awoke, fed and cleaned the baby, adding another soiled cloth to the pile of laundry and moving the basket outside to avoid the foul odour. As the sunlight struck her eyes, she realised she could also be free of this. She had the means of escape. Her children could have a better mother, one who would love them, one who was happy and could help them. It was a moment of insight, and of inspiration.

Returning inside, Isabella poured herself a glass of amaro, adding the rest of the viscose liquid and throwing the vial into the fireplace. She listened as it cracked and then started consuming the drink. It took several sips for Isabella to finish it, and brought her an instant sense of relaxation.

When the labourer arrived, the nausea had begun. But she covered over it with feigned distress. Isabella called the labourer inside, allowing him to witness what had happened, and demanded that he collect the dottore. Antonio was white and cold and surely dead. She wept behind the labourer, seeing him off into the rising sun and pleading for him to make haste.

While Isabella awaited another witness, between bouts of vomiting, she got the boys some breakfast. The children did not see what was happening to their mother; she kept it hidden, so there was no need for concern. However, when the dottore arrived, she was too dizzy to stand and collapsed as she opened the door. Isabella could not see past the halos around her eyes. Were these the angels coming for her? She was so thankful that they were finally here.

Isabella felt the dottore by her side but was distracted by her heart, which was flying with the angels, taking her away from this place. Her chest hurt, but no more than anything she had felt at the hands of her husband. And this pain was her own doing, which made her feel so proud. There came a time when she could no longer think, and simply allowed herself to ride on the wings under the warm sun. And then the day went dark.

Paulo

The Count denied Paulo's vacation with Vittoria. Despite pleading and promises, the opera could not afford a holiday.

"No, Alessio. With the Pope's edict, we have to keep the pressure on, to maintain a public face. We must show that despite the formal condemnation, castrati will continue. If we create space now, there will be questions and concerns. It will breed doubt that we can ill afford. Our audiences have remained faithful, and we must honour that. We must show them that the Pope's message is meaningless.

Our people need to be inspired and entertained, Alessio, and that is what you offer. Besides, some of the King's family and maybe even the King himself will be in town, so we will put on a very special show.

And Alessio, if you impress, who knows, perhaps you may be offered a place in the palace."

Of course, everyone knew the King already had his own castrato. Rumours were rife about how the King's own eunuch played a key role in political affairs, unnerving people with his unique style and even acting as a concubine for the Queen. The castrato was the perfect courtly companion; there was no ability for them to produce heirs which could usurp power and their unique appearance added to an air of mystique. Castrati, it appeared were assets on many fronts, and the count was now suggesting that Alessio could play an integral part in a much greater drama.

Such a future did not interest Paulo, though. His thrill came from the music, not the politics behind it. The show that would be presented to royalty would have his composition performed, and this meant more to him than any possible court posting. This news was bittersweet, knowing that this was the success he had worked for, and yet it came at the cost of time with Vittoria. The preparations for the royal performance meant there was no time on the weekends for the couple to meet and only sparse time to send apologetic messages. There was no chance to come together before she departed for her holiday, and Paulo missed Vittoria so much it hurt. He only had a few minutes in the dark each night to remember Vittoria and pine for her until the opium took hold, and he slumped into sleep.

Instead of being with Vittoria by the beach, Paulo spent long days and nights with the opera master and the orchestra, arranging his piece to perfection. The schedule though, and all the standing, was wreaking havoc on his knees and back. The escalating tension in his neck created a constant headache. Most days, he was balancing a fine line between the love of his music and the battle with his body. Sometimes, he would step back and look at the count to assess what ailments affronted his patron, seeking some comparison. The count was almost double his age and yet appeared more healthy. Only gout would goad him, and usually only into surliness, not submission.

Paulo had learnt his lesson and took heed from the count's reliance on the dottore. Paulo called the dottore for his counsel and to oversee an increase in the dose of opium to match the rising intensity of both the performance preparations, and the pain. Peace was still possible; it just took more medicine to achieve it, and unfortunately, the more it took for relief, the greater the ramifications for the rest of his body. The nausea was almost constant. The dottore delivered digestive tonics to help settle the stomach and stir the appetite, but Paulo was still not eating much, and his ribs were still protruding. The constipation was also causing problems, creating extended absences from rehearsals. The dottore prescribed balms for the fissures that were bleeding, and Paulo only hoped they would heal in time before Vittoria's return. Otherwise, he would be so embarrassed. The pain relief also seemed to come at the expense of his concentration. Focusing was becoming more of a challenge, distractions were becoming disturbances, and a haze was his constant companion. It was excused away as a symptom of exhaustion, but it did not improve with rest, and so it was another thing he learnt to mask.

Paulo was managing the physical pain, although, on some days, his hold over it felt tenuous. No medicine, though, could help him overcome how much he missed Vittoria. The tincture was a poor substitute for her touch, her acceptance, and her enlightenment. Still, he would seek to capture her essence in his work and make the time go quickly through concentrated effort. Paulo would bear these burdens and see the beautiful Vittoria again soon. Then, they would continue to write her opera.

There was a hearty congratulations and a feeling of great achievement when Paulo's arrangement was finished. He only wished Vittoria could be there to see it on the stage. She had come regularly to watch him perform, sitting in the balcony with her father, stealing glances and sending sneaky smiles. In the hours laying naked together, they had come up with their own sign language. Paulo would lift his eyes to see Vittoria and place one hand on his heart. In return, Vittoria would raise her handkerchief to her eye. This was the way they shared their love in public, and this would warm Paulo more than the repeated ovations ever could.

Paulo tried during each performance to scan the audience to find Luca. But it was too difficult to find any one person in the crowd. He imagined Luca there, though, and the thought of his lover and brother both being there made him feel complete.

Opening night of the performance, with the balconies decked with dignitaries, Paulo's body felt beaten, but his spirit was buoyed. This was his song. He strode onto the stage, the orchestra struck up, and the audience hushed. While Alessio was being adored, Paulo dug into the depths of his wounds, wrestling with its darkness, almost bringing himself to tears with the agony of the words and the memories they evoked. Then he climbed out of the pit of despair into the heights of the heavens. His cantata was the carriage transporting the people from misery to courage and then on to strength. Paulo's song lifted them all above their lives, and, for a moment, above his.

The applause for Alessio was thunderous and overwhelming. Flowers were thrown onto the stage, and he received a standing ovation from the balconies. Paulo's joy, though, was tinged with sadness, for those who were not there to see the success, and for all the sacrifices he had made to get to this stage. His bows were deep and genuine. He was truly blessed.

The count came onto the stage to cease the applause and signal for Alessio to leave. More was to come, and they must keep moving. Alessio departed with dignity, then staggered to his room and slumped into a chair, enjoying the buzz that was reverberating through his body and the sense of being whole. Paulo came forth to whisper prayers of gratitude, and the count came in to congratulate him in person. Paulo had never seen the count looking so pleased. Yes, in fact, he would suggest it was pride that emanated from the man's face.

"Alessio, you have impressed many, including the King's cousin, the Duchess Anne-Marie de Bourbon. She has requested your company tomorrow evening and made a fitting donation to the opera in return. You will dine with her, and I have approved for you to spend the night at her lodgings.

I trust you have now had suitable practice with Vittoria to provide her with pleasure. She is an older woman, a widower, in need of some safe satisfaction. And you should be honoured, Alessio; she has chosen you."

Paulo felt like he had been smacked down onto soggy ground. He tried to protest. Did the count not understand the relationship he had formed with Vittoria?

"There are no excuses, Alessio. You are a star. Satisfy her Alessio, and she will give a good recommendation to her cousin. This woman could take you to the palace."

Paulo was so confused and tried all he could to challenge the count's commandment.

"Don't be stupid, Alessio. It is not as if you can have any future with Vittoria. You are a stupid child if you think she would give up marriage and children for a castrato. Anyway, I heard her father has already found an advantageous match. Realistically Alessio, it will not be long before she is wed and you will not see her again. You need to find yourself an alternative, and the duchess is a very wise choice. You will be thanking me for this in the future, I know it."

Until now, Paulo had been able to cast away his concerns with the Pope's edict. He had parked the idea that his castration was condemned and that, by extrapolation, he was an agent of the amoral. He had found meaning in the music and found purpose in his performances. He revelled in the crowds' reactions and used them to assure his actions were right. But now, with the count's assertion that his power came from providing another kind of pleasure, that he could be bought, and that he should be glad for it, he was heartbroken.

Paulo knew that this was how it began with Vittoria, but it became so much more. It was a coupling, a companionship that went beyond money. But now the count was happily selling his body to others to create opportunities for his opera, and obviously, and for himself. How wonderful it would be if one of the count's castrati was placed in the palace. What power that would afford him. And then Paulo realised he was not just an inspirational performer; he was also a pawn.

"Oh, and I will advise the dottore that he can provide an overnight supply of tincture for you. I would not want your ability to please the duchess to be compromised with pain."

With that kindness, the count departed, leaving Paulo in disbelief and back in the depths of despair.

And yet, the next afternoon, Paulo arrived at the villa where the duchess Anne-Marie was staying. It was far more magnificent than the count's lodgings, with peacocks roaming and roses blooming. The sights and the scents were marvellous, but by now, Alessio was used to majestic embellishments, and he was feeling embittered and mean. However, he donned the Alessio mask and was utterly charmed to meet the duchess, which his low and long-held bow testified to. The smile was well-practised, as was the sly attention he paid to the wrinkles around the woman's face, which no amount of powder could cover. Her hair was high, fake, like a fluffy façade. She was weighty, with rolls of fat bursting out above her corset. Her voice was polite, yet stern, like she was used to giving orders. The duchess instructed Alessio to join her in the parlour, where they drank tea and she plied him with praise and asked about his past. He diverted the conversation as much as possible by enquiring into her interests. She, however, was interested in him.

This woman was so different from Vittoria. She was staid and serious. Her demeanour was stiff and appeared even defensive. Paulo wondered whether this was what happened when you became a target. For everyone knew there were others in the shadow plotting to steal her title. After tea and some superficial talk, she suggested the afternoon was lovely, and that they should take a walk. Alessio agreed. It was a wonderful idea and he called the duchess wise, which resulted in a wry smile from the host.

Their outing was much less of a walk than a shuffling, with the duchess' dress swooshing with every movement. She held out her hand for Alessio to hold, which he took reverently, and placed his other behind his back. She was so much shorter than him, so he tried not to stoop. Luckily, he did not have to bend to make conversation, for she had a bold, almost booming voice, apparently used to speaking strongly. She was not one to ask for what she wanted, rather to announce when she expected it to be delivered.

As they walked past the front gate, a troupe approached. Paulo had driven past a few in his time but never heeded them much mind, considering them merely touring entertainers. This group carried a few simple musical instruments, a juggler and a singer. They were actually quite good, and Paulo was surprised by the quality of the voice that arose from the man in front. There was something, though, about this man that made Paulo investigate further. Perhaps it was the long limbs that were scarily familiar or the eyes that brought back memories. This man was a castrato, but if he recognised Paulo, he did not let on. The singer stopped at the gate, gave the duchess a wink and a smile and asked if he could be of service. Paulo was waiting for a response of shock and anger at the assertion that sat behind the asking. Instead, she simply replied that she was already taken for the evening. So, the rumour was true. Castrati, who could no longer perform and who had no place else to go, survived by being gigolos for rich widowers. And here he was. In truth, he was no better. Just a far more expensive version and conveniently free from the dirt of the streets.

Paulo downed one dose of opium before dinner, which was more of a feast. The duchess did not restrain herself, enjoying what Paulo would have described as an excess and a stark contrast to his nibbling. She did not take his restraint personally, for she understood his need to keep his performing physique. Alessio assured her that the food was delicious and praised her perceptiveness. However, Paulo did indulge in the wine, each sip being used as a form of self-punishment, for he knew that it would make him feel sick the next day. Then there were the digestives at dessert, and so by the time the duchess declared it was time to retire, Paulo was feeling quite tipsy. In a slightly slurred voice, the duchess alerted the ladies to ready her boudoir and to escort her to the necessary room. Paulo was taken to the garderobe to prepare himself.

Alessio and the duchess met at the base of the stairs. He took her hand, told her that it was his honour, and let himself be led all the way up by a woman who was subtly swaying. The fire was roaring in the room, making it almost uncomfortably warm, with the heat being exacerbated by the serving of more spirits. The duchess went behind a screen where she was undressed, her hair disassembled and where her body was draped in a delicate robe. With the attendants dismissed she sat on the bed, told Alessio to undress, and then to join her.

Paulo did, calling on Alessio's courage look confident sitting opposite and being observed. The duchess ordered Alessio to show her the scar from the surgery, which he did, lifting the sagging flesh away to show the thick fault line. The duchess was fascinated, not hesitating to reach out her hand to feel it, to fondle it.

"Now, Alessio, show me what else you know."

CRUCIFIXUS

Paulo

Paulo was awake, listening to the duchess' substantial snores. He should have taken her offer for another room, but Alessio had stepped in and played the role far too well, not wanting to insult one of such influence. It would be his pleasure to awaken with her, or so he said. What a lie. Alessio was taking on a life of his own, well over and beyond Paulo's sensibilities. And yet, what else could he do?

Paulo snuck out sporadically and took some more spirits, hoping it would send him off to sleep. It did not. He took another dose of opium, which made him feel heavy and hazy, and he thought he might have slept for a moment but could not be sure. He heard the birds and arose to take in more spirits and wash before the duchess awoke, readying himself to play whatever role was required.

A repeat performance was ordered, and Alessio pleasured the duchess just as she instructed, to her immense delight. Paulo, though, was feeling decidedly qualmish, with a large gulp of spirits doing little to quell the upset. He excused himself to the garderobe and threw up his excess consumption, then returned, not bothering to mask his breath, merely swilling his mouth with more spirits and spitting it out into the pot. His mother would be disgusted, and in his heart, he knew Alessio was crossing the line between alluring and loathsome.

Politely and generously, Alessio refused breakfast, for there was a lengthy workday ahead. The arrangement must be further fine-tuned for the next performance. But Alessio promised that he would come again soon, for it would be his pleasure to spend more time with one so worldly and wise. He dressed and departed, singing the praises of the duchess and leaving her in no doubt of his admiration. Alessio disappeared when the villa went out of view, and Paulo slumped in the seat, the curtains closed, head in hands, trying to stop the pounding. His heart hurt, too. What would Vittoria say if she found out? She would return in a few days. How could he tell her that he had been with another woman? He would have to force it down, forget it happened, and petition for the count's secrecy.

The day Paulo arrived back from the duchess was filled with torment. Paulo tried to slip into Alessio and dismiss the dread he felt, but it was embedded too deep. Instead, he captured the suffering of his spirit into song. The flow started slow, a cacophony, so much so it was hard to hear the notes. It was like the orchestra tuning, grinding, trying to come into unison, searching for the notes amongst the noise. As he wrote, his reality unravelled and was laid before him, out of his heart and onto the page. By the end of the day, after another dose of opium, more spews and spirits, a short nap and some soup, his head became clearer. He was just doing what needed to be done. This did not make him evil. He was giving pleasure, and for this, he should be proud. Paulo's time with the duchess did not lessen the love he felt for Vittoria; in fact, it had reinforced it. Paulo would meet with Vittoria again in a few days, more determined than ever to give her all of him, all that she deserved. Until then, he would do whatever was necessary to keep himself well and in good spirits. For Vittoria would not find him flagging.

By the morning of Vittoria's planned arrival, Paulo was excited, if not ecstatic. He had cleared his stomach of the toxins taken with the duchess and settled his mind. Now, he could not wait to let his heart loose with his lover. The thought of being close to Vittoria made Paulo's heart thump hard. He had vowed to show her all she meant to him on this day and love her like nothing and no one else ever would.

However, instead of a carriage, came a messenger upon horseback. Instead of his princess, came a parcel. Paulo held his breath. She could have been called away by her family. She could be ill, or her father could be indisposed.

It was none of these things.

She was to be married.

The letter contained little friendliness or frivolity, only fact. Vittoria had returned from holidays to be told of her betrothal. It had been a surprise, and she was still in shock. She would marry in the late autumn, at the Feast of All Saints, and then move to the north, to her husband's estate.

Paulo sat, stunned.

The messenger asked if he should wait for a response, to which Paulo said no. There was far too much to process to reply quickly, and he wondered if he would at all.

Vittoria would be wed on his birthday.

And all she had left him was a book.

Paulo opened it, tearing at the plain wrapping. It was a bible.

Inside was written a message.

May this give solace and reassurance that my spirit is with you always.

There was no solace to be gained from this inscription. The only feeling Paulo had was fury. The count had been right. Paulo was simply a pleasurable placeholder. He had survived these past weeks only thanks to the thought of being in Vittoria's arms again. He only wanted to go out into the world because he knew she was in it. He only wanted to be on stage to see her smile at him. But now it was clear that she did not share his sense of commitment. He was genuine, but for her it was a game.

The Bible was hurled towards the wall, with his mangled wrist hurting from the force with which it was flung. He screamed, one so awful, so agonising that it would have scared the angels if they had been around. But Paulo needed to be clever to deal effectively with this pain. He quickly called the dottore and complained of a new, intense and acute affliction, which was actually the truth. He shed tears telling of the stabbing in his chest and the tension in his limbs. He skilfully led the dottore to prescribe a plethora of sedative treatments, asserting all the time that his concern was being able to continue delivering for the count. As a patient, he was conscientious, calm and so appreciative of all the dottore was doing for him, even more grateful when the prescriptions were filled. Alessio's mask was coming in very handy.

Then, when the dottore left, Paulo let the evil embrace him and sink through his skin. He began to breathe embitterment and began to take in the treatments he had slyly extracted. Paulo spent the next two days drunk and doped out on opium. It was the weekend and he was missing nothing except for mass, and he did not care for this anymore. There was no God. Or perhaps there was, and the Pope was right, and now he was being punished for the vile creature that he had become. It did not matter. There was no place for him in a church. He could not even bring himself to read the Bible on Sunday, for every sentence would remind him of Vittoria and stab at his heart. He was godless now and completely alone.

Paulo did try to write, but nothing would come. He was either too broken or too incapacitated. He could only cry and whisper Vittoria's name. As the day drew to a close, the sad declarations of love were increasingly replaced with curses, and Paulo's pining was replaced with spite.

The attendant came into Paulo's apartment Monday morning, opened the curtains, and advised Paulo that the opera master expected him at rehearsals after breakfast. There was talk of a new opera and a tour to capitalise on the success of the recent shows.

Paulo stumbled out of bed, with spew on his shirt, shit on his pants and saw the evidence of several missed hours all over the floor. The books that Vittoria had given him, and the drafts of her opera were ripped into pieces and thrown around the room. He did not remember doing any of this, but he assured himself his rage must have been relatively sedate, for no guards were called. Or were they, and he just did not recall? Oh well, if there was a ruckus, he would be sure to hear about it soon. The count would come and condemn him, but they both knew that Alessio was of great value, so just let him try to take him down. The Count's opera would be nothing without him. The count could threaten him with being usurped by all the new young men coming out of the college.

There were hundreds supposedly vying for his place. But it would take them time to rise to his heights. He was a star, and the count knew it. Besides, he could easily run back to the duchess if the count dismissed him.

Feeling sick and acidic, Paulo called his attendant to run his bath. He would play their game but play it to win. Paulo would take all he could from the Church, the count and his lackeys, for they had taken everything from him. His family, his dignity and now his best friend. He would get revenge and become the victor. He would show them what it means to suffer. Paulo had made a plan; spend the day as usual so they did not suspect a thing, and then that night, he would begin his scheme. He would suck them dry until they were one sad saggy sack, like the one he had between his legs.

The warmth of the water eased the pounding in his head but did nothing to soothe the hatred in his heart. Attempting to remove that was now useless. He had crossed a line now and could not look back. He could only wash away the superficial stink of the spirits and the stench of his self-pity. Despair was now a dye embedded into his entire being, and nothing would extract it.

Paulo stood to exit the bath, feeling somewhat refreshed but also a little shaky. The breeze that met his bare body was stirring, but the floor was slippery, and his foot was infirm. Paulo's attempt to clutch the side of the tub came too late, and he landed hard on his hip and then his head. He felt the stab in his side and screamed for help. Then everything went dark.

Francesca

Messengers were a rare occurrence at Francesca's farm and so spying one approach from the road caused anxiety. Her husband's family did not need them as they all lived nearby and had enough labour to deliver their own communications. But Francesca's family was fractured. Each sibling was in a vastly different place, and this message could bring news about any one or more of Antonio, Luca, Paulo or Maria. It could be a matter of business, but this was done mostly face-to-face at the market, leaving Francesca to worry for the worst.

Maddalena was crawling around with the cats when the messenger came close. Francesca was relieved that the child was also not in need of attention for when the messenger announced the sender as the Ferrara family, her worry turned to fear. What could they possibly want? Why did the letter not come from Antonio or Isabella?

Francesca signalled for the messenger to come into the house, where she would provide refreshments. She picked up Maddalena, who protested at leaving her friends and went inside, calling for Rosa, who was in her room. She placated the toddler's tantrum with some bread and honey and supplied the same for the messenger along with some watered wine. Then, as her mother was seated with her at the table, she took the letter and braced herself for its contents.

As she read of Antonio's death, and of Isabella's, Francesca heard her mother howl. Rosa's heartbreak did not come out in words but in wails. What of the children? They were currently with the Ferrara family but as is law, must be fostered to the family of their father. And so, the message came as a summons. Francesca was to come and collect the children, of which there were three, two boys and one girl, Antonio, Matteo and Lydia. Isabella's father would arrange for a stipend for the children's schooling. The funeral would likely be held before they could arrive as the conditions of their death had led to fears of disease. The farm, owned by Antonio, was currently being overseen by another son-in-law, but they must arrange an alternative landlord promptly, or it must be sold.

With tears falling down her face, and hands over her mouth to hold in the anguish, Rosa repeatedly called for her son, Antonio, whom she adored. Francesca watched as she crumpled over the table and thought for a moment that this news might just kill her mother. But she knew that deep inside, her mother was stronger than this and that it was likely the shock that caused her to lose her composure. Rosa could be broken because Francesca was there to figure out what to do next, and Rosa trusted her to do it.

The daughter did not hold the same heartache for the loss of Antonio as the mother who bore him. He was a brute, and while she would not wish ill on anyone, Francesca believed this world may be better without him in it. She did feel, though, for Isabella, his wife. Perhaps now, though, she could be at peace. But what about the children? She must consult with her husband. Before leaving to find him, she brewed a calming tea for her mother and wrapped a blanket around the old woman's shoulders. Then Francesca wrote two letters for the messenger to take. The first was to the Ferrara family. She would be there within the week. No more needed to be said. It would be all sorted when they could speak in person. The second letter asked Luca to be the farm's landlord and appoint an administrator. It will be held in trust for Antonio's son when he comes of age. Francesca saw the messenger off with some dried fruits for his trip and then went to test the mettle of her man.

Francesca found her husband in the shed, sharpening his axe. His voice, drenched in disbelief, boomed, filling every corner and making Francesca doubt her ability. Then came the questions that quelled her concerns. How was the house to hold three more children? She had already solved that one on the walk out of the house. The girls would sleep in with her mother, and maybe they could even create a partition to give her mother some privacy. The boys would have the storage room, and they would find other places for their possessions. It would be a short-term solution until they could put on another room for the girls, which they were always going to do anyway as they planned for a larger family.

Then came the stress around money. How could they support three more children? Their means were already minimal. Francesca was also ready for this point of protest. They would come with a stipend that would cover all of their expenses. And did he doubt his wife's ability to use their resources wisely? She promised that her husband would not suffer for want with the extra children, and she would see to it herself that they earned their keep.

And what of the farm? Was he expected to care for this too? He already had so much to do. No, she explained calmly.

She had already written to Luca to deal with this and would discuss this with the proctor. For every one of her husband's arguments, she had an answer. And then, she added, there was the blessing of boys. He would have sons, and these sons would have their own farm to tend when they came of age. He could show them and teach them to be great farmers like him, and their family would have a much larger legacy. Francesca knew this would work. His eyes lit up like he was already hoisting them up on a horse and leading them out to fix a fence.

Her husband gave a huff and shrugged his shoulders, his usual sign of reluctant assent. Francesca advised that they would leave to collect the children in two days' time. Until then, she would work on creating space for the boys and making some interim bedding.

Francesca returned to the house to find Rosa still huddled over the table, but with Maddalena pulling at her skirt. Francesca swept the little girl up in her arms and blew bubbles on her cheek, making her giggle. Holding the child, Francesca sat opposite her mother and wondered why she did not feel the same sadness. It was because Francesca saw the blessing embedded within this disaster. She would now be a mother to many more, and this thought of duty and gain overshadowed all other loss. Francesca counselled her mother, calling on her to be strong for the children and to help her prepare a place for them. She was their Nonna, and they needed her. Francesca's words echoed those her mother had used to rouse her after the loss of her first baby and the dispiriting birth of the second. The wisdom of the women was weaving down through their family, and now there would be another girl to share it with.

The afternoon was spent finding suitable spaces for what was in storage. Some items were placed in the marital room, lined against the wall, waiting for a future cupboard. Other things were taken to the shed, and those able to endure the weather were stacked by the barn. Dust and spiders were swept outside and the clean room provided some relief for the grieving Rosa. The next morning, they went to the market to gather the ticking and enough food to satisfy her husband for the next few days. Back home, the horsehair, wool and hay were gathered, and with much rustling and Maddalena's meddling, four small mattresses and pillows were finally made, sown tightly shut to withstand the children's movements. Her mother asked why four when there would be only three children. Francesca feared that with the trauma these children had been through, bedwetting was to be expected, and so she would be prepared.

Arriving at the Ferrara's, Francesca and Rosa stepped into a chaotic scene. Maddalena was asleep, strapped to Francesca's back, but awoke suddenly when she heard the crying. Both Nonna's were wailing, supporting each other in their distress, sharing their agony at the loss of their children. There were desperate discussions about what had happened and the nature of the disease that took them. Sobs and shouts also rang out from the back room, with one boy running through, pushing past the other people and into the garden. The shrieks of a baby could also be heard.

That was when Signora Ferrara explained that they were at their wits end with the children. The eldest, who had just escaped, was, if they were being truthful, evil. He would tease and torment his brother and sister, hurting them and making their home one living hell. They would try to punish him but did not have the stamina for one as out of control and quick as him. Perhaps Francesca and Rosa may have better luck. And while they hoped he would settle in time, and one day take over the farm, the Ferrara's would also understand if this boy would be better placed at an orphanage or monastery that catered for wayward children. Francesca was told bluntly that Isabella's family would support any choice she made.

Right then, her romantic notion of an instant extended family faltered. It was as if she was dealing with her elder brother all over again. She was distracted by the need to attend to Matteo and Lydia, with Matteo explaining that Antonio had kicked him and pinched Lydia until she screamed. Rosa's arms were wrapped around Matteo, and the injuries were examined. Francesca took up Lydia and inspected her for wounds. When all was well, they just sat together and let Maddalena meet them. Matteo reminded him so much of Paulo, so sweet and cuddly. Lydia's loud cry scared Maddalena, but once the baby was fed and settled, Maddalena was happy to pat her. After some time, Antonio returned inside, and Francesca could see how he still seethed. This boy had no desire to meet them and just sat by the window. Francesca shared a glance with her mother and saw guilt written all over her face.

The old woman stood as straight as her aching body would allow, and she stomped over to the recalcitrant grandson, grabbing him by the ear and pinching him hard. Francesca felt both fearful and joyous when she said in a stern voice that he would show respect to his elders just as God had commanded, or he shall be struck down by lightning. Even despite her age, Francesca had to admit that her mother in a rage was terrifying. The young boy tried to slap this new Nonna, but she grabbed his hand and twisted it tightly. He tried to run, but picking up on the need for concerted effort, Nonno Ferrara closed the door, conveniently, with him and his wife on the other side, safe from the ruckus.

Rosa shrieked for Antonio to sit, and when she did, Francesca could have sworn that she looked like a banshee. But this was not a devil, this was a mother who had realised where she had gone wrong, and was driven to make amends. Nothing had been said, and nothing could be proven, but there was shared doubt about whether Antonio and Isabella had died from disease. And Francesca could feel her mother's desperation to prevent the same mistakes she made the first time around. This child would not be shown any slack.

Antonio sat, and Rosa signalled to Francesca that now was the time. Francesca pulled the small bag of marzipan from her pocket and saw the boy's eyes light up. Francesca thanked him for coming to join them. She confirmed the expectation that there would be no violence or Nonna would get mad again. He nodded his understanding and the boys ate their treats while Francesco explained how they would be moving to a new home. Matteo cried for his mama, and Antonio went to push him, but not before Rosa could pull him back and shoot him a look that even gave Francesca shivers and made Maddalena snuggle further into her mother. She did not know her Nonna as a monster; this was just one of the many adjustments that would need to be made for their family.

As they all went to wash for supper, Francesca thanked her mother. Rosa replied sadly that she was committed to making things right this time. This time she would help Francesca raise a boy the Lord would be proud of, who could control his fear and treat all with respect. But as they spent that night dealing with Antonio's tantrums, Matteo's desperate cries in the dark, Lydia's need for regular changing and feeding and Maddalena's madness at shared attention, it seemed so easy to say, but far more arduous than Francesca could have ever expected. It was then that Francesca began to doubt herself.

Luca

The letter arrived as Luca was about to leave the lecture hall. He had been spending an increasing amount of time there since Bianchini had suggested he would make a great teacher. His friend, supported by other peers, had seen how he mentored the new students and held their respect. Last month, in recognition of the esteem with which he was held, Luca received the post of Ricerrcatore Senior. So, now the career path of a lecturer had become a possibility. Luca truly loved undertaking his own lines of enquiry, and he already had one piece published on the latest developments in tracking lunar phases. There was a line of sight to become a professor, and that made him deeply proud.

Although lately, Luca was gaining even greater delight in sharing his knowledge with those younger than him. Luca's heart would sing when he saw the spark in a student's eye, showing their appreciation for the magic and the mystery around them. He would watch their frowns as they attempted to grasp the more complex details and smile when one finally came out of their shell, asked questions and challenged other's conclusions. As their minds expanded, so did his whole being. Not only did he feel physically lighter and bigger, but he also felt like he belonged. More than anything, he wanted this for every boy under his tutelage. He would work with each one individually to find the ideas that would inspire them. He could not deny that the added income from teaching was also helpful, allowing him to afford his own lodgings beside the Accademia and to begin entertaining a lady.

Caterina was the daughter of a professor. Her petite size would make many think she was fragile, but she had one of the fiercest and most impressive minds Luca had ever met. Their first encounter was in one of the salons run by the senior researchers on the weekends. All who sought knowledge were welcome, and within smoky air, spirits and jokes were shared, and ideas were debated. Unlike the Accademia, women were allowed at these events, and Luca was constantly amazed at how, despite being deprived of the opportunities for formal studies, the females knew so much.

Caterina had a deeper understanding of alchemy than he did and used it to inform all about the importance of internal transformation in the process. Simply, Luca was enraptured, and he felt blessed that there was evidence that she also found him attractive. Her wit was sharp, but her heart was warm, and she was desperate to follow in the footsteps of Elena Cornaro Piscopia and receive a degree. Luca supported this pursuit, even if it meant that soon he may lose her, for this was only possible in Padua, several days travel to the north. Until such time, though, she was happy to sit in the wings and listen to his lectures when she could, ploughing him with questions afterwards.

The room was empty on this day, though, when the messenger appeared. Luca was sharing the space with only the scent of burning wax, oil lamps and the subtle acrid aroma of sulphur. His first thought as the paper was presented to him was that Paulo had recognised him and had found a way to make contact. Luca went to see Alessio perform whenever there were spare funds and time, wriggling to the front near the stage and trying to make eye contact. It was clear that the crowd loved him. He had such a beautiful blend of confidence and humility, bravado and honesty. Of course, rumours were circling of Alessio's drunken antics. It was said these indiscretions were why he would always wear gloves. But it was hard to believe any of these seeing him sing, with the strength, the spirit that came from his body and how it moved the masses. He could not be sure, but he thought that Paulo had spied him on more than one occasion. Now, maybe Paulo had decided to reach out, and Luca was overcome with a sense of elation.

However, when Luca turned over the folded page and saw Francesca's name, his heart hesitated, and his body took a deep breath. The messenger stood in front of him as Luca raised his head and asked if he should await a response. Luca advised it was not necessary. He would leave almost immediately and may make it to Naples even before the messenger could. In a fluster, Luca found Bianchini and asked him to secure a lecture replacement for the remainder of the week. Then he scribbled a quick note, taking it to the Professor and asking for him to pass it on to Caterina on his behalf. The Professor was a champion of Luca's work and was happy to help. Then he went to his apartment a few blocks down, quickly packed the essentials and raced to catch the afternoon coach.

Bumping along, Luca brought his mind to think how long it had been since he was last at the farm where he spent his childhood. Antonio had advised him when Maria was being sent to a convent, although he did not explicitly invite him to attend on the day of her departure. Luca did want to see his little sister again, and to wish her well for the life that would then be spent behind the convent walls. However, he was sitting his major exams at the time and so had to compensate with a heartfelt message and a hand-made handkerchief. Luca hoped that Antonio had seen fit to pass it on. And as the man beside him reeked of stale beer and belched, Luca reflected on the animosity between him and Antonio. It went so very deep, and that is why, despite his brother's death, Luca could not feel sad. Though he would pray for Antonio's soul, he was unsure where it would be sent.

Luca exited the coach feeling battered and dirty, but he was glad to be out in the fresh air and away from the offensive odours. He secured a small room in the tavern, ate a hot meal, washed, and then retired early, for he knew the next days would be full of activity and emotion.

There were plenty of horses available for hire the next morning, and Luca chose the one that looked the most solid. The first stop was to Isabella's parents where he was met with a great disappointment. His mother and sister had departed the day before, wasting no time returning to what would be the children's new home. The women were eager to settle the children as soon as possible to prevent further ruptures in their sense of stability and in their behaviour. They had already met with the solicitor, and the land agent, signed the land transfer deed, and informed the administrators of Luca's impending arrival.

After some refreshments and assurances about his family's health, Luca headed into town to begin the process of becoming a landlord and securing a tenant. The solicitor pointed out the amendments made to the deed, now declaring the land and equipment held in trust for the sons but with all profits until transference to be held by the landlord, Luca. A bank account was required, and extensive time was taken to establish this, with details being taken back to the solicitor for recording.

Once oversight of the farm was confirmed, a visit to the agent was necessary. Fortunately, he knew of a family already looking for a leasehold, and they were known to be solid workers and upstanding citizens. Luca waited while the paperwork was prepared, and then they visited the prospective tenants together. They were a lovely family, which made Luca feel both happy and sad at the same time. In so many ways, they reminded him of his own. He allowed the agent to negotiate the details and take them to the farm, politely declining the offer to join them. He could not bear to be back in a place where there were very few fond memories and where those that rose to the surface were of being lost and alone and of Isabella's tiny corpse. Then, there was the knowledge that Antonio and the older Isabella had died there, too. He could just not do it. There were far too many ghosts.

Instead, he went back to the solicitors confirming the agent's details and preparing a letter to Francesca advising her that all had been settled. He also mentioned his sadness at missing her and his mother and expressed his sincere desire to see them again soon. It was late afternoon before all the tasks were complete, and he made his way back to the Ferrara family to provide an update. They generously offered for Luca to stay with them that evening, but he had to excuse himself.

His explanation about needing to return immediately was, in part, a lie, but it did allow him to have the night in his own company, which he much preferred. Besides, it would allow much easier access to the morning coach, and now that the solicitor and agent had all of his details, and he theirs, there was no more reason to stay. The rest could be managed at a distance, and this place no longer felt like home.

On the long journey back to the Accademia, Luca was wedged beside a newly married couple headed to visit relatives near Venice. They were excited about the adventure, and Luca found it impossible not to join their conversation. In fact, it lightened his spirits substantially, allowing him to arrive back weary but with renewed hope in the good of the world and in a possible future with Catarina.

Still, Paulo should know about his brother. Everything had happened so fast there was no time to fuss about before he left. After a well needed night's sleep, Luca went to visit the count, asking him for access to Alessio so that updates may be provided about the loss of his brother. Luca even offered payment of his current savings for the chance to converse with the castrato. The count only mocked him.

"Thanks to me lad, you have risen well in the world. Your presence here gives me great pride. However, you seek something that is still far beyond your station and need to be reminded of your place. Alessio is already greatly stressed with his success and is now in disciplined preparations for his next show. He cannot be troubled with such trivial family matters. Go back to the Accademia Luca, and your lessons, and come back again when you too hold the title of Count."

With that, the count walked away, and Luca was shown the way out.

Luca though was not going to give up. He began taking Caterina to every possible concert, engaging her beauty and her brains to help him find a way to see his brother. They had developed a plan that would allow Caterina to scout around the security and at least get a simple message through. It would happen that night, and they were both thrilled with the trickery they were about to enact. But Alessio was not there. He was listed on the program, but the opera master announced there had been a last-minute change to the schedule. No explanation was given, but people quickly made their own suppositions, and the whispers began. Perhaps Alessio was ill. Surely, he would return soon.

For almost a year, Luca followed the count's opera, fitting in attendance whenever his teaching commitments would allow. But still, Alessio did not reappear. Luca felt sick with worry. Where was his brother? Had he died, too? Or was he simply on tour again? Maybe Paulo had secured a place in the royal court and was now playing politics. Without anything said at the opera, Luca was left with numerous possibilities for where Paulo could be.

Caterina and Luca enacted their plan, but now with a different target. Caterina got close to the opera master and flourished him with compliments. When he was suitably taken, Caterina turned the tide of the conversation and asked where Alessio was. Was he ill? Was he on tour?

"No girl, he has been let go."

Then began Luca's long search.

CRUCIFIXUS

Paulo

Nothingness.
Numbness.
A sense of something solid.
An ever-expanding experience of pain.
Bound.
Trapped.
Crashing.
Piercing clarity.
Calls and cries.
Explanations.
Excruciating movement.
Numbness.
Nothingness.

This was the process that played out for Paulo: the hours, the days, the weeks and the months following his fall. He spent his time living through snippets of consciousness, wrapped in wooden splints, immobilised and inconsolable. After three weeks, there was no more energy left for weeping. There was only enough remaining to order more opium and to sleep. Paulo had no hope left, and he could hear no song; there was only silence or screaming. He could not even hear his own heartbeat, for it was buried too deep, broken like his bones, but with no one or no way to wrap them.

There was no knowing the exact span of time Paulo spent in the hospital, except for knowing he had felt the transition from sweat on the sheets, to shivering through the night. With the cold would have come another birthday and Vittoria's nuptials. Paulo could not even conjure sadness with the thought of Vittoria being taken to her marital bed. He was beyond feeling anything but physical pain, for this was the only one for which there was a remedy.

The bonesetter had held out hope that he could push the limb back into its proper position. When done, Paulo would regain the full function of his leg. But the procedure was a failure. Paulo had to be restrained and gagged to prevent his torment from disrupting the dottore. He was dosed well and in a daze when it began, but even the extensive sedation could not assuage the agony. Paulo could feel his bones crunching together and, with muffled screams, fell into madness. More months of waiting went by until the dottore determined Paulo would never again be able to walk well on his left leg. It was no consolation to hear from the dottore that breakages such as these was a common occurrence for those of his type. Crumbling bones was a known outcome of the castration, and Paulo should have eaten better to prevent it. His demise, it seemed, was his own doing.

Paulo had decided prayers were useless. They could not undo the situation. God had given but now decided to take away. All Paulo could rely upon was the opium that would let him crawl back into his little cave, under the covers, in the dark, where a wretch like him belonged. Coming out made him feel sick, and so he had one simple wish - to sleep in this hole and never awaken again. For what use was life as a cripple castrato. The count would not take him back. And this was confirmed by the opera master who appeared when the weather was again becoming warm. Alessio was too fragile for fame and had become unreliable and useless. He was meant to bring beauty to the people, to lift them up to the heavens. How was this possible when he now looked like a demon crawling out from the fires of hell? Paulo could not argue with the opera master's assessment. He could not even stand properly. Paulo's muscles had wasted away, and were now devoid of form and of function, forgetting what they were made for. His skin was covered in seeping sores, punishment for the sin of sloth. And Paulo's face was grey, the colour of ashen flesh.

In the hours in which he was awake enough to think, Paulo had decided that he would die. They would not allow it here of course, for his body was owned by Christ. He would have to escape so that he could end this pathetic life, and to do that, he would at least have to be able to hobble. Over weeks, then, he worked through taking step after step, supporting himself on the crutches, wincing through the shooting pain that would come whenever he applied pressure, and finally came to some sort of basic, shuffling movement. The medicine still came to calm the chaos within, and Paulo began to see the day when he could finally depart and die.

Perhaps, with his savings, he could secure a small apartment close by and enough opium to make sure he would sleep for eternity. That sounded like a solid plan but was quashed when the opera master advised that his savings had been used for his treatment. It had been over a year, and all of the medical attention he was receiving was expensive. There was no money left. But Paulo would not be distracted from his plan. He asked the opera master about his possessions, his costumes, clothes, books and bric-a-brac with which he had decorated his room. Perhaps these could be brought to him so they could be sold or swapped for food and lodging.

"Did you not read the contract, Alessio? It was a condition of your appointment that all goods and chattels were the possession of the count. Keeping you in such a life of luxury was pricey, Alessio, and your medicine even more so. The count needed to be adequately compensated. These things are long gone."

There was a part of Paulo that was glad. He was not sure he could see the clothes he wore with Vittoria or the battered books she had given him. Yes, it was best these were never seen again, lest they stir something in him that would dissuade him from his determined path.

Paulo pleaded with the opera master for some funds, just to secure a shelter for the short term, until he could contact his family. However, he had no intention of using the money for this purpose and certainly no desire to show his poor mother, if she were still alive, what a monster he had become. If she was not dead already, the sight of him would surely kill her quickly. No, Paulo's asking came with the knowledge that any funds granted would be spent immediately on the vials that would send him to a grave. He would crawl into a dark crevice, consume the lot, lay down and let the end come.

The opera master relented and advised that a small sum would be available to him on departure. But only if he left within the week. Otherwise, this would be kept by the hospital for further payment. Paulo agreed and provided his sincere thanks. He could not risk losing this, too, so he decided to leave the next day. While he wedged himself into a position where he could find some ease, Paulo wondered what happened to those who had no means or no mind to commit the sin of suicide. Then he remembered he had seen them before. These were the men, the women, and the children huddling in the dark beside the church, asking for alms, hoping someone would hear their pleas and have some heart to help the poor. He would not allow this to happen to him and to destroy his family's honour. He would slink away and never be found again. That was a fitting end for this castrato.

That night, on the eve of his end, as always, Paulo felt pain but also at peace.

And finally, he heard a song playing through his mind, the Crucifixus he had learnt in the church choir.

He was crucified for us
Under Pontius Pilate,
He suffered and was buried.

CRUCIFIXUS

Rosa

Rosa gave thanks for her son-in-law. He was strong and fair. He could be fierce but matched it with a sense of fun. He was solid, stable, respectful and kind. Of course, he had his bouts of being choleric and cranky, but he would let Francesca care for him and come back to a place of calm. He gained no pleasure in hitting the children, preferring rejection and removal as a more effective means of punishment. And Francesca would be there with small honey cakes to provide rewards. Rosa was happy to support them both, playing the hard old hag when hard lessons needed to be learnt, but also handing out the honey cakes and adding hugs in between.

This consistency worked to ease little Antonio's attacks. Rosa saw the soft side of the boy arise subtly, in small ways. He would start patting the cat, rather than twisting its tail, celebrating at his sister's first steps, rather than scowling and slapping her whenever she was the centre of attention. The boy had stopped getting mad at Maddalena when she came to cuddle him. He had hurt her in the past, pinching and pushing her over. Now he would just sit and take her embrace, lately, even beginning to return it or reach out to tickle. Antonio was becoming a wonderful big brother. She did worry about making him soft, but then he would stride out alongside his new father, and she knew that he also had a great role model for what it meant to be a man.

They were all fearful for how Matteo would settle in, but he bloomed quickly in this space, finally sensing safety. Francesca tempered her anger over his bedwetting, accepting it with patience and choosing not to condemn the boy. Rosa would have taken a different path, but she was so proud of her daughter for not damaging the boy further with fury, as his father would have done. Nightly episodes of damp, stinking sheets became weekly, and then there were only random occurrences. Then, across months, there was no more wetting the bed. Francesca did not have the same faith in God, the Holy Spirit and the Saints as she did, but her daughter had faith, nevertheless.

Little Lydia was a worry. She seemed so small for her age, and was a fussy feeder. Rosa kept reminding her daughter that a child will not starve itself, and so to be guided by her mood rather than what her mother thought she must eat. Rosa and Maddalena had joined up to dote upon the littlest child. Maddalena would amuse her by playing peek-a-boo and blowing bubbles on her belly. Rosa enjoyed embroidering the hand-me-down smocks to make them special for Lydia, changing out the coloured flowers that adorned the collars.

There were sleepless nights and days that felt cursed; still, there was progress. Rosa tried to tell her daughter about the challenges of having more children. Yet, all the advice Rosa provided could never have prepared Francesca for such a struggle. Rosa was well versed in the juggle and showed her how to assign, delegate, and push each child to become independent as soon as possible. She loved her role as grandmother and guide and provided a strong foundation through the first few months until there was a natural flow.

Life was not without its difficulties, however, for Rosa was ageing, and the aches would sometimes cause her to be crotchety. There were days when she was too tired, and her breathing was so laboured that she almost wished for death. But then her daughter would bring her tea, the little girls would crawl onto her bed, and Rosa would feel a renewed will to live. Her back was making it more difficult to travel to mass, and in the cold weather, she missed some services. When this happened, Francesca would always organise the priest to visit during his ministries to the sick so that Rosa could receive the Lord's blessing and share in the Eucharist. But when Rosa missed mass, she would still yearn for the singing. She missed the music desperately. Although part of her was happy when she could not hear the hymns, for while they would stir her spirit, they would also stir the shame she felt for sending her son to be a castrato. Every happiness, it seemed, was tainted with some horror.

Rosa tried to console herself with the news from Luca that Paulo was an acclaimed performer and was achieving great success. Luca would also provide regular progress reports on Antonio's farm, assuring them that it was secured with good tenants and was making a small but stable return. When a letter arrived that morning from Luca, Rosa assumed it was another update on the farm or on Paulo's achievements.

It was a bitterly cold day, and there was a fear of frosts, forcing them all to stay close to the fire. The messenger was invited in and provided with hot broth and spirits while he waited, genuinely thankful for such a generous welcome. Francesca read the letter by the fire, declaring that it was not news of the farm. Rosa could tell from her frown and the pauses she took as she read ahead that something terrible had happened.

Luca had found Paulo, almost dead. Luca had, with the help of his friends, restored him, but Paulo was crippled and in need of constant care. The dottore advised that he may not last long. Could Luca bring him to be with them?

The cry that came from Rosa's chest was like a chasm opening. It scared the children, with Maddalena hiding behind her mother, and it caused Lydia to cry. Rosa, through sobs and calls for her son, began pleading with her daughter to let him come. Rosa would care for him.

Francesca's husband walked in, hurrying towards the fire, seeking warmth. He had seen the messenger arrive and glanced at the guest awaiting awkwardly at the table. Rosa composed herself, for acting frantically would not help her case. She shooshed her sobbing and let her daughter speak. Francesca could convince her husband of anything.

However, when Francesca explained the situation, Rosa saw him change. She had known him as a generous man, but his decision was clear. He would not have such a disgusting creature, such a monster, in his house. This man, who Rosa had viewed as placid, now fought hard against Francesca's request. In his mind, castrati were amoral beasts, and this did not change if the castrato was her brother. No eunuch would enter his house and bring bad omens onto his boys. Besides, he had enough mouths to feed. Francesca looked frightened. This was also the first time she had seen him this hateful, and despite the assurances that Luca would provide funds to support Paulo's care, it appeared that his decision was final.

Rosa had no option but to risk his ire and to speak her heart. She explained that she was old, and her days were now numbered. It was she who sent her child to be a castrato. It was she who had sinned. Rosa pleaded with the man to not deny her the chance to seek forgiveness from her son for the suffering she had caused him, to allow her to make amends with her child and the Lord. He could hate her for what she had done, and she would accept that, but asked that Paulo not be punished any further. She pulled on this husband's heartstrings, asking him to imagine if his own child was suffering through his own mistake. Would he not want to make it right? She begged him to please give her this chance to make amends before she and her son died.

Francesca, strengthened by Rosa's petition, calmly added another condition. Her husband could see what this meant to her mother. And so, if he could not permit Paulo to come, she would take Rosa and the children to Luca and stay as long as necessary to allow the reunion of mother and son and to provide the care that her brother needed.

Francesca's husband bowed his head. Between them both, they had succeeded.

He could never deny a dying woman her wish.

He could never neglect his own son.

And he could never live well without his wife for weeks.

Paulo could come but must stay in the room and not be seen. Did the women understand his order? Of course, they did, and then they congratulated him on his generosity and wisdom, which made him sigh and roll his eyes.

Francesca quickly prepared a note and briefed the messenger, sending him off with some honey cakes. Now, they would be the ones waiting.

Francesca

Francesca had thought that Paulo coming home to them would ease her mother's worries, but it seemed only to enflame them. Rosa spoke of the concerns regarding the journey and whether he would be strong enough to endure it. She shared her fear that Paulo could not or would not forgive her. Her mind and words wandered off to surmising how he had ended up destitute, but she would not speak of his death. To settle her mother, Francesca employed her in the making of more mattresses, which the woman did while reciting the rosary. As each day passed, Rosa's nerves seemed to grow more uneasy, and she spent more time smelling lavender, sipping chamomile tea and whispering at the shrine.

Francesca's mother was always near the window and was the first to see the carriage arrive, alerting all with a shriek. That was when Francesca began to fret. If Paulo had not survived the distance from the Accademia, her mother would be inconsolable. It was likely that she would lose both her brother and mother on the same day. She saw her mother, one hand on her heart, and the other clutching a handkerchief, hurry as fast as her old body could take her out to where the horse had stopped. Francesca followed cautiously, waiting back to see what may be needed.

Luca opened the carriage door and stepped down, dressed in finery. He was such a handsome fellow. Rosa let out a yelp and opened her arms to the man, who called her mother and gave her a long embrace, before turning to help a young woman down the carriage steps. This was Catarina, Luca's friend and fiancé. This guest was graceful but generous in her salutations, although keeping them short and stepping aside so that the old woman could see her son.

Even with Luca's hand offering support, scaling the carriage steps was too difficult for his mother. Luca would bring Paulo down, for he was not able to walk.

Francesca moved forward to stand with Catarina, and they all watched as Luca removed the straps that held the tightly wrapped bundle of a body onto the seat. With gentleness and care, Luca carried the package down to them, struggling with its length but not its weight. Rosa cautiously pulled back the blankets, revealing a face they could barely recognise, but for his eyes. His skin was ashen, his cheeks sunken and his body was covered in scrapes. The way Luca held him, Francesca could tell that he was nothing but bones and that his limbs were limp. One of Paulo's hands wriggled softly from the wrapping to take his mother's, and he mouthed the word mama. Paulo was alive, but it appeared only just.

Rosa instructed her sons to come inside, shuffling ahead to show them the way. She led them into the boys' room and signalled to the largest mattress. Luca lowered Paulo toward the floor with great care, the broken body finding a soft home. When Paulo was safely down, Rosa replaced the travelling covers with clean, warm blankets. In the process, it became obvious how distorted Paulo's body had become, and there were many tears and lamentations for her poor boy. Even Christ's gaunt, tortured body, pulled dead from the cross was not as wretched as what lay before them. Francesca was told to bring broth, which she did. After she handed it to her mother, Francesca sat beside her younger brother, taking his hand and kissing him on the forehead. As she sat back, Paulo's eyes followed hers and they looked at each other, saying so much with only silence. It was heaven having Paulo so close again. But how his body had been destroyed; so cruelly changed. His condition would haunt her until the day she died. And yet, within him, Francesca got a glimpse of something eternal. Her mother then ordered Francesca to fetch warm water, and then the two siblings left their mother to wash her lost son.

Francesca prepared food and introduced the two girls and Matteo to their uncle and soon-to-be aunt. She had never seen Luca so happy, hugging each one and Catarina doing the same. Maddalena cuddled on Luca's lap, and Lydia held onto Catarina's fingers. Matteo excitedly told them of a new litter of kittens and then ran off to find one, bringing back a tiny grey baby for Caterina to pat. The children were settled with treats while Francesca joined the other adults at the table and poured wine. She had so many questions, which Luca graciously answered one by one.

Luca had not seen Paulo for almost a year and thought he was on tour or posted to the palace. But when more time passed without his return, they found a way to speak to the opera master. The master informed them that Alessio, that is, Paulo, had been let go. It took them time to track down an attendant at the count's estate, but he was helpful, telling of the fall, broken bones and Paulo being sent to a hospital. The attendant also counselled Luca about Paulo's dependency on opium and warned them if he were to be found withdrawing from it. This man had witnessed Paulo's wretched state once before and told Luca to start praying that he was well.

By the time they had made it to the hospital, Paulo had already left. The staff said that Paulo, though, would not be hard to find, for he could only move with the aid of two crutches. Luca and Caterina scoured the streets near the hospital until they found him in a stench-ridden corner behind a church; the crutches gone, convulsing, coughing, crying, and already losing consciousness. Luca carried his broken brother to the college, where he was cleaned and a dottore was called. It appeared the opium had largely left his system, but the damage was done. How he survived withdrawal the dottore did not know. The diagnosis now was peri pneumonia, pleurisy and impending death. Paulo could hardly talk; he was too breathless, could not move and mostly slept. But Paulo could hold your hand, and the look he gave said more than any words ever could.

That was when Francesca started sobbing, and Catarina came to put her arms around her shoulders. Caterina said nothing, but her support was strong. Caterina reached her other hand over to take Luca's, creating a link between them. She was so gentle and so smart, and it was clear she simply adored Luca. Just then, Francesca could sense some lightness in this very dark day, and she smiled with pride, listening closely as they shared their love story.

Francesca made tea and took some to her mother. Standing at the door, she could hear Rosa sobbing the word "sorry", with only silence as a response. When she entered, Paulo's hand was on Rosa's, and his gaze was gentle.

In the early afternoon, after much conversation, time with Paulo and play with the children, Luca and Caterina said their goodbyes and began their trip to town. They would lodge at the tavern overnight before returning to the Accademia in the morning. They wished for a longer stay, but both had college commitments that would not wait. The three children gave them cuddles, and Maddalena asked them to come back soon, which they promised they would, whenever they could. But they would also write and perhaps, if the children were good, send some gifts from faraway places. Catarina giggled when she saw the girls' eyes light up and Matteo take a little leap. Yes, there was light here too.

Francesca took the three small children in to see Paulo, piling the two girls on her lap and tucking Matteo close beside her. The two girls gave Paulo's hand a little pat, and Matteo touched his leg. That was when more tears appeared under Paulo's tired eyes, and Maddalena ran to get a handkerchief to wipe them away. Francesca was glad she had spent some time warning the children that Paulo could look strange but assuring them that their uncle was safe. However, Francesca was surprised that they were not scared. For despite his frightening form, he still exuded the same energy she remembered, and which created a very special space for anyone embraced within it. Francesca found it hard to imagine this gentle man wild on opium or raging through the withdrawals. However, after the death of her elder brother and his wife, she realised that there was no way of truly knowing what was in the depths of a person's heart.

It was quite some time after Luca and Caterina left that Francesca's husband arrived home with Antonio riding on his shoulders.

"Is he here?" was all that the husband asked. Francesca nodded, and nothing further was said.

After Antonio had washed and while his father poured some wine, Francesca took the boy's hand and led him in to meet the man sharing his room. She could feel him pull back a little and then, slowly, lean forward. It may have been through curiosity that he crept so close, but he did so calmly, and so Francesca let him be. Looking into her brother's eyes, Francesca explained that this was Antonio, his brother's son, and a streak of recognition and then hesitation spread across Paulo's face. Rosa excused herself, stating that she must go and start supper. Before she left, though, Rosa motioned to Antonio, asking the boy if he could stay and make sure Uncle Paulo was comfortable. Antonio wriggled closer, carefully clasping his fingers around the fragile man's hand.

"Yes, don't you worry, Uncle Paulo. I will take care of you."

Paulo let out a small moan as more tears welled in his eyes and flowed forth down his face. Antonio picked up the handkerchief that Maddalena had left and gently wiped them away.

With his other hand, Paulo reached upwards and touched his lips, then moved the fingers away ever so slightly, gesturing his heartfelt thanks.

That was when Francesca decided to sing. She did not care if her mother got mad. Nothing was going to stop her. There would be no more suffering.

CRUCIFIXUS

As she began, she saw Paulo give a small smile.

Queen, mother of mercy:
Our life, sweetness, and hope, hail.
To thee do we cry, poor banished children of Eve.
To you, we sigh, mourning and weeping
In this valley of tears.

And Francesca smiled too when her mother returned, joining in the hymn she adored.

Turn then, our advocate,
Those merciful eyes
Toward us.
And Jesus, the blessed fruit of thy womb,
After our exile, show us.
O clement, O loving, O sweet
Virgin Mary.

Pray for us, O holy Mother of God.
That we may be made worthy of the promises of Christ.

CRUCIFIXUS

Epilogue

Paulo's story is but one of around half a million boys who became castrati between the mid-16th and late 19th century, when the practice was finally prohibited.

At the time, the Pauline Dictum within the Catholic Church forbade women from singing in public. Yet heavenly voices were needed for the choirs. Castrati became the solution to meet both these needs: they successfully supported the continued suppression of women and the gratification of the flock.

The castrati had the lung capacity and strength of a male physique while also being able to deliver the high vocal range of a woman. The result was awesome, enchanting, and described as the voice of an angel.

And so, scouts roamed the country, finding prospective castrati on behalf of wealthy patrons and chapels. Many were recruited from families struggling financially, convinced that this was their chance for fame and freedom and that such a severe sacrifice would find great favour with God.

Because of the patrilineage system at the time, only the eldest son would receive an inheritance of land or business. Therefore, families with multiple sons had to find sources of work and support for all other boys. Becoming a castrato was then seen as a sound option for their future.

Boys were typically castrated between the ages of seven and twelve before reaching puberty to ensure their voices did not deepen and their potential was lost.

The castration process involved the removal or crushing of the testes, often without anaesthesia, and was performed by surgeons or barbers. Sometimes, the boys would be drugged with opium before the procedure, or the carotid artery would be compressed to first render them unconscious. It would take several weeks for the wound to heal strongly enough for them to be able to sing.

The bloodletting was an important part of the surgery, as it emulated the crucifixion of Christ and strengthened its mystery and meaning.

The practice of castration was done secretly, as it was illegal and bodily mutilation was classed as a sin by the Church, with the only exception made for medical necessity. However, while some Popes went as far as publicly condemning castration, it continued. Some boys were supported by doctors who declared that castration was necessary to avoid future accidents. In other cases, it was stated that the boys gave consent and wished for this sacrifice for the glory of God, the Church and the King. It is unknown whether coercion was applied to the boys or the parents for this consent to be given.

The boys were taken from their families before the surgery. They were kept at a training college for at least ten years, where they underwent rigorous vocal, composition and general musical training for around ten hours each day.

As the castrati also did not develop secondary male sexual characteristics, they also had an androgynous appearance that added to their enigma. Some researchers also claim that schadenfreude may have played a role in the fascination with castrati, with audience members possibly gaining pleasure from imagining the torturous procedure the castrato had undergone.

However, despite the claims that castrati would find fame and fortune, only around twenty per cent of castrati progressed to be prominent public figures, and many of these did not reap the full rewards due to their patrons' exploitation.

Some boys died in surgery or afterwards from infection. Others suffered from physical abnormalities and pain or psychological torment that plagued them throughout life. Some were deemed too unattractive for the stage, dealing with unsightly fat deposits or excessively elongated limbs. The lack of testosterone also contributed to higher rates of osteoporosis, diabetes, and urogenital complications, which would have made life challenging. Of those who did not find fame or positions within rich parishes, some eked out a comfortable existence in local church choirs, while others whose talent did not pass the test ended up on the streets.

At the time, the only reason for marriage was for procreation. Because castrati could not sire children, they were also banned from taking a wife. Nevertheless, they were sought after by wealthy women who found their sexuality both a curiosity and a safe source of pleasure.

Despite their inability to bear children, the identity of castrati as men was not questioned, with their castration lauded as proof of their extraordinary masculine courage.

Castrati lived in a world of contradictions. They were created by a church that also condemned them. They were intended to be a source of spiritual inspiration, but many became embroiled in their patron's materialistic pursuits. They were not able to marry but were still able to partake in physical pleasure. Some saw them as angels, others as purely abhorrent. They were welcomed into palaces as singers and sages and some became influential trusted advisers. At the same time, they were shunned and stigmatised by some who considered them amoral creatures. They were made to entertain the masses but never truly belonged. Their influence and inspiration on the world of music was vast, but one must ask, at what cost?

The last castrato, Alessandro Moreschi, also known as "The Angel of Rome", sang within the Sistine Chapel Choir at the Vatican until 1913 and died in 1922. His was the only castrato voice ever recorded. Though his recordings capture his unique vocal quality, they were made late in his career and are said to not fully reflect the peak capabilities of a castrato voice during its prime.

Sources:

Feldman, Martha. *The Castrato: Reflections on Natures and Kinds*. University of California Press, 2015.

Victims and Seducers: The Fate of the Castrati. 2003. Directed by Stefan Schneider, featuring Cecilia Bartoli. Medici.tv

About the Author

Belinda Tobin is a researcher, author, producer, and avid explorer of the human experience, with all its challenges and complexities. Her works span fiction, non-fiction, poetry, tv series and film. However, they all share a common purpose, to foster a more conscious, compassionate and connected future.

Find out more about Belinda and her projects at www.belindatobin.com.

CRUCIFIXUS

For more titles go to:
www. heart-led.pub/bel-house-books

Milton Keynes UK
Ingram Content Group UK Ltd.
UKHW041121121124
451035UK00019B/301